'We dance, therefore we are.'

African Proverb.

For Mary, dearest spouse and dancing partner.

Miss Esther Scott's Fancy

Lorn Macintyre

Best wishes
Lorn Mac[...]

First published in Great Britain in 2012 by
Priormuir Press
St Andrews, Fife KY16 8LP

Phone: 01334 476428
e-mail: priormuirpress@btinternet.com

ISBN 978-0-9567681-3-1

Typeset in St Andrews by Print & Design, University of St Andrews
Printed and bound in Great Britain by Elanders Ltd, North Tyneside

Dying to Live

Jessie Mackenzie passed away in the Isles of the Deep Nursing Home in Wester Ross, in rural Scotland, on a calm day with a whiskered seal lifting its head in the bay outside her window. She was one hundred and one. For a year she had been confined to bed, having to be turned constantly to prevent sores. In the beside cabinet were two books, a Gaelic Bible, and stories by Katherine Mansfield, inscribed on the title-page: *from Kass with love*. Jessie retreated further and further into her own world. She kept calling out a word that sounded like *gurev*, and the staff assumed that it was Gaelic, a language none of them understood, though their parents had had plenty. They changed her incontinence pad and continued to hug her while she uttered this word that seemed to have become a mantra.

Cuthbertson the lawyer was her executor. He had already sold her house to pay the nursing home charges, and after she died he visited the home and took away the few contents of the bedside locker. The Gaelic Bible looked old, so he offered it to the museum, but they weren't interested. As for the inscribed copy of the stories of Katherine Mansfield, Cuthbertson didn't include the book among Jessie's assets. His wife tried to read the stories, but they weren't to her taste, so he gave the book to a church sale of work, where it went for fifty pence to a tourist.

Jessie belonged to a family that had never had cremation as an option, and would never have chosen it. She was buried in her parents' grave, and there was enough money left in the estate to add her name to the headstone.

Jessie Mackenzie was the daughter of a hill farmer in Wester

Ross. Even at the age of three she was dancing over two crossed wooden spoons on the flagstoned floor of the kitchen, as she had seen dancers doing at the Highland Games. When she was five her mother enrolled her in 'Dancie' Grant's class in the village hall. He was an itinerant teacher of music and dance who served the area on a bicycle. After one session it was obvious that Jessie was a born dancer. While the other children beat out the 1, 2, 3 of the *pas de basque* to 'Dancie's' fiddle Saturday after Saturday in the church hall, Jessie's step was already perfect. 'We have a champion here, Mrs Mackenzie,' the dancing master told Jessie's mother. 'Give her plenty of milk to drink to strengthen her bones.'

It was her spinster aunt Mairead who encouraged her niece Jessie to become a competitive dancer. She bought the girl her first pair of pumps, and paid for a kilt. The cairngorm brooch which fixed Jessie's plaid to her shoulder when she was dancing in local ceilidhs had come from her aunt's jewel box. Mairead produced an eagle feather and pushed it through the diced band of the balmoral Jessie wore when she danced.

'There now, you're a wee Highland chieftain, Jessie.'

Two years later Jessie was taking the prizes at the local Highland Games. Her mother started to take her further afield to Braemar, where she danced in front of the royal family, and had a trophy presented to her by His Majesty King George V. Mavis treasured a snapshot of her daughter dancing at Braemar. The fact that it was out of focus added to its charm, as if the petite girl in the feathered bonnet had dropped into this world from a mystical place.

Jessie was intelligent as well as a wonderful dancer. Her aunt wanted her to train as a teacher, but Jessie didn't want to leave Wester Ross to go to college. At the age of fifteen she started work in the local post office. Because she had only a week's holiday in the summer she couldn't compete on the Highland Games circuit, and had to be content with dancing close to home.

Mairead gave her niece books for her birthdays, because she was a firm believer in the improvement of the mind. Jessie received a history of North American Indians for her seventeenth birthday, with pencil marks against certain passages in the chapter on the importance of dancing in Indian ceremony. Six months later her aunt was found dead behind her door where she had lain all night following a stroke. In her will everything went to Jessie. A month after her aunt's funeral an elderly woman came into the post office and pushed a parcel across to Jessie.

'It's for my daughter in Glasgow,' she explained. 'Will it get there tomorrow?'

The plucked hen had been wrapped in brown paper, but the claws were sticking out, and Jessie had to make it up again. That afternoon she walked out of the post office and the following day was seen taking the bus. She wrote to her parents: 'I have obtained a passport and am going to France. I'll write later.' Her brother John would help them on the farm.

A year before her death Mairead had given her niece a magazine. Above an article called The Genius of Gurdjieff Mairead had written: 'Jessie, this will interest you. I hope that one day you can meet this man. I am sure that he will help you with your dancing and the general balance of life. Never forget that we are only the shadow of what we can become with the proper guidance.'

Jessie, who had never been out of Scotland before, was shivering on the cross-channel steamer, and thinking about her aunt. Was this really what Mairead wanted her to do with her legacy - to go to France to meet a man called Gurdjieff, a 'Master of Dance,' as the magazine article called him?

Jessie felt bad about walking out on Mrs MacLennan in the post office. But when she had put the parcel on the scales and seen the claws of the chicken sticking out, she asked herself: *is this really what I want to do with my life?*

Jessie hadn't studied French at school. She took Gaelic, against the advice of her parents, who said it was a dead language. But her aunt encouraged her, maintaining that Gaelic was a vital part of her heritage. Even Jessie's English wasn't proving of much use to her across the Channel. She wrote out the name of the place she wanted to go to: Fontainebleau. The man at the French port tried to explain how she would get there, but Jessie couldn't understand a word he was saying. He pushed her into a train and slammed the door behind her.

Jessie arrived in the Gare du Nord in Paris. A porter tried to take her suitcase, but she resisted, because she would have to tip him. She couldn't squander her aunt's legacy, which was intended for her development both as a dancer and as a person.

She held up the printed Fontainebleau plea for assistance in the station. A woman took her arm and led her into a waiting-room where she drew a diagram on the other side of the paper, showing Jessie that she had to get to the Gare de Lyon station, from where she would get a train for Fontainebleau. She wrote out the letters 45. Was this minutes or miles, Jessie wondered?

On the train Jessie sat opposite the first black person she had seen in her life. He smiled at her, and she was amazed at how white his teeth were. Then she saw his tongue, pink like a cat's. Across his knee he had a black case from which he took out a saxophone. He played Jessie some jazz before he alighted at a station with an unpronounceable name.

Within the hour Jessie was in Fontainebleau. This time it was even harder to make herself understood.

'I want to go to the Prieuré,' she told this man.

He put his hands together. 'You mean pray. The church.'

'You speak English,' she said in astonishment.

'I fight beside Scots at Somme.' He twiddled his fingers as if he were playing an imaginary set of bagpipes.

Jessie took out the magazine with the article on Gurdjieff which her aunt had given her and pointed to the line with the address Prieuré des Basses Loges. The man began to wave his hands. 'No! No! No go there!'

'Why not?'

'Bad man!' the excited Frenchman shouted.

'Who's a bad man?'

'Bad man,' he repeated. 'Many women. You no go.'

'I'm going, now I've come all this way,' Jessie told him, and turned to ask a woman passing by. The woman took her arm and led her to a line of vehicles. She spoke to the front driver and he opened the door for his passenger. Jessie watched the countryside of woodland and pasture passing the window. It wasn't unlike the Highlands, and it made her homesick. They drove through a village, scattering a flock of geese, an old woman by a pump shaking her fist at the speeding vehicle.

'*Ici*,' the driver said, braking at gates.

Jessie didn't know the value of the fare, because she hadn't found out how much the franc was worth, but it seemed a lot of money she was counting into his palm.

Sonnez fort, it said beside the bell of the Château Le Prieuré which housed the Institute for the Harmonious Development of Man, as the Prieuré was called. She didn't know what the French phrase meant, but she knew that bells were for pulling. She tugged three times, but nobody appeared, so she opened the gates. The large building two storeys high reminded her of the laird's house at home. Men and women who were working in the grounds straightened up and waved to the young woman lugging her suitcase up the drive. She set down her case by an ornate pool and sat on its edge for a few minutes before making her way to the front door.

No answer again. It was open and Jessie walked in. A woman was sitting on the floor, her legs folded in front of her.

'Excuse me,' Jessie said. 'I'm looking for a Mr. Gurdjieff.'

'I Gurdjieff,' a voice behind Jessie said, giving her such a fright that she dropped her case.

With his moustache and bald head he reminded her of the seal that had appeared each day in the bay outside the post office, lifting its head to stare inquisitively at her as she stamped letters. He led her into the faded splendour of a large salon, mirrors in flaking gilt frames round the walls.

'Come far?' he enquired.

Jessie had the feeling that he was mocking her, the way he was smiling.

'From Scotland.'

'Ah, Scot-land,' he said, nodding.

'I'm a dancer,' she told him.

'Show me.'

'*Now*?'

6

'Yes, now.'

'But I don't have any music.'

'Music in here,' he said, touching his heart.

Puirt a beul, as it is called in the Gaelic language, is musical rhythm produced with the mouth. Jessie made it as she danced the Highland Fling, having kicked off her brogues.

'Not dance,' Gurdjieff said, waving a finger.

'It *is* a dance,' she insisted. 'A very old dance, done by Highlanders.'

'Dervish dances even older. Watch.' He spread out his arms and began to whirl across the floor, stamping his shoes, duplicating himself again and again in the mirrors. Jessie had never seen a dance like it, and she was dizzy just watching.

'I teach you this dance. What's your name?'

'Jessie.'

'Jay-see.'

'How much does it cost to stay here?' she enquired.

'How much you got?'

'I've brought fifty pounds of a legacy from my aunt. She wanted me to come here because she had read about you in a magazine which she gave me.'

'What you pay.'

'What does that mean?' she persisted. She didn't want to part with all her money there and then, because she needed to keep some back in case she decided to go home.

Gurdjieff picked up her suitcase and led her up two flights of stairs. The room under the roof was very basic, with a covered mattress on an iron frame. When she had unpacked she went downstairs. And then it was time for dinner. Jessie was timid about going into the big room where Gurdjieff sat, with his pupils around him, with a sheep's head steaming on a plate in front of him. Jessie loathed sheep's head, having been made to eat it whenever her father killed an animal. It was as if Gurdjieff knew this, because he was watching her as he picked up a knife and extracted one of the eyes, holding it out to her on the blade.

Jessie knew that this was her second big test. She had passed the first, with her dancing. Now she had to take that horrible object from him and eat it. But she went up, watched by all the others, who had probably had to do the same, as a kind of initiation rite. Jessie picked up the loathsome eye from Gurdjieff's blade. For a moment she thought she was going to bring it back up again, but she returned to her seat as Gurdjieff started to applaud.

During the meal he seemed to start quarrels among the diners and then sat back, enjoying the arguments he had provoked. He also picked on people and insulted them.

Who was this man Gurdjieff? Jessie made enquiries among his disciples, and was told: he had been born in Armenia to an Armenian mother and Greek father. He had served as a spy and was a former stage hypnotist. At various times he had made reference to: Chitral; Tibetan monasteries; Sufi schools in Persia, Bokhara and eastern Turkestan; Mount Athos; and a good deal about Dervishes.

Gurdjieff was certainly a carpet dealer, because Jessie had to take a woman from Paris who had arrived in a limousine driven by a chauffeur into a room where Persian carpets were laid out on the parquet floor, and later Jessie had seen Gurdjieff rolling up one and carrying it out on his shoulder to the limousine.

Jessie was told that when Gurdjieff was trying to establish

his first Institute in Tiflis the Russian Revolution had broken out and he had fled to France.

'A very wealthy English woman gave him the money to purchase this place,' a woman from Somerset told Jessie as they were working together in the kitchen of the Prieuré. 'She's a Theosophist.'

'What's that?' Jessie enquired.

'A follower of Madame Blavatsky,' the woman volunteered as she scraped the carrots, but Jessie was none the wiser.

The disciples did all of the tasks around the château, the housework, the repairs. In her first week Jessie found herself acting as kitchen maid. She was required to rise at 5 a.m. and go down to the kitchen to prepare to feed the entire community. The sun was coming in the window as she stirred the vast pot of porridge and thought of sunny mornings in Wester Ross when she had risen early to practise her Highland dance steps for the Games, while a sandpiper calling from the shore provided the music. Was this a daft idea, coming to this place? But Gurdjieff fascinated her.

After she had served the breakfast Jessie had to join some of the other women to sew the white trouser suits that would be used in the dance classes. Jessie was skilful with a needle and had made some of her Highland dance outfits herself.

Gurdjieff himself never rested. He laid bricks for a new building in the grounds and the next time Jessie saw him he was in the forge, beating glowing metal which was reflected in his eyes. After breakfast one morning he announced that a steam-room, hot-room and cold-room would be built, so that the pupils could relax after the dance exercises.

The brickwork seemed to go up as if by magic, and one night

after dinner Gurdjieff announced: 'women have bath.' Jessie went with the others to sit naked. She was particularly taken with a dark-haired beauty. Jessie understood that Olgivanna had joined Gurdjieff when he had had the Institute at Tiflis. She was a graceful dancer who seemed to float across the room, followed by Gurdjieff's admiring eyes.

'Gurdjieff is a mystic,' she told Jessie as they sat in the cloud of steam. 'He knows things that other men don't.'

'What kind of things?' Jessie wanted to know.

'Have patience and you'll find out. One thing is certain, this place will transform your life.'

Gurdjieff usually made his important announcements at the evening meal, where the disciples sat in several dining-rooms. He had told Jessie to stay in his, since she was a new pupil, and would benefit from what he had to say.

'Who like pigs?' he asked the company after the appetizing stew.

'I like pigs,' Jessie spoke up. 'We have six of them on the farm at home.'

'Then Jay-see is pig-girl,' Gurdjieff announced with shining eyes, before he turned to his neighbour and insulted him to provoke a response.

The pigs arrived the next day, and were put into the sty that Gurdjieff himself had built in the grounds. Jessie had fed the pigs on the farm, and had always found them intelligent and affectionate creatures. She loved her charges at the Prieuré, and would spend a long time talking to them as they rooted in the French soil.

Some evenings, when she carried the bucket of swill from supper on the crook of her arm, she would find Gurdjieff leaning over the sty, talking to the pigs in a foreign language.

'Pigs know more,' he said, tapping his head. 'People very stupid.'

'In what way?' Jessie asked to be enlightened, because she was there to learn.

'No understand powers they have. I learn in monasteries in the mountains. Man has powers he not know he has. He lives dull life. You need bring out these powers.' He was watching her with his hypnotic eyes across the grunting animals. 'You very beautiful.'

'Thank you,' Jessie said, and dug her fingers into another handful of swill for her charges.

Jessie loved the dance sessions, especially learning the movements of sacred dances which Gurdjieff claimed were derived from ancient Dervish dances. Gurdjieff himself would demonstrate, arms outstretched as he spun across the room to the haunting Sufi music.

'You become superhuman!' he shouted, raising his arms as his disciples repeated his movements. He appeared at Jessie's back, lifting her arms above her head. 'You fly, Jay-see! You a bird! Eagle over mountains. Higher higher! Down below you see leetle people who never rise.'

Jessie was exhausted after these classes, but there were still the chores to be done, helping to prepare supper, then taking the bucket in the twilight to feed the pigs which seemed to know she was coming, because she heard them before she saw them. When she went back to the house she discovered a new arrival standing in the hall. What struck Jessie about the small young woman was that she seemed to be square everywhere, as if the contours of her body hadn't been completed. She had brown hair and brown eyes, set very far apart.

'Can I help you?' Jessie asked.

'I've just arrived, but there doesn't seem to be anyone about. Do you know where Gurdjieff is?'

'Who shall I say is calling?

'My name is Katherine Mansfield, otherwise Mrs Murry,' the stranger introduced herself, holding out a hand.

'What a nice voice you have,' Jessie complimented her.

'I'm from New Zealand, but I've lived in England for a long time. And you?'

'I don't expect you'll have heard of Wester Ross,' Jessie said. 'It's in Scotland.'

'I know Scotland,' Katherine told her. 'I went to Glasgow with the Moody-Manners Opera Company years ago. Have you heard of it?'

'We don't get opera in Wester Ross.'

'I had kippers in the boarding house in Glasgow. I adore kippers.'

'So do I,' Jessie told her. 'I'd get my mother to send us some, but they wouldn't keep in the post. Are you joining the course, Mrs Murry?'

'I've a health problem which I'm hoping Gurdjieff can help me with. He said that I could come for a fortnight, under observation, and then we'll see. What about you?'

'I'll be staying, if he'll let me. I'm learning a lot from him - especially about dancing.'

'I don't think I'll be dancing,' Katherine said. 'Don't call me Mrs Murry. Call me Katherine. No.' She hesitated. 'I like you, and I know we're going to get on. Call me Kass. That's what my family in New Zealand call me.'

Gurdjieff asked Jessie to show the new arrival up to her room. After climbing the stairs Kass had to sit on the bed because of a fit of coughing, so Jessie unpacked her case, folding the clothes into the squeaky drawers.

'Did you write this?' Jessie asked in admiration, lifting a small book from the bottom of the case and studying the cover.

'They're short stories.'

'I'd like to read them,' Jessie said eagerly.

Kass took the book from her, wrote an inscription and handed it back.

'For you, as a gift.'

'Should you be doing that?' Jessie asked solicitously when her new friend lit a cigarette.

'I'm addicted to the damn things, but I hope I can give them up here. And I hope I can give up other things here as well.'

At supper that night Jessie noted that Kass wasn't put through the sheep's eye test by Gurdjieff. She was sitting on his right hand, and had pushed away the plate of cabbage that the Master, as some of the disciples called him, believed was so nourishing. Kass was listening to the Master maintaining that most people exist in a state of 'waking sleep.'

After supper there was a dance session. The music would stop suddenly, and Gurdjieff expected his pupils to hold the pose until he clapped his hands for the music to start again. Kass wasn't well enough to dance. She sat and watched Jessie and the others. After the dance session she went with Jessie to feed the pigs, taking her arm because she felt weak.

'Gurdjieff has ordered me not to smoke,' she confided.

'Will you stop?'

'I haven't had a cigarette for three hours twenty seven

minutes,' she said, consulting her watch. 'I'm desperate for one, but I daren't disobey in case he sends me home. I need to stop smoking, to change my life. That's why I'm here. I'm hoping for so much. I need to die, you see.'

Jessie almost dropped the pail of swill.

'I don't mean die, and that's an end to it. I need to die so that I can live again, just as we died and then lived again after the war.'

'My uncle died in the war,' Jessie informed her. 'He doesn't live again. He's buried somewhere in Belgium.'

'Don't you remember how life became intensified and illuminated during the war, Jessie? The zeppelins came over and we were bombed. Things were lit up in a new light. I need to get that feeling back into my life. I need to get my health back, Jessie, so that I can live a full adult-breathing life.'

'What's the matter with you?' Jessie asked, aware that she was being inquisitive, a trait of folks back home, with the post office the centre of gossip.

'I have tuberculosis.'

Jessie rested the pail on a wall and had to sit down. TB: the abbreviation brought terror to Wester Ross. When someone who had it came into the post office Mrs MacLennan would warn Jessie: 'don't touch the letter before you lick the stamp, otherwise you could get consumption.'

A young woman whose sweetheart lived in the south came to the box every afternoon to post him a letter, telling him that she was getting better in the pure air, and that he could safely come soon to visit her. The next time she passed the post box it was in the hearse.

'I feel that I've a flat-iron in my chest tonight,' Kass told her friend. 'I need to get rid of it, to be in contact with the things that I love - the earth, the sea, the sun. I want to enter into the external world, to be part of it.'

'You can begin with these pigs,' Jessie said. 'Look at the welcome they're giving us. Sometimes I like pigs better than I like people.'

'Do you like me?' Kass asked as she hesitantly touched the rough back of the swine.

'I like you very much. I want this place to cure you. Or rather, I want Mr Gurdjieff to cure you.'

Kass had given Jessie a lot to think about. She could see what her friend wanted from the Institute, but was afraid that she might not get it. Most of the residents were healthy, dancing and digging, but Kass didn't have the strength to join in either activity. Gurdjieff obviously appreciated this and didn't give her any duties. She was an observer, not a participant. When others were beginning to make supper she would come into the kitchen and sit on a chair in the corner which the Master said was hers. Jessie prepared the vegetables while chatting to Kass.

One night when Jessie was taking the swill down to the pigs she heard a hammering sound coming from the outbuildings. Gurdjieff was up in the open loft, and took the nail out of his mouth to answer her enquiry.

'Building couch for Messus Murry.'

'But why up there?' Jessie asked, mystified. 'Is she not better to be in the house, where she'll be warm? You know she's not well.'

'Get better soon, drawing in breath of cows,' Gurdjieff said.

'What cows?' Jessie asked, wondering if this strange man was going out of his mind.

'Coming tomorrow,' he told her, and resumed hammering.

Next afternoon a dozen cows were driven up the avenue. Gurdjieff was establishing a small farm at the Prieuré, where there were already the pigs, goats, sheep and poultry. Obviously he intended the Institute to be as near sufficient as possible in food.

'The good thing about the couch in the cowshed is that it shows Gurdjieff wants you to stay,' Jessie told Kass when they were out walking in the gardens.

'I couldn't leave now. I need to be reborn so that I can go back into the world to resume my writing.'

'Will you go back to London?'

'That's where my husband and friends are, Jessie,' she said in a subdued tone.

'Don't you yearn for New Zealand?'

'Oh I do, but that's another story, one I've still got to write up.'

That night Gurdjieff called Jessie up to his room after supper to tell her how pleased he was with her progress, and what a far better dancer she was since she had come to the Institute.

'You one of my best dancers, Jay-see. No mechanical now.' He put his arm round her waist but she removed it.

Gurdjieff had completed the couch above the cowshed. It was covered with fine oriental rugs and cushions, and one of the men had painted the roof in bright patterns of trees, flowers, animals and birds. He had given the creatures some of the faces of Institute members. Jessie was a bird of paradise, and Kass did not feature.

The German girl who had been detailed to milk the cows couldn't master the technique, so Jessie volunteered. She liked cows, and after the day's work in the post office she would bring them in for milking. Her new chore - she still had the pigs - meant that she could spend more time with Kass.

Jessie sat on the three-legged stool which Gurdjieff had made for her, tugging the cow's udders as she conversed with her dear friend on the loft above.

'It's so therapeutic, lying here, inhaling the cows' breath and listening to their milk hissing into the pail,' she called down to Jessie. 'Tell me about your life in Scotland.'

'There isn't much to tell. I worked in the post office, handling His Majesty's mail, and badly made-up parcels of chickens and rabbits. There's nothing more disgusting than a gift that has gone off in the post. I used to throw such parcels into the sea rather than have them delivered. Was that wicked of me?'

'Very practical, I'd say,' Kass called down.

'They weren't wasted. The seals ate them, then sang to me.'

'Do seals sing?' the invalid on the loft wanted to know.

'They do, if they like you. Often when I went for a walk by the sea seals lying on the skerries seemed to be singing a song for me.'

'I must use that image in a short story.'

'I'm glad,' Jessie told her, carrying her stool to another cow and settling beside its laden udders.

'Have you ever had a love affair?' the voice from the loft enquired.

'Not yet. And you?'

'Several.'

'I'll hear about them after I've finished the milking,' Jessie called back.

She went up the steps and sat on the boards beside the couch on which Kass was reclining.

'You're so beautiful - and healthy,' she told Jessie as she stroked her hair. 'I'm going to tell you something that very few people know. I like women better than men. Are you shocked?'

'No,' Jessie said earnestly.

'I had affairs - including a Maori woman - when I was in New Zealand. I'm not ashamed of it. The only thing that saddens me about it is not recognizing that it was a natural impulse. I made a hasty marriage, then became pregnant, but I lost my baby when I tried to lift a trunk from the top of a wardrobe.'

Kass's eyes were brimming with tears as Jessie held her hand.

'Then I married the writer John Middleton Murry. There's a rousing English name for you, if ever there was one. He's a good caring man with a temperamental wife. You see this wedding ring?' She held up her hand in the gloom as the cows shifted in their stalls below. 'It's not mine. It was the ring that Frieda Lawrence wore when she was married to her first husband, before Lawrence took her away from him and her children. I was with the Lawrences when they were living in Cornwall. He may be a great writer but he was beastly to Frieda, and used to beat her up. That's why I prefer women. We're a much more gentle sex.'

After these conversations in the cowshed Jessie was coming to believe that she was in love with Kass. She had never contemplated the notion of love for a woman before, but now it seemed possible and desirable. But she sensed she had a rival in

Olgivanna, who carried armfuls of logs up to Kass's bedroom in the château and sat talking with her. When Jessie came up she was treated like one of the many servants this haughty woman must once have had.

Gurdjieff was obsessed with the building of a study house in the gardens of the château and demanded the same commitment from his disciples. He had bought an old aircraft hangar from the French army, and the residents worked into the wee small hours of the morning, lining the inside and outside walls with uprights of rough laths, then stuffing the space between with dead leaves which Jessie helped to carry in sacks from the gardens. The laths were then covered over with a mixture of mud and straw, like a native hut. Stoves were lit in the building, so that the walls would dry and harden before painting.

The dried floor, which had been pounded, then flattened with a garden roller, was covered with matting, over which were spread some of Gurdjieff's impressive carpets, and the walls below the windows were hung with rugs in what was the oriental fashion, the Master told his disciples.

But Gurdjieff wasn't finished with his embellishments.

'This my special place,' he told Jessie as he created a curtained booth at the far end, facing the stage. 'I sit in here and watch performances.'

His disciples were to occupy a low divan covered with oriental carpets which ran round the room, men on one side, women on the other.

Kass hadn't had the strength to help build the study house, but Jessie took her in to see it.

'This is very impressive,' she enthused, looking up at the

collection of musical instruments hanging on the balcony.

Jessie pointed to inscriptions which Gurdjieff had had painted around the eaves, in a peculiar script that was difficult to read.

We can only strive to be able to be Christians.

Remember that work here is not for work's sake but a means.

Gurdjieff came in as they were deciphering the next inscription.

'You like?' he asked eagerly.

'I like it very much,' the New Zealand writer told him. 'It has a special atmosphere - like a magician's tent.'

'No finished,' Gurdjieff disclosed, wagging a finger. 'Special organ being built. No other like it. Octaves in quarter tones. And this.' He put his hand on the fountain. 'Every hour different perfume. All for meditation. Body and emotions in harmony.'

'That's what I want,' Kass said.

Gurdjieff asked Jessie to go with him for a walk in the gardens, taking her arm as though they were lovers.

'No too friendly with Meesus Murry,' he cautioned, stopping suddenly.

'What do you mean?' Jessie asked, wishing their Master had better command of English. He sounded like some of the old Gaelic speakers who had come into the post office, trying to use the little English they had to send a parcel overseas.

'Meesus Murry ill.'

'Then why have you moved her to that cold room in the workers' quarters?' Jessie demanded to know.

'Letters to write,' Gurdjieff said abruptly.

A week before Christmas, when she was lying on her ornate

divan above the cows, Kass asked Jessie if she would bring a pair of scissors.

'What do you want them for?' Jessie enquired when she came back with them.

'I want you to cut my hair.'

'But I'm no good at that sort of thing.'

'You've got a steady hand. I want you to cut off my fringe. I'm tired of it. I want to look different, in the same way as I want to *feel* different.'

She closed her eyes as Jessie snipped, catching the brown hair in her palm and blowing it away as if it were thistledown.

'I'm changing everything, even my writing,' Kass announced. 'I'm going to make the virtues of life as attractive as the vices. In other words, I'm going to write about goodness. You're a good person, Jessie. When I'm well I'm going to write up your story, because I've been listening carefully to what you've been telling me. A girl from Wester Ross who throws stinking parcels of game into the sea for the seals who sing to her decides to come out to France to study dancing under a strange man called Gurdjieff who offers his guests a sheep's eye as an appetizer. What do you think of that for a plot?'

'It's true to life,' Jessie conceded.

'She comes to this old château and there meets a writer who's consumptive and who lies for most of the day inhaling the breath of cows. This is beginning to sound like a fantasy.'

'Go on,' Jessie encouraged as she snipped hair, finding Kass even more attractive without the fringe.

'This writer won a lot of praise for her short stories. But really, she was only a camera, observing, recording situations. Now she's going to be a participator.' She clenched her hand

and raised her arm. 'Let good triumph!' she shouted, startling the beasts below. 'I'll write a romance. The woman on the couch falls in love with the maid who comes in to milk the cows below. When she's better they depart and live together in a country that is tolerant of such behaviour.'

'And are they happy?' Jessie wanted to know.

'Blissfully happy.'

'Don't get yourself too excited,' Jessie cautioned. 'You must save your strength. Then we'll go away together. I'll keep a few cows and pigs while you do your writing, and when you're tired I'll dance for you.'

'You promise?'

As Jessie promised Kass broke out in a burst of coughing that disturbed the cows below.

Gurdjieff was boisterous at supper, as usual provoking some of his pupils, then sitting back to see their reaction. Kass and Jessie were in his dining-room, holding hands under the table, and Jessie became aware that his gaze was on her. Afterwards he called her up to his room.

'How is Jay-see?' he asked, stroking her hair.

'I'm fine,' she said nervously.

'Jay-see very beautiful,' he continued.

'I don't think so.'

'Jay-see has many admirers. Meesus Murry. She love you.'

'We get on well together,' Jessie said, embarrassed, wishing he would remove his hand from her hair, because it was giving her a queer feeling.

'Only normal person in sex has any chance in this work.'

'Say that again,' Jessie requested him.

'No strange desires, otherwise I cannot teach, and you no

learn.'

Jessie knew what he was saying. He couldn't work with lesbians. Well, she knew she wasn't that way inclined, though she loved Kass. She wouldn't lie on the couch beside her, or go to her bed. But what did Gurdjieff's words mean with regard to Kass? Was he telling her that he couldn't do anything for Kass because of her lesbian tendencies, which he had picked up, because this man who was still stroking her hair seemed to see through people with his piercing stare?

Or was he telling her something more sinister? Was he warning her that Kass was going to die, and so she shouldn't form a romantic attachment to her? But there might of course be a simpler explanation. Gurdjieff desired Jessie himself. That was why she was watching his door nervously, in case Madame Ostrowska, Gurdjieff's wife, came in and found him stroking her hair.

Jessie went to Paris for the day and found a fishmonger who sold kippers. She fried one and carried the golden fish on the plate under the stars to Kass's room in the workers' quarters where she was writing letters.

'This is wonderful,' Kass told her, picking the bones from the succulent flesh with her fingers. 'It reminds me of Scotland. You must take me to Wester Ross when I'm well. I want to meet this friend of yours.'

'What friend?'

'The seal that comes into the bay outside the post office.'

'It probably doesn't come any more,' Jessie said sadly. 'There's nobody to throw it parcels. What kind of Christmases did you have in New Zealand?' she asked her friend.

'Not like here,' Kass said, continuing to write her letter.

Jessie noticed that she didn't like to speak about her family, and gathered that there had been some disagreement about her going to England to make her way as a writer.

'I have a letter that I've never answered,' she confided to Jessie, and went to a drawer. She smoothed it on the table. 'I got this from Lawrence when he was in Capri. This is what he wrote: "I loathe you. You revolt me stewing in your consumption."'

'That's a terrible thing to write,' Jessie said, aghast.

'There's worse. "You are a loathsome reptile - I hope you will die." I feel now that I can reply to this letter, and I'll do it in the next few days.'

'What will you write?' Jessie asked.

'I'll tell him that I've died as a reptile, but that I've been reborn as something better.'

There was no sheep's head at the Christmas party. Gurdjieff presided over a selection of fowls and sides of meat, and there was much wine. After the feast he called upon various people to perform. A woman from Italy sang an aria by Puccini.

'You dance, Jay-see!' the Master ordered.

She went up to her room to put on the kilt and plaid she had brought with her. There was now a piper at the Prieuré. He had fought with the Gordon Highlanders in the war, but couldn't settle in Aberdeenshire after the Armistice. There was something lacking in his life, so he decided to go back to France, and heard about the Institute for the Harmonious Development of Man.

He played for Jessie as she danced the Highland Fling while the others clapped and Gurdjieff leered at her. As she turned she caught sight of Kass, who looked so pale, almost transparent.

The cows still had to be milked on New Year's Eve. Kass came with her and rested on the couch above while Jessie filled the pails. Afterwards they went back through the frosty grounds arm in arm. Jessie asked her if she were writing again.

'I won't do anything until the spring,' Kass told her as they passed the almost completed study house. 'I'm tired of my little stories, like birds bred in cages. I want to do something bigger, more ambitious, and this time I want to be inside it. I'll write up your story, Jessie.'

Kass had gone back to her big bright bedroom on Gurdjieff's instructions. Jessie banked up the fire and Kass sat writing a letter to her father in New Zealand, telling him about the couch Gurdjieff had built for her above the cows. 'I feel I must look like a great Pa-woman, perched up aloft.' She told him that she was going to stay at the Institute for at least six months, and then she sealed the envelope with her contaminated spittle.

She began a letter to her husband, apologizing for having to write in pencil because she had mislaid her fountain pen. 'I have asked Mr Gurdjieff if you can come to stay, and he says that you are welcome. Come on January 8th or 9th for a few days. The new study house is being opened on the 13th. It will be a wonderful event.'

The finishing touches were being put to the study house under the excited supervision of Gurdjieff, who kept rearranging the carpets for his booth from which he would observe the performers. Jessie was helping with the painting when Kass brought her husband John Middleton Murry into the study house, to introduce him. Jessie thought he was reserved, until he took up a brush and painted beside her.

'Kass tells me how good you've been to her. I hope you'll

come to see us in London.'

Jessie's brush stopped embellishing the glass.

'Is she leaving?'

'She was going to stay, but feels she's probably got as much out of this place as it can give her. It's made a tremendous difference to her. She seems so calm, so full of love.'

Jessie resumed painting, saddened that her friend would be leaving, and resentful that her husband was taking her away. For the first time she was having to face up to how much she loved Kass.

After supper everyone assembled in the dancing room for the exercises. Kass was at her favourite place by the fire, but was restless and irritable, calling Jessie over and telling her: 'I want music. Why don't they begin?' She seemed to be remote, and Jessie had a premonition that something was wrong as the music struck up. She couldn't concentrate on the rhythm for thinking about her pale friend sitting by the fire, her body with the same transparency she had noticed before, as if she were a ghost that had wandered in from the winter chill.

Jessie was following Murry and his wife up the staircase when Kass began to run ahead.

'Be careful!' Jessie called up, knowing that Kass didn't have the strength for such exertion.

At the top of the stairs Kass's body was racked with coughing. And then, as she spun round to look down on her husband and Jessie, blood spurted from her mouth.

'I believe I'm going to die!' Jessie heard her call down to Murry.

They carried her up to her bed, and someone rushed down the stairs for the resident doctor. Jessie gave Kass a towel to try to stop the blood flowing from her mouth. The rest of that night became a dream to Jessie. She found herself hurrying up the stairs with hot water bottles as the doctor was trying to save Kass. On her way up once again the door was barred to her.

Jessie ran wailing through the grounds of the château, past the study house with its perfumed fountain that was due to be opened with much ceremony in a few days' time, and which Kass had been so looking forward to. She ran into the cowshed and stumbled up the steps, throwing herself on Kass's couch, stuffing the edge of the valuable carpet into her mouth to stifle her anguish, the cattle below lowing in distress.

Why did she have to die? She seemed to have been making such good progress. Jessie heard a noise below which was not an animal. Gurdjieff was standing there with a lantern, looking up at her.

'So you knew?' she called down.

He nodded.

'And you did nothing?' she wailed.

'I let her live here. What she wanted.'

Next day Jessie went into the small chapel. Kass's white coffin looked so bare that Jessie went back up to her room and brought back her tartan plaid, the one she danced in, to spread on the coffin.

Jessie was walking beside Murry behind the hearse drawn by two black horses adorned with funeral plumes.

'She was happy here,' she told him.

'It's not for me to pass judgement on Gurdjieff's Institute,' Murry responded. 'I don't know if her life was shortened by her coming here. But I do feel that she was reborn here in some way, and that she entered the Kingdom of Love. You helped her in that process, Jessie, and I'm very grateful.'

When they returned from the funeral Gurdjieff announced that the study house would be opened that same day.

'Surely not' Jessie protested, horrified. 'In Scotland we respect the dead. We don't do any work for the rest of that day when someone is buried.'

'Dancing not work,' Gurdjieff said with a shrug. 'Dancing is life. Death is death. Meesus Murry knew.'

'Knew what?' Jessie asked, becoming exasperated by this obtuse man.

'Knew she was going to die.'

'So why did you go to all that trouble to build her the couch above the cows?' Jessie challenged him.

'Prepare her for end. A good death.' He clapped his hands. 'Dance!' he shouted, before he went into his carpeted tent.

That night Jessie left the Institute for the Harmonious Development of Man and returned to Wester Ross and her job in the post office. Hens continued to be handed over the counter in inadequate wrapping, claws exposed, and when the seal surfaced it reminded her of Gurdjieff. Jessie never married, though she had several proposals. She read her inscribed book of short stories until she almost had them by heart, like the Biblical passages she had learned in Sunday School.

Dance with your Soul

Esther Scott travelled by steam train from her home in the Scottish Borders. It was the era where there were porters with barrows at stations to convey one's luggage to the appropriate platform, touching their peaked caps when they were tipped. Esther gave hers a shilling, a fair sum for 1936, when her wages from the hosiery mill she worked in in Hawick amounted to thirty five shillings a week. The twenty year old, whose braided blonde hair enhanced her classical beauty, had been saving for two years for this holiday to St Andrews, not to lie on the sand and eat kippers in a boarding house, but to join the Scottish Country Dance Society's Summer School.

Esther's mother was one of the first members when the Edinburgh branch of the Society was formed in 1924. Dancing was in her blood, because her people had been farm workers who, after the harvest had been cut, used to dance Corn Rigs among the sheaves in celebration. She travelled by train to Edinburgh to classes, learning how to dance reels and to turn elegantly with two hands in a strathspey. Esther was nine when she was taken up to the hall in Edinburgh and, wearing her first pair of pumps, participated in the class while her mother sat close by to give her confidence. The 1,2,3 beat of the *pas de basque* came naturally to Esther, and somehow she knew where to go in a complicated reel, as if the information were stored in her genes. As the train conveyed her home to the Borders the child would beat out the rhythm of the *pas de basque* to the cadence of the massive wheels below.

Esther's second train of the day pulled out from Edinburgh

with a sharp expulsion of steam and clanking of metal. Her suitcase (actually her mother's) was in the netting above her head. There were three other people in the compartment, one reading a newspaper. Esther saw the headline that Adolf Hitler had opened the Olympic Games in Berlin the previous day, but she had no interest in athletics. Dancing was her passion, and she had saved up for a wind-up gramophone on which she listened to her growing collection of Scottish dance music records by William Hannah and his Band. When she played his recording of the Petronella she danced in her room, and lay on her bed listening to the strathspey Loudon's Bonnie Woods and Braes, dancing it in her head with a handsome expert partner.

The train rumbled across the Forth Bridge and through the flickering spars Esther saw yachts tacking in the breezy afternoon. The world was a beautiful peaceful place to this young woman, who had her weekly dancing, her Guide group, her church where she helped her mother to arrange the floral offerings on the altar. For her first visit to the Summer School Esther was wearing a becoming straw hat, and she had on a blue dress and carried a matching bag. Though she spent most days at her machine in the hosiery mill, that didn't mean that she couldn't appreciate nature, the fields of Fife where a man on a combine pulled by a pair of horses, blinkered against distractions, was cutting an early harvest in the exceptional weather. Esther was interested in everything she saw, including several mottled cows which had stopped grazing to watch the passing train. Esther waved to them, and the woman sitting opposite her smiled.

'You evidently like cows,' her fellow traveller observed.

'I like all animals.'

Esther estimated that the woman opposite must be in her early forties, but had watched her figure. The young mill worker had a curious habit of studying a person's feet, as if she could read character from them. When she was walking through Hawick she would watch the feet of a female in front of her and say to herself: *she's a dancer. Her feet are dainty, and she moves gracefully.*

The feet of the woman who had spoken to her in the carriage were small, in sling-back two-tone shoes, white and blue.

'Where are you going on holiday?' the woman asked in an educated voice.

'To St Andrews,' Esther replied in her gentle Borders brogue.

'Is this your first visit? You'll enjoy it. It's a really beautiful place – especially in this weather.'

'I'm going to dance,' Esther informed her.

The woman leaned forward.

'At the country dance Summer School? So am I.'

'Have you been there before?' Esther asked eagerly.

'This is my ninth year. I was at the very first Summer School in 1927. I'm one of Miss Milligan's very first dancers.'

'I've heard my mother talking about Miss Milligan,' Esther said. 'She used to come through from time to time to the dance class my mother attended in Edinburgh.'

'Well, you're going to see plenty of her at the Summer School,' her fellow traveller predicted. 'She's a very inspirational lady who has been instrumental in reviving country dancing.'

At this stage in the conversation they introduced each other. The lady's name was Martha Armstrong. They alighted at Leuchars Junction to join the connection for St Andrews, and as the train curved round by the sea she pointed out their destination in the distance. For the rest of her life Esther would retain that first sight of the towers and spires of St Andrews, and would come to regard the town by the North Sea as Camelot. Even when she was working among the clattering machinery of the mill she need only close her eyes to see that cherished vista.

'Do you play golf?' Mrs Armstrong enquired as the train ran alongside immaculate links by the sea.

'I don't.'

'I'm a devotee of golf myself, and if I can slip away tomorrow from Miss Milligan's eagle eye I'm going to watch Miss Dorothy Pearson competing.'

'I haven't heard that name before,' Esther confessed.

'Miss Pearson has been English golfing champion, and is the only female competing in a field of over four hundred males in the Eden Tournament which starts tomorrow out there,' Mrs Armstrong explained, pointing out of the train window. 'She's no stranger to St Andrews. She played with the Prince of Wales before he became king.'

At the station a taxi summoned by telegram was waiting to convey Mrs Armstrong and her two hefty suitcases, and she invited Esther to accompany her on the short journey to University Hall, where the Summer School was located.

'I love this building,' Mrs Armstrong announced as the driver unloaded their luggage. 'I was a student at St Andrews over twenty years ago, during the war.'

Esther looked up at the large building with its towers and long windows. It reminded her of a mansion house in the Borders, not far from Hawick, but it looked far less sinister. When they went to register a woman with hair parted in the centre, and with round spectacles approached and embraced

Mrs Armstrong.

'Welcome back, Martha! It's wonderful to see my loyal girls again. And who is this?' she asked, turning to Esther.

She spoke her own name nervously.

'Ah, you're a new student. Welcome. I'm Miss Milligan. We'll find out which room you're in and then we'll have a chat later, Miss Scott.'

Esther was led up to her accommodation on the first floor. The single bed against the wall had been converted into a sofa, and there was a small armchair by the fire, a toasting fork leaning against its tiled surround. Hanging from the mantelpiece were different coloured tassels. At first Esther wondered if she was in the room of a foreign female, because she had seen such adornments in a film on African tribal customs. But later, when she asked Mrs Armstrong for enlightenment, she was told that a different colour of tassel was worn on a female student's trencher each year, and that they were retained as trophies. Esther was conscious of her lack of education, and so didn't ask for the definition of a trencher.

After tea and biscuits downstairs she was asked by Miss Milligan to come into the common room, where she was interrogated about her dancing experience and her background. She explained that she had been taken up to Edinburgh for lessons as a child.

'My mother attended a class you used to take. Her name before her marriage was Marion Dalgleish.'

'I never forget a good dancer,' Miss Milligan maintained. 'I'd like to see your *pas de basque* to show me you're your mother's daughter.'

Esther felt self-conscious, but with the founder at the piano, tinkling out eight bars of a reel, the new arrival did as she was requested.

'That's excellent,' she was complimented. 'You keep perfectly to the one, two, three beat, and both your feet have good turn-outs. That's something that irritates me, feet pointing straight ahead when they should be out to the side, but not too far out, as in a ballet step. In fact we have ballet dancers at the Summer School who never quite get the hang of a *pas de basque*. But you've been well taught, and I look forward to seeing you dance in a class tomorrow. I expect absolute dedication and concentration from my dancers. Do you have a brother?'

'I've two.'

'And are they interested in dancing?'

'I've tried to interest them, but they won't give it a try.'

'Keep at your brothers to join us. There are more men than ever before at the Summer School, and many of our male members hold the teaching certificate,' Miss Milligan said proudly. 'But I want more men. There are four hundred of them gathering in St Andrews for the Eden Golf Tournament, and I've a good mind to send a demonstration group of women dancers on to one of the greens to show them the country dances and persuade them to lay down their clubs and join in. I tell my dancers: you are missionaries; go out and spread the word about how wonderful Scottish country dancing is and how important a part of our tradition it is.

'We collect our national songs and tunes, so why should we neglect one of our most beautiful national possessions, our dances?' the major-domo continued. 'We collected the first dances by word of mouth, and now we do research work in the libraries, and find many interesting new tunes. Some

34

old families have presented us with tunes from their family chest, and we're always getting new ones. Country dancing has become a recognized form of social activity.'

Miss Milligan went to greet a new arrival, and Esther wandered along the corridor, past an open door where a group of women were sitting chatting. She was too shy to go in, but fortunately she met Mrs Armstrong.

'Do you like your room?' Esther was asked.

'It's very nice. It must be very cosy in the winter.'

'We wore red gowns, which were very warm because St Andrews can be a bitterly cold place. I still have my gown. I came here to study in 1913, and the following year, when the war broke out, the Hall was turned into a hospital. There were beds in the common room and the dining-room. Miss Dobson the warden told the military authorities that barriers would have to be erected to shut off the hospital to protect her female students. But it didn't come to that because the Hall wasn't required after all. There were only thirty six of us in residence. Some students had left to take up nursing and other work, thinking that the war wasn't going to last and wanting to do their bit. We planted potatoes and kept hens for their eggs as part of our war effort, but there was a shortage of coal for the fires, so the Hall was bitterly cold, and you had to wear a hat indoors. We knitted socks and gloves and sent them out to the soldiers, and to this day I've never taken up a pair of needles again. It was so sad, going to classes and realizing those male students who had been your friends wouldn't be coming back.'

Esther was put into Miss Milligan's advanced class, with a Mrs Shand from Aberdeen on the piano. The founder commented on the footwork of individual students, and one young woman started to cry when she was told that she was 'grievously off-beat.' But Esther received encouraging smiles from the dumpy major-domo, whose eye glasses flashed with the sun streaming in the window and who, like a female version of the Pied Piper, led the class round the room for skip-change steps. There was much more criticism of sluggish feet, and one young woman was told: 'the way you're swinging your arms, you would think you were a traffic policeman. Dancing is about the deportment of the whole body. It's not enough to get from A to B on the dance floor: you must move with grace and precision, but at the same time with what I call controlled abandon, to express the spirit of the dance. Come here, please, Miss Scott.'

Esther wondered what her shortcoming was, but Miss Milligan wanted her to demonstrate the *pas de basque*.

'Note how lightly the feet tread the floor, but how beautifully they are in tempo to the piano. And when Miss Scott moves into a figure of eight – eight bars please, Mrs Shand - the right foot is extended without loss of balance or grace. Show us please, Miss Scott.'

Esther described a solo figure of eight on the floor and, as she passed the watching faces, saw envy as well as admiration. However, at the end of the class Mrs Armstrong was generous enough to compliment her.

'You're going to be one of Miss Milligan's special girls.'

'What does that mean?' Esther asked apprehensively.

'It means that you can do no wrong and that she'll use you to demonstrate what she wishes lesser mortals like myself to achieve.'

The mill girl wasn't sure that she welcomed Miss Milligan's attention, and would have preferred to be left alone to dance.

36

But the other members of the class were nice to her at meal times. A young woman from another class asked her if she would be prepared to give her private lessons in the art of the *pas de basque*.

'I'll pay you.'

But it wasn't a matter of money. Suppose that Miss Milligan found out that one of her students was giving lessons to another? Wasn't that the founder's task, and that of the teachers she had trained, to improve their footwork? Esther understood that Miss Milligan was autocratic and wouldn't tolerate interference. But this young woman had appealed to Esther for help, so how could she refuse? In a whisper she invited the dancer up to her bedroom that evening before supper.

Her name was Judi Macpherson from Canada.

'The fair-haired man in your class is my brother Gregor. I'm in the beginners' class.'

'You've both come all the way from Canada?' Esther asked in wonder.

'From Vancouver. There isn't a Scottish Country Dance branch there, but we visited Edinburgh three years ago and went to a class out of curiosity, and caught the bug. There are other people in Vancouver who dance. We thought we'd come to the Summer School because we want to train as teachers of country dancing. But my teacher doesn't like my *pas des basque*.'

Esther gave her a lesson in the bedroom, and within the hour there was a marked improvement in the attractive Canadian's setting step and also in her confidence.

'You're wonderful,' she enthused. 'You demonstrate so well and are so patient. You should train as a teacher.'

Esther had never considered this possibility, but didn't tell her pupil that she didn't feel she had the confidence. Instead she refused the payment proffered and swore her to secrecy about her tuition. The following morning the teacher commented on the improvement in Miss Macpherson's *pas de basque*.

'You must have stayed up all night practising.'

Esther was studying Judi's brother Gregor across the set in her class. At twenty five he was two years older than his sister, with close cropped fair hair and a frank appealing face. He was wearing a kilt of his clan tartan, and as Esther watched him taking his turn she saw that he was a natural dancer, with a most pleasing light tread of a setting step, and an attractive way of smiling at his partner when he turned her by the hand. When Miss Milligan taught a strathspey Esther was paired with the Canadian dancer, and found that their rhythms seem to meld.

Miss Milligan sought out Esther after lunch.

'Her teacher was telling me how much Miss Macpherson's *pas de basque* has improved. It's your doing, isn't it?'

Esther was overcome by fear as the eyes behind the round lenses fixed on her, and her thought was: *she's going to send me home for daring to take over as a teacher, when I'm not qualified.*

'She asked me to, Miss Milligan, and I thought there was no harm in it.'

'No harm in it? It's worked wonders. I've been thinking about you. You're such a gifted dancer that I want you to train as a teacher.'

'A teacher, Miss Milligan?' she enquired apprehensively. 'What would that involve?'

'I'm not talking about training you as a teacher of Scottish country dancing, though of course that would come into it. I'd like you to study to become a primary school teacher, so that you can teach our kind of dancing to children, because I'm sure you have the skills and patience to be a big success. Who knows, you may become a lecturer in physical education, one of my team at Jordanhill. Will you think about it?'

'I can't afford it, Miss Milligan.'

'Don't worry about that side of it. There are ways and means of finding money. You'll come to live in Glasgow, to study with me, and I'll arrange accommodation for you. Now tell me: what qualifications did you take in school?'

'I was studying for my Leaving Certificate examinations when a job came up in the hosiery mill, and I took it.'

'Then you can pick up your studies again and sit your examinations next spring. It's a challenge, but life is full of challenges – like reviving Scottish country dancing.'

Esther was in a daze at the implications of this transformation in her life. Her head thumping from the incessant machinery, how many times had she wished herself out of the mill? How many times, in the dark Border nights, going home through the eerie historic streets, with only a torch to light the way, had she wished that she lived in the city? But this momentous move would have to have the approval of her parents.

She had taken a liking to Mrs Armstrong and confided Miss Milligan's plan to her over supper in the dining-room where the older woman had eaten her wartime rations over twenty years before, dancing with the other females afterwards in order to keep warm as well as to keep up their spirits.

'It's an excellent idea and I'm sure you'll make a splendid success of it,' Mrs Armstrong reassured her. 'In fact I may be able to help. I've a large house in Glasgow with a garden flat which I thought of renting to students. It's in a very pleasant location, overlooking Kelvingrove Park. I'd be very pleased if you would occupy it – at no charge. I'll give you my telephone number and you can come through to Glasgow to see the flat.'

For the first time Esther Scott felt that life held exciting possibilities for her. She had found two people who believed in her, and who wanted to open doors into a new world for her. But that wasn't the only thought that made her dance with even more grace and 'controlled abandon' in Miss Milligan's exacting class: she was attracted to the male Canadian dancer who stood opposite her, his feet turned out, arms relaxed by his side, listening to the teacher's instructions for a complicated reel and dancing it with ease, except for one addition – he winked at her as he passed her. Fortunately Miss Milligan's eyes were elsewhere at the time, on slipshod steps. Gregor's sister Judi came up to Esther's room each evening for cocoa, telling her that the family had been cleared from the Highlands ninety years before and been shipped to Canada, finding it so hard to exist in Nova Scotia that they moved to the west coast, to Vancouver, where they prospered sufficiently to own a hotel. Gregor was studying engineering at university and also learning to fly.

'To fly?' Esther asked.

'Yes, he has an obsession with planes, and his ambition is to own his own plane. He says that he can fly himself to engineering projects all over Canada. I love my brother dearly. He likes you.'

This last item of information was added so swiftly that Esther was taken by surprise.

'He's a very graceful dancer.'

'He said to me: "try to find out about her."'

'To find out what?' Esther asked apprehensively.

'Where you come from, and what you do.'

Before she replied Esther pondered: *if I say I work in a mill he won't be interested in me.*

'I'm going to become a primary teacher, studying in Glasgow under Miss Milligan.'

'That's wonderful. Where is your home?'

'I live in the Borders with my parents.'

That amount of information seemed to satisfy Judi for relaying to her brother.

'And what do you do?' Esther asked her interrogator.

'I help my parents to run our hotel. My mother doesn't keep well. We have thirty letting bedrooms and a restaurant that's very popular, with a view over the water. I have to do with the restaurant, to make sure that the diners are satisfied with our service and our charges. Oh God, that sounds so pompous. Basically I show people to their tables and open bottles of wine, and when someone has had too much to drink I go up to their table, put the cork back into the bottle and call a taxi. I'd have liked to go to university to become a veterinary surgeon, because I adore animals, but my compensation is that I have four cats and two dogs, not to mention a very garrulous parrot.'

It was time to go to bed, to be fresh for Miss Milligan's class the following day. Esther stood at her window, looking out into the grounds of the Hall where Mrs Armstrong and other students had planted potatoes in the shortages of war. This had been a momentous day, with Miss Milligan's proposal for the transformation of her life; and there was the image of Gregor flying his plane across the Canadian prairies to retire with.

The following afternoon she went for a walk with Judi and Gregor along the West Sands. A large crowd were cheering the competitors in the Eden Tournament in which the sole female entrant Miss Dorothy Pearson had knocked her first drive only fifty yards, but had redeemed herself, thrilling the crowd as her spoon club lifted the second shot on to the green, the third holing it. The three dancers returned to the town, to afternoon tea in the elegance of the Victoria Café, its garden with a pergola covered with roses alongside the street, the three-tier silver plated stand on the table offering scones and cakes. This was the best week of the mill girl's life, and when it was time to go home she was tearful, hugging the Canadian brother and sister.

'We must keep in contact and come again next year,' Gregor said.

Having brought her suitcase downstairs, Esther stood in the common room which was deserted, most of the dancers having left. The sight of a discarded pump on the floor made her want to cry, because she could have stayed dancing in the elegant building with the same friendly folk for the rest of that summer.

'I'll make enquiries about your course and write to you,' Miss Milligan said at her back. 'And I hope when you return here next summer you'll be ready to start training to be a primary teacher.'

When she trudged home from the mill through rain and snow in winter Esther was weary, but somehow she found the energy to open the text book which would help to take her to Glasgow and a qualification as a primary teacher. One night a week she went out to a class in mathematics, which had never been her strong subject, though she seemed to know instinctively where she should be at a certain bar in a dance set without having to count them. Fractions proved particularly tricky, and some nights she couldn't get to sleep for seeing them looming in her anxious mind. When it reached the stage of tearfulness she went to her old teacher, Miss Hardie, and begged for assistance. But she liked reading, so writing compositions was a pleasure. There was a young man, Martin Elliot, a mechanic in the mill, to whom she was attracted. The lace frame machine she operated made delicate lingerie, the pattern determined by a rotating belt of punched cards, and when the belt broke down she called for the mechanic, because idle time was money lost.

'I see you reading a book at dinner time,' he remarked as he worked on her machine.

'That's because I'm studying.'

'Studying for what?'

'I'm going to become a primary teacher,' she told him proudly.

'So you'll be leaving the mill?' he asked, genuine disappointment in his voice.

'I hope that June will be my last month.'

He wanted to tell her: *I'll miss you*, and that, as he serviced his motorbike in the garden shed in the dark night, he thought about her, and wondered, as he polished the chromium reverently until his pensive face showed, how to ask her if she would like a ride on the pillion. He prolonged the repair to her machine so that he could admire her by side glances as she stood by, waiting to resume work. But the supervisor came up to warn him to hurry up, and as he got the belt going again he knew that it was hopeless: she would go on to a new life elsewhere and he would age, a mechanic for life in the mill.

Which came first, the love of a man or dancing? she asked herself as she finished another pair of embroidered knickers. Could one have a husband who didn't dance, and go out in the evening, leaving him until she returned from her exhilarating reels? It wouldn't be fair to him, especially if there were children to look after. She couldn't give up dancing. If she married, it would have to be to a man she loved and who was a good dancer.

'Would you like a ride on my bike on Sunday?' the voice from the floor asked tremulously.

'I'd love to, Martin, but I have to study, if I'm to pass my exams and become a teacher.'

She was truly sorry as she watched him going away among the clattering machines in his overalls and cap, a decent young man who deserved a nice girl who didn't have a selfish obsession.

The light burned late into the night in Esther's bedroom under the snow-laden eaves, and one of the enterprizing supervisors went to the mill on skis. She worked out fractions on the frosty window with her finger. The night school classes had been cancelled, but she bent over her text books. She had a Christmas card from Miss Milligan. 'Dance with your soul!' it exhorted. In the first week of January the temperature dropped drastically. The streets were treacherous sheets of ice, and coming home chilled to the bone from the mill she slipped. As she lay under the statue of the Cornet holding the standard aloft in Central Square, depicting the Riding of the Marches, she was crying, not only at the searing pain in her right ankle, but with fear that if it were broken, that was the end of her dancing. She lay on the pavement, the cold going through to her bones as she called out for help, but the street was deserted on such a night, the curtains of houses closed. She heard a jig being played on a piano in the tenement at her back, as if to taunt her immobility. Was she going to contact pneumonia and die? Ten minutes later, when she seemed to be drifting into sleep, she heard the clip-clop of a horse. She called out and the cart pulled up beside her. The animal's warm breath was on her face as the driver jumped down.

'What's happened, lassie?'

She told him that she feared her ankle was broken, and he lifted her carefully on to the cart and conveyed her to the Cottage Hospital. She had to wait on a bed because another casualty of the ice was being attended to. When the doctor eventually saw her he diagnosed a break and told her that she would have to remain in hospital overnight so that she could be X-rayed in the morning.

'But my parents don't know I've had an accident.'

He brought her paper and pen, and she wrote them a note, telling them that she was 'all right,' and warning her father not to venture out in such treacherous conditions. The note was delivered by ambulance, and when it returned half an hour later her father was in it. She didn't want a fuss. She wanted to sleep in the bed they had put her into, and she worried about him getting home, but the doctor said that the ambulance would take him back.

The X-ray confirmed a fracture, and Esther's leg up to the knee was put into plaster. Fellow workers from the mill came bearing gifts of fruit and sweets. Martin the mechanic arrived, handing her a bag of tablet his mother had made for the invalid, but it burst over the bed covering before she received it. Scarlet with shame, he gathered up the pieces and put them on the bedside cabinet, then sat by the bed, kneading his cap between his hands as if he had a morbid fear of hospital. She asked him how work was going at the mill, and he told her that they were very busy with festive season orders. She had to do most of the talking, as if he had a speech impediment. She saw him take a pencil from his pocket and tap it against his teeth pensively. Then he leaned over and printed on the plaster: GET WELL SOON.

'I like that!' Esther said laughing, 'and when I'm well you can take me for a ride on your motorbike. Will I be safe with you?' she teased this gentle visitor.

'I never go above forty.'

But when he had gone and the ward was settling for the night she became very depressed. Miss Milligan had complimented her on her perfect balance at the Summer School in St Andrews, but she wouldn't have it any more after her fracture. Perhaps she wouldn't be able to dance again because of the damage, though the doctor assured her that it would heal, with rest. She was taken home by ambulance the following day and hobbled, half carried up to her bedroom by her father. She lay on the horsehair mattress under the sloped ceiling, writing to Miss Milligan, telling her about her fractured ankle.

'I'm afraid that I won't make a good teacher of dance now, after my accident, so I won't come to Glasgow to be a primary teacher.'

The following weekend Jean Milligan climbed the stairs in her brogues to Esther's bedroom, bearing chocolates and a book of new dances.

'What's this nonsense about you not coming to train as a primary teacher under me? Of course you're going to come. I had a girl who broke her ankle falling from wall bars in the gymnasium a few years ago and she's still a beautiful dancer.

How long are you going to be off work?'

'About six weeks. I said that I could go in and work my machine, but the foreman said it was too dangerous.'

'Quite right. Will you get paid?'

'No.'

'Then I'm going to help out.'

'I couldn't take it, Miss Milligan,' the invalid said earnestly.

'You'll do as you're told, young lady. Don't think you're going to lie there dozing all day. You've got exams to sit, so get your text books out. I'll be back in a fortnight to check on your progress.'

The doyen of Scottish country dancing reappeared on the due date, in a fur coat, and with Christmas gifts for her protégée, a dressing-gown and a pair of knitted gloves. She wasn't a woman for small talk, and instead utilized her visit by taking a French textbook from the bedside table and questioning the invalid on nouns.

If I asked you: *ouvrez la porte*, what would you do?'

'I would go to the door and let you in or out,' the pupil replied.

'Good. Now how would you say: I wish to dance?'

Esther felt sad when her tutor had departed. She had grown fond of the middle-aged woman and regarded her as a kind and caring aunt. But at the Summer School she had seen the determination of the woman who would brook no opposition in her crusade to revive Scottish country dancing. She was inspirational, but she was also intimidating.

Several weeks later the plaster-cast was removed at the hospital. Miss Milligan had motored through for the occasion, but instead of giving Esther a lift home, she walked with her through the streets. 'You need to get that ankle working again. It'll feel weak at the beginning, but it'll strengthen. I'll show you some exercises you can do.'

Esther duly performed these in the back yard among the dustbins in the late winter sunshine. She returned to the mill, and on a Sunday afternoon Martin's motorbike arrived to take her for a run. She clung to his waist as they drove through the Border countryside, stopping at a tearoom with a tier of cakes in the centre of the table, and a silver pot.

'When will you get back to your dancing?' he enquired.

'I'm going up to the class in Edinburgh next week,' she told him apprehensively.

She was in a state of trepidation as she bent to tie her pumps round her ankles. The teacher always had a warm-up session and advised Esther 'to take it gently, and sit down if you feel your ankle beginning to trouble you.' The big test was the *pas de basque*. She felt that there was a lack of lift in her step, and this worried her, but the heaviness disappeared, and in the reel the Flowers of Edinburgh she moved with her former grace and with perfect timing as though her ankle had never suffered injury. That night she wrote to Miss Milligan to tell her of her triumph.

'It's thanks to your encouragement and care that I've recovered so quickly. I'm working hard for my examinations because I'm looking forward so much to studying under you. My only worry is that I'll let you down in some way. Love, Esther.'

In reply she received a card on which Miss Milligan had drawn her likeness as a dancer doing the *pas de basque*, and enclosing a ten shilling note. 'Do buy yourself something to celebrate your triumphant return to the world of Scottish country dancing.'

On a spring day Esther walked into a classroom and sat down at a desk to take her Leaving Certificate examinations for entry to Jordanhill College. She placed on her desk beside the inkwell a tiny dance pump which Miss Milligan had made for her out of felt as a good luck charm. As she was writing the series of papers she had the strange feeling that her mentor was standing behind her chair, encouraging her to concentrate, to draw from memory all that she had learned from the textbooks over the previous year. When the envelope arrived with the results she was very nervous about opening it, but her father encouraged her.

'I've passed!'

She ran to the phone box to call Miss Milligan with the news.

'Well done! I knew you could do it.'

In early August Esther was back in St Andrews for the Summer School.

'Didn't I tell you that there would be no lasting effect from your broken ankle?' Miss Milligan said to her after the morning class, when a new difficult dance had been learned, though not without a show of frustration on the teacher's part. 'When you are standing in the set, please keep your feet turned out, Miss Davidson! It's so much more elegant, and makes it much easier when you are called upon to set. And you, Miss Clark, as you're travelling round the set, don't keep looking at your feet. That's a sign of lack of confidence. Your feet will still be there at the end of the dance. Hold your head level, look straight ahead, smile as you engage with other dancers. Scottish country dancing is not a solitary recreation. We work as a team – a harmonious team, alert, alive, considerate of our fellow dancers.'

Mrs Armstrong from Glasgow was also attending Summer

School, and she and Esther took walks along the West Sands in the afternoons. She repeated her offer of the use of her garden flat in Glasgow when Esther came to college.

'What do you think of Miss Milligan?' Mrs Armstrong asked.

Esther repeated how Miss Milligan had encouraged her to study to become a teacher, and revealed how, after she had broken her ankle, the queen of Scottish country dancing had driven over treacherous Borders roads to visit her.

'She has a very good heart, though she doesn't always show it,' Mrs Armstrong conceded. 'But then again, she's taken on a formidable task, not only reviving, but also expanding Scottish country dancing. She doesn't do it single-handed, of course – she has Mrs Ysobel Stewart our co-founder to help her, and also Lord James Stewart Murray - but she comes across as a one-woman band. It's her whole life.'

The Canadian brother and sister Gregor and Judi Macpherson had crossed the Atlantic by liner to attend Summer School. Gregor told Esther proudly that he now had his wings and that he was considering joining the Canadian Air Force after he graduated in engineering from McGill.

'You must come across to Vancouver to visit us,' Judi urged. 'And bring your dancing pumps, because people, especially those of Scottish descent, are beginning to show a big interest in Scottish country dancing over there.'

Esther loved being back in University Hall. It was full, with a hundred and twenty dancers attending the Summer School, and every available room in the Hall used for teaching, as well as the University's gymnasium. She sat in the dining-room with the Macphersons, and in the evening she either went to Judi's room for cocoa, or else invited the Canadian to hers.

'My brother's very fond of you,' Judi revealed. 'When he's home from university he never stops talking about you. "What do you think Esther will be doing in Scotland? Will she be dancing? Will she have learned new dances?"'

'I like your brother very much,' Esther told her friend without any show of embarrassment. 'But I worry about him flying.'

'So do I, but he assures me that the design of planes is improving all the time and that they're becoming safer and safer. Besides, he has a parachute if he has to bale out. You *must* come to Canada to see us. You can stay at our hotel – a room with a view of Vancouver Harbour. When will you come?'

Esther saw no necessity to tell her that she couldn't afford the fare by sea or by air on her wages. It was hard enough, putting money aside for the Summer School after she had paid her parents her board and lodgings, so she responded: 'it's difficult for me, with my commitments,' and then she changed the subject to dancing.

Years on, those pre-war summers in St Andrews would be preserved in a special light, like sepia photographs, and long afterwards, she would lie in a room with the window open in another place, scenting the honeysuckle in the garden of University Hall. Even the fork by the tiled fire which she used to toast the muffins she bought in the bakers in St Andrews would come to have mystical properties, like a holy relic. For the rest of her life she would recall these conversations with the Canadian brother and sister about glaciers and grizzly bears and whales that sprayed their damp breath from their blow-holes. And, at times of sorrow and loss she would be so grateful for these memories that had become inviolate.

As she made the last pair of embroidered knickers on the frame Esther felt sad about leaving the mill where she had worked since leaving school at fifteen. As the punched card created the pattern on the fabric she saw Martin the mechanic moving among the machines with a spanner sticking from the back pocket of his overalls. Though her machine was working perfectly, he came across.

'I'm sorry you're leaving, Esther.' It was the first time he had found the fluency to address her by her name.

'So am I. I've made good friends here – including you.' She wanted to say: *I'm going to better myself*, but that sounded cruel, because where was the betterment for this earnest young man, a slave to the machines? *Why don't you leave and get yourself a job in a garage*? But that was easier said than done in the Depression, with idle men leaning against the walls of Hawick.

'You'll come back?' he asked anxiously.

She laughed. 'I'm not going to abandon my parents – or Hawick. I'll be back in the holidays, looking for a ride on your motorbike.'

'I don't have it any more.'

'Why? It was your pride and joy.'

'I've bought a horse.'

This news was so momentous that discussion of it had to be postponed until the lunch break, when they sat together, eating their sandwiches.

'All my friends have horses and I felt out of it,' he confided to her. 'I like horses.'

'Where did you buy it?'

'From a local farmer. It's a young mare called Susan. His daughter rode it but she got married and went to live in a city in England.'

'Riding a horse is very different from riding a motorbike,' Esther cautioned the novice.

'I like it a lot better, because it's a living thing – and it's much cheaper to feed. I go riding in the hills with my friends on Sundays.'

'I'm glad you've found such an interest, with your friends.'

'Would you like to meet Susan?'

She almost burst out laughing, because it sounded like an invitation to be introduced to his sister. But he was a sensitive soul, so she said: 'of course I would. When?'

'What about Sunday morning, by the war memorial in the park?'

'All right. What time?'

'Half past nine?'

'That's fine, because I can still go to church.'

When she arrived in the park on the Sunday, her Bible in her gloved hand, a straw hat pinned to her hair, he was standing beside his horse at the war memorial, transformed by a hard hat and breeches into a different person from the mill mechanic.

'Hullo, Susan,' she said, patting the neck of the chestnut mare which regarded her with a shrewd eye. 'She's very docile.'

'She's a darling.'

It seemed a strange word to use for a horse, but he had no girlfriend, and found communicating difficult, so Esther could appreciate why this creature towering above her was his ideal companion. As he watched Esther's face as she spoke to the horse, he remembered a ballad that his grandfather used to recite about a Border lad who had fallen hopelessly in love with a local lass, to the furious opposition of her parents. He had ridden up to her house and lifted her on to the saddle in front of him, galloping away to bliss in another shire. But the mill mechanic knew that he didn't have the courage for such a deed, riding with this lovely young woman through the streets of Hawick as the church bells called the faithful. Nor did he have the skill, because he had walked his horse to the park, and would walk it back to the place where he was to meet his friends before going riding with them in the hills around Hawick.

'We'll meet when I come home on holiday from college,' she promised as she went to answer the summons of the bells.

Esther Scott arrived in Glasgow on a balmy day in September 1937. Miss Milligan was at the station in her car, to convey her to Mrs Armstrong's residence in the Park area, a most imposing townhouse overlooking Kelvingrove Park and with commanding views of the city. Mrs Armstrong, left wealthy by her stockbroker husband's intuitive investments, had had the garden level flat renovated and redecorated for the young dancer she had befriended at St Andrews. The walls were white, the single bed in the bright room with a new mattress and linen. The lounge had a sofa, a wireless, and there would be constant hot water for the bath. When she had unpacked she was taken upstairs to supper by her hostess.

'I want you to be happy when you're with me,' Mrs Armstrong began after her maid had served the high tea of haddock, to be eaten with silver cutlery. 'At the same time I would like to be told if you go out in the evening to dance classes or lectures, because I feel a certain responsibility towards your parents. Unfortunately there are undesirable people, even in areas of this city you would think were safe. Only last week I witnessed a vicious attack with a razor down on Sauchiehall Street. There are rival gangs in the poorer areas like the Gorbals who sometimes come into the centre to battle and cause trouble and damage to people as well as property, so do take care, Esther.'

She slept on a horsehair mattress, on a pillow stuffed with feathers, and on the first morning puzzled for fifteen minutes how to operate a gadget she had never seen before, an electric kettle. There was porridge in a cupboard and a bottle of milk in a chilled white compartment. She had been told to go down to Sauchiehall Street, to get a tram that would take her out to Jordanhill. Everything about this city was new and exciting. Horses and carts and motor vehicles manoeuvred on the congested streets, and women and men swung on and off the trams with amazing agility, as though they were accomplished gymnasts. As she walked up the avenue to Jordanhill College she felt intimidated by its sheer size. How would she fare in this new environment? Would she make friends, and would she understand the lectures?

Miss Milligan was waiting to introduce her to Jordanhill, to some of the lecturers who would help her to become a primary teacher, and to remind her that Scottish country dancing was to be an essential part of her training and her career. The new student was also told that she was expected to attend Miss Milligan's Tuesday dance class from 5.30 p.m. to 7.00 p.m. 'I'll be calling on you from time to time to demonstrate steps.'

Within the week Esther felt that she had been at Jordanhill for months because her fellow students were so friendly. At the end of the day they went down the driveway together in the autumnal darkness, and on the tram Esther looked out on to the lighted streets, citizens hurrying homewards, men with umbrellas and bowlers marching purposively, women with shopping bags to feed families. She made her own supper and settled on the sofa to an evening of study, but left free half an hour before bedtime so that she could absorb the new Scottish country dances in Book 9 pocket edition. She was pleased to note that the Duchess of Atholl's Slipper had been 'Collected in the Border country,' and she went through the steps of the elegant strathspey with an imaginary partner. Miss Milligan had taught the very old reel Cadgers in the Canongate in her Tuesday class, concentrating on bars 17 to 24 because 'the timing of the *pas de basque* steps has to be precise, otherwise you end up behind the music.' Esther was led into her sleep on her comfortable bed by the Canadian pilot guiding her with firm hands in the square formation of the poussette in My Love She's But a Lassie Yet.

When snow covered the driveway to the college Esther took great care, holding on to the arm of a friend, her briefcase in her other hand. She loved the diverse subjects they had to study in order to give young children an all-round education, but Miss Milligan's physical education class was easily her favourite. The major-domo directed the class from the centre of the gymnasium as they hung from the wall-bars, 'like a tribe of monkeys,' one of the young women remarked. But there was always time to teach dance technique, or a new dance. Esther could appreciate why Miss Milligan was strict with them, and sometimes severe, because she wanted them to pass on skills to their primary pupils so that the dances she had helped to revive would endure in coming generations with elegance and precision. This was the agile spinster's mission in life, and it replaced any disappointment that she hadn't married. After all, didn't she have her 'boys,' the male students of physical education and hygiene whom she was turning into accomplished dancers by a combination of discipline and sarcasm? 'You, Harry, are not leaving this College to shame me with such dreadful footwork. Stay behind at the end of the class and I'll give you some exercises to do. Feet turned out, heads up: look as if you've spotted a pretty girl across the street, and not as if you're going to the dentist with an abscess!'

On Saturday afternoons Esther went shopping with her friends. She had a generous bursary from a Hawick mill owner who wished to see the young of the town improve themselves, though it would take them away from the machines that had made his fortune. Also, she didn't have to pay anything to Mrs Armstrong for her garden flat. Esther was conscious that her friends didn't have the same resources, so she was careful to buy clothes for the same prices which they could afford, though one luxury she allowed herself was a fur-lined hat which came down over her ears. Once a month, on a Saturday afternoon, Esther descended from the heights of Park Terrace to meet Miss Milligan in James Craig's tearoom on Sauchiehall Street, with its tempting confections, and appealing Scottish paintings on the walls. The conversation was confined to Jordanhill and dancing, with the elder woman satisfying herself that her protégée was applying herself to her studies, and that her missionary zeal to spread Scottish country dancing would be perpetuated through her young friend.

When Esther went home for the Christmas holidays she felt she no longer belonged in that drab house in Hawick, and as she lay on the bed under the sloping wall she thought of her bright spacious bedroom in Glasgow. She felt ashamed of these sentiments, and excused herself from her parents' company, maintaining that she had to study.

'Surely you can take time off your books for Christmas,' her mother remarked as she brought her up a cup of tea. 'Mr Hogg is coming to see us this afternoon. Will you come down and tell him how you're getting on at College? He's always asking after you.'

She went down reluctantly to say hello to the middle-aged minister whom her parents venerated with a respect almost approaching fear.

'What church do you go to in Glasgow?' he began.

'I go to the one at Park with Mrs Armstrong, who owns the flat I live in.'

'And are the sermons stimulating?' he persisted.

'Very stimulating,' she answered, though her mind often wandered during them to the dance she had attended the night before.

'It's important to keep up your faith,' the solemn visitor decreed. 'You'll be teaching children when you qualify, and they have to be told about God, because some parents neglect their religion, and some have abandoned it.'

'Esther's a very good dancer,' her mother told him proudly.

'That's all very well, but prayer is far more important, and besides, dancing encourages sin.'

'What do you mean – sin?' Esther challenged him.

'Couples hold each other too close.'

'The kind of dancing I do, we don't hold each other close, Mr Hogg. The only parts of our bodies that are touching are our hands. Surely that's allowed.'

She went with her parents to the watchnight service and

endured a long bleak sermon in the chilly church with its forbidding stained glass windows. Surely worship was supposed to be more joyful, like dancing, with people leaving the church exhilarated, instead of cold and depressed. She gave her parents the presents she had bought for them in Glasgow – a warm cardigan for her mother, the first pair of slippers her father had ever owned. She met one of the mill girls in the street, but the machines and the lace-patterned lingerie belonged in a world she had left behind, almost as if she had never worked there. On Hogmanay Martin Elliot the mechanic came to first-foot her, bringing the traditional lump of coal and whisky for her father.

'How are you getting on at the mill?' she asked the shy visitor as she gave him a kiss and cake.

'I miss my talks with you. Some of the girls have been paid off because of the slump.'

I might have been one of them if I'd stayed, Esther thought to herself.

'How is your horse?'

'She's fine. I went to see her this morning before work.'

'Do you still go out riding at the weekend, even with snow on the hills?'

'We were out last weekend. It was cold, but the horses seem to like it.'

She was making all the conversation, and she saw that he would never develop as a person, because he accepted his situation.

'How are you getting on in Glasgow?'

'I love College.'

He wanted to say: *I suppose you've got a boyfriend*, but the answer would be too painful.

'Have you ever been to Glasgow, Martin?'

'Never.'

'You should come through to see me one weekend.'

But she knew that he wouldn't, because he wasn't adventurous, his life contained by the Border hills.

She returned to Glasgow early in the new year, to her bright warm flat, supper with her hostess, and tea with Miss Milligan in James Craig's.

'This is going to be a very busy year,' the doyen pronounced as she quartered her scone. 'I've been asked to provide dancers for the Empire Exhibition which will be staged in Glasgow from May until September, and I want you in one of the teams, Esther. It's going to be a tremendous opportunity to show off Scottish country dancing to the world.'

Miss Milligan trained her teams hard for the Empire Exhibition, going over the smallest details of the dances again and again until she was satisfied with the coordinated performance. The teams were drawn from other branches of the Society as well as Glasgow, so she was travelling constantly. On fine spring evenings Esther took her dance books down to Kelvingrove Park and worked at the movements until they came naturally to her, those taking the air stopping to admire the good-looking young woman with the graceful steps. Male students from Maclay Hall came down to sit on the slope and applaud her, and one of them brought her an ice cream cone. It was wonderful to be alive on such an evening, in the balmy air, with her audience of appreciative students and citizens. Could life ever get any better, she wondered as she went home in the dusk to make herself cocoa before bed, massaging her feet before she lay down, because Miss Milligan said that it was vital for a dancer to take care of his or her feet.

Esther was in the demonstration team for the opening ball for the Exhibition, and she danced in a white dress at the Clachan, the recreated Highland village. It was a disappointing summer of frequent downpours, but she loved performing for the crowds among the sleek towers and cascading fountains, with Miss Milligan sitting watching for shoddy footwork, the failure to acknowledge one's partner with a smile.

Martin the mechanic came forward.

'You came to Glasgow!' she exclaimed in delight. 'How did you know I was dancing in the Exhibition?'

'I met your mother in the street and she told me.'

'Did you come by horse?'

'I came by train,' he said solemnly.

'Let's go and have some tea,' she said, linking her arm through his.

They went to a tea room in a pavilion and ordered cream horns. As she licked hers Esther was studying her companion. Was he in love with her? He must be very fond of her, to make such a journey beyond Hawick. But was she in love with him? Could you be in love with two men at the same time, because she was very attracted to Gregor the Canadian aviator? He seemed such a romantic figure, flying a plane over the snow-laden forests of Vancouver, dancing reels and strathspeys with such style and joy at the Summer School. But it wasn't fair to compare Gregor and Martin. This was a sincere young man sitting opposite her, wondering how he should eat his cream horn (there was some cream on his nose) until she took it from his hands, and, using her teaspoon, scooped out the contents and fed it to him. Afterwards they took a tram to the station where she saw him off, and before his head disappeared into the window he had blown her a kiss, or was he checking his mouth had no cream on it?

She went home to Hawick. On the first Friday after the first Monday in June she was wakened by the bells of St Mary's striking six as the drum and fife band marched through the streets, blowing and beating out the Hawick anthem 'Teribus.' It was the day of the Common Riding. The first history lesson Esther had in secondary school was about the Common Riding. She had to copy from the blackboard into her exercise book: *the ceremony dates back to 1514, and represents both the capture in battle of an English flag by the youth of Hawick and the ancient custom of marking the boundaries of the common land.* She put on a cotton dress and straw hat with azure and gold ribbons, the Common Riding colours which were hung from balconies and strung across the streets. Esther had been attending this ceremony since infancy, sitting on her father's shoulders, and it was still a thrilling spectacle.

'The Cornet's coming!' the crowd shout.

The young man chosen to lead the riders as they move on horseback round the boundaries of the common land is carrying the flag, representing the one captured from the English centuries before. Esther sees that it's Martin the mill mechanic, the young man who had such difficulty consuming a cream horn at the Empire Exhibition the previous month. How has this shy slow man transformed himself into a swift graceful rider, the flag streaming in the cloudless sky above him as he sits on his mare outside the town, singing the 'Old Common Riding Song' in a clear pleasant voice, reading the words from inside the top hat he holds in front of him. He sees Esther, waves the hat at her before galloping off through the streets. Later, when he returns from Riding the Marches, he has the Cornet's Lass, a local girl who had been in school with Esther, sitting in front of his saddle, his arm round her comely waist. Esther is both glad and jealous.

She returned to Glasgow for her second year of study, attending Miss Milligan's class, learning an exciting new dance from Book 10, General Stuart's Reel. In late October, Esther, with over a thousand others, processed into the vast elegance of St Andrew's Halls to pipers from the 2nd Battalion the Seaforth Highlanders, for the ball to close the Empire Exhibition, an unforgettable experience of superb music and elegant dancing. Afterwards, Miss Milligan, who was also present, took her arm.

"I'm afraid that you won't be able to go to the next Summer School in St Andrews. There's an International Folk Dance Festival in Stockholm in the first week of August, and I want you in the dance team I'm sending to Sweden.'

Esther tried to visualize the map slung over the blackboard in her primary school. Wasn't Sweden far in the frozen north?

'These will be the most important demonstrations of Scottish country dancing we've given so far,' Miss Milligan enthused. 'It's an international stage, and we need to spread word of our wonderful dancing tradition to as many countries as possible, so that they feel inspired to set up branches.'

Esther was awed by the size of the world and enchanted by the experience when she went to Sweden the following year. One of the male dancers carried the St Andrew's flag as they walked out to perform in the Auditorium in Stockholm. Eight nations were participating, the Swedes in their swirling brightly coloured costumes, the dark Norwegian costumes embroidered with a brilliance that Esther's machine in the Hawick mill could never reproduce. The male Morris dancers from England had bells at the knees of their black breeches and black silk hats. The diversity of colours of the national dresses and the different dances were breathtaking for the young Borders woman as she waited to take part. A male dancer demonstrated the Highland Fling to the pipes, and then Esther was on the move in a reel, with the sensation that she was floating and would take off in her white dress. When the Scottish dancers bowed and curtseyed to the audience, the applause was thunderous.

Afterwards one of the women in the Rumanian team sought Esther out and, using her hands, tried to express her appreciation of her wonderful dancing. She fingered the tartan sash Esther was wearing and in a spontaneous gesture Esther lifted it over the young dancer's head, receiving in return a silk flower pinned to the young woman's bust.

Though the Swedish experience was thrilling, Esther was sorry that she hadn't been able to attend Summer School in St Andrews. A letter from Canada awaited her on her return home, informing her that the Macpherson brother and sister wouldn't be coming to St Andrews. As a trained pilot Gregor hadn't been allowed to leave Canada because of the fragility of the international situation.

Esther went through to Glasgow to visit Mrs Armstrong, and to hear her news of the Summer School over afternoon tea in the Grand Hotel at Charing Cross.

'Everyone was very subdued this year,' Esther's hostess recalled. 'I looked around the table at supper and asked myself: how many of these men will be in uniform soon, and how many of them will we see at next summer's School, if there is one?'

On the morning of Sunday 3 September 1939 Esther and Mrs Armstrong were preparing to go to the nearby church when Chamberlain was announced on the wireless. Mrs Armstrong called her guest upstairs to the drawing-room, and both women peeled off their gloves and sat at the set to listen to the declaration of war with Germany. This momentous Sabbath would be fixed for the rest of her life in Esther's mind because as the Prime Minister was addressing the nation in his sombre tomes, she was looking out of the window, the trees in the park below in their russet autumnal colours, the spire of the university clear and distinct against the blue sky.

But the news didn't come as a surprise to the two listeners. There was already an Anderson Shelter installed in the back garden, and they had watched the demonstration in George Square of a searchlight. Mrs Armstrong spoke about her only child Alasdair. When he was ten his father, a keen sailor, had ordered a new racing yacht from Fairlie's yard on the Clyde, and the boy had become addicted to the sea, crewing for his male parent in the weekend races and soon becoming so skilled that he became helmsman, manoeuvring for wind and passing precariously close to other contenders in the race so that the Armstrong yacht could take the lead. His father had always assumed that the son would follow him into his stockbroking office in Glasgow, but the boy didn't want to stride out from the heights of the Park district in the mornings with bowler hat and umbrella. At Glasgow University he had joined the Royal Naval Volunteer Reserve, and on graduating in economics (a subject he hated, but which he had taken to please his father) he signed up for the Royal Navy. He was now a sub lieutenant on a destroyer, and that sunlit September morning in her elegant town house, his widowed mother articulated her worries about him to the young woman sitting beside her at the wireless that had just delivered the catastrophic news.

'It may not last long,' Esther tried to reassure her.

'That's what they said in 1914'.

The following morning Miss Milligan phoned. Would Esther please meet her outside Central Station at noon? Esther wondered what this mysterious summons was going to entail. Were they taking a train journey? When she reached the station there were hundreds of children with little cardboard suitcases and gasmasks, labels with their names round their necks. Some were anxious, other excited. The two sons of a neighbour of Miss Milligan's were being evacuated into the country, and she had come to see them on to the train, and to give them comics and sweets for this journey into the unknown. Esther took a small hand and led her charge along the platform, the anxious mother with the other child. The doors were slammed shut, leaving bitter steam and tears.

By the time the new term began at Jordanhill College there were gaps in Miss Milligan's Physical Education class because some of the students had volunteered.

'They were some of my best dancers, but patriotism comes first,' Miss Milligan told her favourite student philosophically. 'Scottish country dancing is going to be important in this war, to keep up morale – and to keep people fit.'

But by November of the first year of hostilities the dancing classes in the city's schools had to be cancelled, principally through lack of blackout facilities. However, there were two classes in the ballroom of Green's Playhouse, and Miss Milligan's Tuesday class continued as usual, the lighting subdued, the windows blacked out as Miss Waddell played expressive reels and strathspeys on the piano. The class was composed mostly of teachers, but Esther had been invited by Miss Milligan. At the end, Esther used a small torch to find her way home to the Park area. Mrs Armstrong had become so nervous about her son on the destroyer that her lodger now took most of her meals with her, and, when she should have been studying in her final crucial year, sat talking to her hostess in the dimly lit large drawing-room, wearing coats because a fire could attract the enemy in the sky.

Esther still went shopping with her College friends on Saturday afternoons, but many of the premises were buttressed with sandbags, the windows of stores taped against shattering glass, so that one couldn't study the latest fashions on the models. The people in the tearooms, parents of evacuated children, wives and sweethearts of serving men, were subdued and anxious looking, even although there hadn't been much fighting.

In the summer of 1940 Esther stood on the front lawn outside Jordanhill College, her mother holding the Brownie box camera at her waist to photograph her graduation, but the snaps would be blurred because of the beginning of the tremors in the photographer's hands which would become palsy, a tragedy because this wonderful dancer who had inspired her daughter would have to leave the floor. It was her father's first visit to Glasgow, and he was anxious that the sparks coming from the tram as it took its power from the overhead wires was a warning that they were about to burst into flames. They had a modest wartime lunch in a city centre café before her parents boarded the train for the journey back to the Borders.

Esther could have applied for a teaching post in the Borders, but decided to stay on in Glasgow, so as to be near her mentor Miss Milligan, and because she loved her garden flat and Mrs Armstrong's maternal ministrations. She worked in a school of well-behaved children in neat uniforms on the south side of the city, teaching them Scottish country dancing, for which their parents bought them pumps. The children brought in tablet made from precious sugar for Miss Scott, and sang songs for her.

Miss Milligan instructed at Jordanhill during the day, and in the evening met Esther outside Central Station. It wasn't to see evacuated children safely on to the trains, but to serve servicemen mugs of tea before they departed for the south and overseas postings, some of them never to return. One night when a train was delayed, she made the men form up into sets and taught them the reel the Duke of Perth to keep them warm, the music provided by an accordion player who appeared every evening to send off the troops with Scottish music, tackety boots keeping time on the station concourse.

When Miss Milligan wasn't serving tea and teaching Scottish country dancing in Central Station, she was instructing on applying bandages at the First Aid Post near her west end home, and late at night her expert needles clicked as she knitted for serving men. She boasted that when the Argyll and Sutherland Highlanders were in China in the early 1930s, they had formed the Shanghai Reel Club, the Pipe-Major instructing them on Petronella and the Flowers of Edinburgh. She hoped that in their new base in Singapore the Argylls were still dancing.

Miss Milligan had a phone call from the secretary of the Perth Branch of the Scottish Country Dance Society.

'My husband Lieutenant Colonel Harris Hunter, who was with the 51st Highland Division, is a prisoner of war in Germany. He and his fellow officers are dancing reels to relieve the tedium. He's sent me the steps of a new dance they've devised. It's called The 51st Country Dance. I'll send it to you, and perhaps you could post me some dance books to send out to them?'

Miss Milligan was delighted with this demonstration of the therapeutic effects of Scottish country dancing. The books were duly dispatched, the St Valery Reel, its new name, taught in her class. The doyen was on the move, undeterred by blackouts and travel restrictions, squeezed into the corners of crowded troop trains as she travelled south to visit branches and to hold classes.

'I don't know when we can hold another Summer School at St Andrews,' she told Esther, 'but we must keep encouraging people to dance, wherever they are.'

Mrs Armstrong had become an air raid warden, standing on the roof of her house in Park Terrace, with a thermos flask, surveying the skies and wondering which ocean her son's destroyer was ploughing through. Esther sometimes climbed up beside her to keep her company, standing back to back, dividing up the firmament between them. The uncountable constellations made Esther wonder if there was life on other planets, and if the inhabitants danced instead of going to war. Some frosty nights, to keep warm, she did a hundred *pas de basque* steps, beating out the tempo on the lead covering of the roof.

'Have you heard from Alasdair?' she enquired.

'All I get is a printed form, saying: I am well. I have no idea where he is, though I hope to God it's not in the Atlantic, with these dreadful U-boats. I have this recurring dream of standing

on the deck of a ship pitching through the waves, and suddenly
I see this object streaking through the sea. I wake up before it
strikes.'

On an evening in mid March 1941 the two women had
finished supper and were listening to the nine o' clock news on
the wireless when the air-raid sirens began to wail. Immediately
they put on their helmets and slung their gas masks over their
shoulders before going up on to the roof for fire watching
duties in case of enemy attack. It had been a spell of glorious
spring weather, and walking in the park in the evening, Esther
had watched the birds building their nests.

The moon was radiant over the city, its lights dimmed. The
atmosphere was eerie, tense, as they listened to the droning
approach of the first wave of bombers, and then the initial
detonations. From the directions of the fires started by the
incendiaries they knew that Clydebank was the target. The
flames would flare in both women's memories for the rest of
their lives.

'There's nothing we can do,' Mrs Armstrong told her
companion. 'If we stay up here we could be killed.'

They spent the remainder of the night huddled in the
Anderson Shelter in the back garden, too afraid to go into the
house for food, because some of the bombs were now falling
on the city.

'There are people living in Clydebank,' Mrs Armstrong
protested. 'Let them bomb the shipyards but leave these poor
souls alone.'

When the last of the bombers departed in the breaking
light of dawn they went into the house to make breakfast.

'We can't sit here and do nothing,' her hostess told Esther, and took her car out of the garage. She had her cheque book with her, and stopped at almost every shop in New City Road, buying up cartons of cigarettes and jars of sweets, as well as whatever food was on offer. But they were stopped at a police barrier.

'You look as if you've been looting,' the constable remarked in earnest.

'We've been buying what we could for the people who've been bombed out,' Mrs Armstrong explained. 'Please let us through.'

'I can't. Most of the streets in Clydebank are blocked by fallen tenements.'

'But we need to get through,' the driver persisted.

'I'll tell you what I'll do. If you pull up on the pavement I'll stop the next lorry.'

The cigarettes and sweets were loaded, and the two women insisted on accompanying their gifts, hanging on to the sides of the lorry as it negotiated strewn masonry and twisted tram lines. What they saw that morning could never be forgotten, and both of them were crying. The sky was showing where tenements had stood, and gables had exposed grates and collapsed floors in rooms where families had cooked and sat talking round the coals.

'I can't get any further, ladies,' the lorry driver informed them.

When they found a policeman to take charge of the gifts they negotiated the hazardous way. People were crying the names of loved ones as they clawed aside rubble with bloodied hands. Salvaged household possessions were heaped on pavements, the miraculously intact mirror of a dressing-table in which a newly wed young woman, lying somewhere underneath her flat, had made up her mouth before setting off for work. The atmosphere was polluted with dust, and masonry continued to fall.

They were directed to the Union Church Hall where a rest centre had been set up. Local school teachers were crowded into the small kitchen, and Mrs Armstrong and Esther helped to distribute small bottles of milk and to comfort the traumatized survivors huddled round the table, one woman with a canary in a cage, the sole item of salvage from her home. But it wasn't singing that morning.

'I need to get back into the city for my ARP duties,' Mrs Armstrong told her lodger at the end of that exhausting harrowing day.

'I'll stay and help here,' Esther told her.

'But they're expecting another raid tonight.'

'I'll take my chance with the people here.'

Because it was going to be a long night Esther decided that she wanted some fresh air, and went out into the street for a walk. The eerie silence was broken by an avalanche of slates from a ruined tenement, and the click click of the buckled wheel of a pram piled with salvaged possessions as a family joined hundreds of others trekking up to the sanctuary of the surrounding hills, though it meant lying down on the ground under the treacherous moon. The sirens went at 8.40 p.m and a cup began to vibrate on a saucer in the rest centre, the first detonation slopping the contents over the table.

Esther knew that she had to find the strength and courage to survive the night. There was no safe shelter to go out to, nowhere to hide from the bombardment. But the fear that the building could come down at any second on top of her was

72

pushed to the back of her mind by the necessity of attending to the new refugees who crowded into the rest centre, children crying hysterically at the loss of their cots and comforting toy animals, the adults dumb with terror, some of them unable to lift the mugs of tea.

She heard the whine of a dive-bombing plane as though it were going to plunge through the roof, but at the last second it banked away, machine-gun bullets drumming on the wrecked streets like a torrential downpour. The All Clear didn't sound until after six, by which time Esther could hardly stand with exhaustion. She was like a sleep-walker going outside, through a dawn of choking dust and hysterical dogs searching for their buried owners.

'You've done every well,' Mrs Armstrong materialized, taking her arm. 'Time for some sleep.'

The crew were hacking at the ice with axes on the deck of the *Matabele*, but no sooner had it shattered than it refroze. The destroyer was escorting the convoy with vital supplies for Russia through the Arctic waters. Under his duffle coat sub lieutenant Alasdair Armstrong was wearing a heavy woollen roll-neck sweater knitted for him by Miss Jean Milligan, but he was still chilled through to the bone, his face protected by a scarf, making him look like a bandit. In the darkness of the Arctic night no lookout could have seen the steel leviathan surfacing, the torpedo ploughing through the water. The magazine blew up under sub lieutenant Armstrong. Even if the depth charges hadn't detonated, the crew couldn't have survived for minutes in the icy sea. The sub-lieutenant wasn't one of the two out of two hundred who lived.

In the spring of 1942 Esther was called into the education offices and told that she was being sent to a house in Argyll, where one of the teachers had become sick. The home for illegitimate children had been evacuated from the city at the outbreak of war, but following the Clydebank raids the authorities had left them in the countryside.

Esther's journey to her posting was a difficult one. Because of the anti-submarine boom across the Clyde at the Cloch lighthouse she couldn't travel by steamer, so she had to take a circuitous route, first on a rickety bus, her suitcase slithering in the boot, the woman in front of her soothing a hyperactive hen in a basket because eggs were a precious commodity. When the decent road ran out Esther transferred to a horse and cart and was taken for two miles along a rutted track, then up an eerie avenue to a mansion house. It was a typical late nineteenth century residence built for a wealthy Glasgow business man who wished to move his family out of the polluted city in which he had made his fortune, contributing to the choking atmosphere. The daughter had decided to offer the mansion to the nation as a hospital. But the access along the rutted track was too distressing for wounded soldiers, so it had become a haven for evacuated children.

There were sixty of them, ranging in age from eight to twelve, and they had been there for over two years. The other teacher was Miss Annabel MacAllister, from Inverness-shire. She was young and compassionate towards her charges, showing infinite patience as she separated fights between the more robust of the male pupils. She met Esther in the cavernous hall.

'Welcome to Glencara. I'm not going to ask if you had a pleasant journey. When I came here I had to go to bed for

74

the afternoon because of the jolting I received. Of course it's intentional.'

'What do you mean?' Esther enquired as her case was carried up the massive staircase by her new colleague.

'The Farquharsons who built this house could easily have made up the road, but that would have brought the inquisitive, so they decided to leave it rough. I'm told that the horses hauling their gigs, which had reinforced springs, had to be shod four times a year.'

The stairs branched, and they climbed left.

'Do the owners still live here?' Esther asked as they entered a long dim corridor.

'Miss Farquharson the owner does, in a wing by herself.'

'Have you met her?'

'She's a very sweet lady. Her cook also cooks for all of us, and her maids wait on table and clean the rooms. There are twenty five bedrooms in the house, and sixty children, so what we've done is to turn six of the biggest rooms into dorms. The children like each other's company because it's an eerie house.'

'Is there a ghost?' the new arrival asked anxiously, since she believed many of the stories of Border hauntings told her by her mother.

'Not that I know of. Several of the children say they've seen a strange lady, but it's probably their imagination.'

'Do they get visits from family?'

'They have no families. They're children who were abandoned at birth. Some of the mothers were prostitutes, others so poor that they couldn't cope. I've never seen the institution they were in in Glasgow, but evidently it's grim, and this place is paradise compared to it. They don't want to go back to the city, the poor wee souls.'

The room Esther was shown into was spacious, with a canopied bed, and a dressing-room off. Flowers had been placed on the marble wash-stand.

'You're overlooking the loch,' Annabel pointed out, leading her into the bay window. The water stretched into the distance, and there was a jetty below.

'That's the main disadvantage of this house,' Annabel explained. 'We can't let the children near the water, so they've got to be watched all the time when they're out in the open. On a sunny day it's a beautiful peaceful place. It seems so far away from the war. Occasionally we hear a plane passing overhead, but that's all. Now, I must show you the bathroom.'

It was two doors along the corridor, its walls clad in marble, a contraption of many perforated steel pipes in a corner.

'That's a shower,' Annabel explained to the bewildered newcomer. 'It has sprays which attack you from every angle, as if you're being stung by a swarm of bees – that is, when it's running hot. The boiler's temperamental, and also (she pointed to the massive bath with the brass taps, the enamel worn by many recumbent bathers) the water is pumped up from the loch, so we're likely to have to share the bath with various forms of aquatic life. As for the toilet, isn't it a masterpiece of design that should be in a museum?'

It was a mahogany box, with a chain with an ivory handle in the shape of a leaping salmon suspended convenient for the right-handed.

The resident teacher closed the bathroom door behind her. 'This is a wonderful house to live in. I've been here since the day before war broke out, and I'm dreading the day that the children have to go back to the institution. Now come and meet our charges.'

The large morning-room on the ground floor had been converted into a schoolroom, with rows of tables and assorted chairs. The children – in temporary charge of the housekeeper - rose when the new member of staff came in, and chanted in unison, as had been rehearsed: 'Welcome to Glencara, Miss Scott!'

Having been introduced to the buxom housekeeper, whose garments seemed to belong in another century, Esther wandered between the tables, looking at the children's artistic efforts. They had been asked to draw the house, but on many of the sheets of precious paper the towers were leaning dangerously, as if about to topple into the loch, and chimneys tilted in similar precarious positions. Having complimented the artists, Esther sat chatting to them, asking how they liked their temporary home, receiving in response many raised arms and snapping fingers. A small girl in blonde pigtails stood up.

'Please Miss, there's a lady in our room,' she announced the momentous news in an excited voice.

Esther glanced at her teaching colleague.

'I don't think so, Rachel,' Annabel replied.

'Oh yes, Miss,' another voice earnestly took up the spooky theme. 'She comes in and tucks us into our beds. She was there last night.'

'What does this lady look like?' Esther asked, knowing she was prolonging a risky topic.

Another girl, taller, with short black hair, stood up. The accent was unmistakably Glaswegian, the delivery assured.

'She's about your age, Miss, and has red hair. She wears a

white dress, and her feet are bare.'

'And she wears a cross here,' a seated child added, touching her chest.

'She kissed me on the forehead,' the tall speaker, still on her feet, disclosed. 'Her lips were warm.'

'And she whispered good night to me.'

'Have any of the boys seen this mysterious lady?' Esther asked.

Fingers snapped, and a small lad asserted that the lady in white had also paid his dorm a visit.

Almost as if on cue to terrify the new arrival, the big brass gong in the hall was struck by a maid with a muscular arm to announce supper. The children filed into the big dining-room where logs were blazing in the cavernous fireplace. The Farquharsons weren't an old landed family, so the persons in the portraits looking down from the walls on the diners weren't intimidating. A tall smiling woman in a fox fur had posed for Sir John Lavery with stunning results. A teenage girl was sitting on a pony, her pleasing face turned towards the room.

An elderly butler in a swallow-tailed coat ladled out the broth for the two maids. Esther could see why these children didn't want to return to their institution in Glasgow. In the economies of wartime, there would be no such generous rations there. But Glencara had five thousand acres of land, and stags were slung across ponies and brought in, to be hung and matured in the huge game larder behind the house, netting over its slatted sides as a deterrent against insects. Tonight generous slices of venison were falling away from the butler's carving knife, two per plate, with potatoes and vegetables. Esther had been served first, with Annabel, but there was too much on her plate, with a silver boat of cranberry sauce now being offered. The sumptuous meal ended with grapes from the extensive hot-houses and real aromatic coffee, served in small golden cups, with lumps of brown sugar lifted with silver tongs.

'It must be costing Miss Farquharson a fortune to keep us,' Esther remarked.

'Miss Farquharson has a fortune, and more coming in every day,' Annabel disclosed. 'She owns one of the largest shipyards on the Clyde, specializing in battleships. It wasn't bombed in the raids on Clydebank. Her brother, who was the heir, was killed in the last war. She never married, and loves children, especially wee ragged ones from the city. Maybe it's her way of paying back the fortune her family has taken from Glasgow, because hundreds of skilled men – maybe the fathers of some of the children here - built their ships. Anyway, it's bedtime for them.'

It's like a well rehearsed military operation. The evacuated are divided into sexes. Annabel leads the girls down one corridor, accompanied by a maid, Esther down another, the other maid accompanying her. There are whispers about 'the lady in white,' but the new teacher ignores them. The children divide themselves into groups of ten and file into their designated rooms. They hang their clothes on their own hangers in the massive wardrobes in the adjacent dressing-rooms. Nighties and pyjamas are retrieved from under pillows. The radiators are warm because the boiler is behaving tonight. The children kneel by their beds, heads bowed, hands together in angelic pose. Until Esther becomes familiar with the house prayer, the maid leads them. They thank God for the safety of the day now ending; for the good food; the warmth; for the infinite kindness of Miss Farquharson. They ask God that people will be kept safe from German bombs in the wartime city and in the turbulent world. And finally, they are asked to pray in silence, with their own requests to God.

The house, too far from the electricity supply, has its own generator, driven by a dammed burn. The brass switches go off, doors are closed, leaving the children with 'the lady in white.'

Annabel and Esther make their way down to the library, which is their staff-room. The walls are lined with beautifully bound books, though it's doubtful if any members of this industrial family had the time or inclination to read the many volumes of the magnum opus edition of Sir Walter Scott's works. But a young woman did cut the pages of Swinburne's *risqué* poems with a knife.

'With Miss Farquharson's compliments,' Annabel said, handing her new colleague a crystal glass of whisky. 'What else but the best malt, and plenty more in the cellar, along with choice wines if we wish any with our meals.'

Esther wasn't partial to whisky, but sipped it out of good manners.

'What do you teach them?'

'Oh, everything,' Annabel replied, her hand sweeping. 'Now the good weather's here, I try to get them out as much as possible, for games and nature study. They didn't get much fresh air in the city. We work from nine thirty until three, with an hour's break for lunch. What would *you* like to teach?'

'Scottish country dancing?'

'That would be wonderful. We can have a lesson tomorrow afternoon.'

When Esther ascended to her bed and unpacked she found to her relief that the Scottish dance records, wrapped in her dressing-gown, had survived the jolting journey. She had also brought books of Scottish country dances. She wondered if, for this first night at least, she should sleep with the light on, in case of a visit from the mysterious lady in white, but decided that would be both wasteful of power and cowardly, considering that the children considered this nocturnal visitor to be like a loving relative, the mother they had never known.

Esther was wakened in the dawn by a knocking sound. She lay rigid with fear, head under the bedclothes, sure that the door was going to swing open and she was about to receive a visit from a presence not of this world. But it was the pipes sounding as the boiler was fired for the day by one of the estate workers.

Esther subjected her pleasing figure to the stinging attentions of the shower, drying herself with the largest towel she had ever seen. She went down to a breakfast of porridge made from oats that had been steeped for the requisite time. There was frothing milk from Miss Farquharson's prize Galloway herd, and honey from her hives. The estate was self-sufficient in almost everything. Cook baked, and a man and horse dragged windblown timber from the wood, halving the trunks on a power-driven lethal circular saw blade, and stacking the logs in the shed, the seasoned ones to the fore. The gardener and his two assistants planted vegetables and tended the fruits in the glasshouses. There was even a woman whose main duty was to sew and mend, including the clothes of the evacuated children.

The large globe of the world had been borrowed from the library, and placed on the teacher's desk in the schoolroom, the former morning-room. Esther was taking half of the children for the lesson.

'Will someone come out and point to Canada?' she

requested.

A girl wearing boots spun the globe so that the class could see the vastness of the North American continent.

'Very good. What's your name?'

'Margaret Mary, Miss.'

'Thank you, Margaret Mary, you can go back to your seat.'

Esther had chosen Canada as the subject of her first lesson because that was where the man she hoped to marry came from. But all she had had in the past two years were a couple of letters from Judi, and a postcard from Gregor. He was on 'active service,' but where, it was not stated, because Canada didn't want Hitler to know to which theatre of war it had sent its squadrons. Judi wrote: 'because of the number of males who have gone to war, dancing partners are scarce, but women dance with women, and since our accordionist has enlisted, we have to make do with records.'

Esther asked some of the bigger boys to help her move the furniture in the drawing-room back to the walls, and to roll up the carpet carefully. The first lesson didn't require music, though there was a wind-up gramophone with a large fluted horn on a table, beside a pile of records. Esther began by teaching them the *pas de basque*, beating out the 1, 2, 3 timing on the floorboards as she had been taught as a child. Some of the children had more or less mastered the step by the end of the lesson, including boys who looked clumsy when they walked, but who became elegant when they danced. One small girl, her legs bowed by rickets, the scourge of the poor in Glasgow, was reduced to tears because her feet fankled, and she almost fell over. Esther took her by the hand and showed her an easier way of doing the step by hopping from side to side.

Esther had intended the lesson to last for half an hour, so as not to tire and confuse the children, but they wanted more, so she spent the following half an hour showing them how to do a reel of three, having chalked the number 8 on the floor.

'Your dance lesson was a great success,' Annabel informed her at supper, beef from a home-killed animal on the gilded platter tonight. 'You're going to be pestered to give them a lesson every day.'

'That would be too much. I'll do it twice a week – if you approve.'

'I approve of anything that interests them and keeps them fit. I hate to think of them going back to a grim building in Glasgow, with no grounds to play in.'

By the end of the next dance lesson the children had mastered the reel formation, and it was time to wind up the gramophone, a task which Esther allocated to one of the big boys. She slipped the precious William Hannah disk from its brown sleeve and laid it carefully on the turntable.

'I'm going to let the record play to the end. Just keep dancing the reels.'

She went among the lines of dancers, taking a small confused girl gently by the shoulders and turning her in the right direction. A boy kept bumping into the two others in the reel with him, but Esther went behind him and propelled him in the figure.

'Now that you know where you're going in the reels, I'm going to teach you the Dashing White Sergeant. You need to stand in a line of three, facing another line of three.'

Some of the dancers hadn't mastered raising arms and moving through to meet the oncoming line of three, so Esther extended the lesson.

'You've done very well. Did you like the dance?'

'Yes Miss!'

Instead of arithmetic and reading, they wanted to dance, but as Annabel pointed out, they needed to be numerate and literate so that they could make something worthwhile of their lives, after such a sad start.

Esther couldn't imagine what it must be like, to be abandoned as a baby and be deprived of the comfort of maternal milk and love. It reminded her to write regularly to her parents, to tell them how happy and fulfilled she was, and hoping to see them soon, though there was nobody to take her place if she took a holiday. Within the month the children could dance the Dashing White Sergeant without colliding with each other, and she had also taught the basics of waltzing, though some of the boys were embarrassed, holding their partners so close.

'We'll have a wee dance on Saturday night before bedtime,' she promised them.

They had succulent lamb for supper, and peaches from the glasshouses. They were dancing the Dashing White Sergeant to Hannah's wonderful music when the door opened. One of the youngest girls screamed. They were being visited by the ghost, because the new arrival had red hair, though not the white dress that had been reported.

Esther lifted the needle from the record.

'Please don't stop!' the figure appealed from the doorway.

The dance began again, the children reassured that this was a living visitor. At the end the stranger crossed the floor to the teacher.

'I'm Laura Farquharson,' she introduced herself, extending a hand.

Esther realized that she was being introduced to their hostess.

'I hope you don't mind us rolling up your carpet and moving your furniture, Miss Farquharson.'

'Not at all. It's wonderful how you've taught them, and how happy they are. I wish I could join them, but unfortunately this doesn't allow me.' She lifted the hem of her long skirt to reveal a calliper on her right leg. 'But do carry on.'

Though she was nervous, Esther told the children that they were going to dance a waltz, 'to show Miss Farquharson how well you can do it.'

She watched the shipping heiress's wistful face as the couples went round, some toes being trod on.

'We used to hold dances in this room,' she informed Esther after the record had ended. 'We brought a dance band down from Glasgow. Do you know the Reel of Tulloch?'

'It's a beautiful dance, but tricky.'

'I loved dancing it, with the men doing Highland steps.'

Annabel appeared to say that it was time for bed, and Esther asked her hostess to be excused.

'When you've settled them for the night, come along and have some tea with me.'

'That's very kind of you, but I don't know where to go,' Esther told her.

'I'll send Alice my maid to collect you.'

Esther was led through the south wing, into a sitting-room, a tray with silver teapot and biscuits set out on the table in the window overlooking the loch. The visitor stopped to study the large oil painting of a yacht above the fireplace. The name *Spirit of Glencara* was clearly visible in gold on the bow, looking as if the two figures leaning out on the side were trying to stop it capsizing in the white-crested waves. What struck Esther was that the two young women, and the third at the big spoked wheel, were wearing blue nautical caps with matching ribbons at jaunty angles on their red curls.

'The painter didn't paint the same person three times,' Miss Farquharson explained at her guest's back. 'My sisters and I were triplets, only an hour between us at birth. We decided that we had come into the world at the same time. We were inseparable, you see. We were sent to school in St Andrews and insisted on being in the same dorm. We ate the same food and wore identical clothes, and we always knew what each other was thinking. And we were obsessed with sport. We skated in the winter, skied in the spring and sailed in the summer. We persuaded our father to commission the Fife yard on the Clyde to build us the thirty ton sloop in the painting. He complained that instead of racing boats we should be going after husbands, but we weren't interested at that stage. The *Spirit of Glencara*, named after this house, had accommodation below, and we stayed on it while we raced on the Clyde throughout the summer.'

'Where are your beautiful sisters now?' Esther enquired, continuing to be enraptured by the dramatic painting, as if she could feel the spray on her face.

The voice at her back faltered. 'In August 1923 there was a big race, with yachts coming from Ireland. One even crossed the Atlantic to compete. It was a squally day. We were out in the front approaching the marker point at Holy Island, when we were dismasted. It struck Catriona at the wheel, and in the confusion which followed, with the deck covered in sails, she was swept overboard. The yacht behind us tried to turn to find her, but she had gone. Her body was never recovered. My leg was pinned under the mast, hence the calliper. We sold the sloop and never raced again.

'My other sister Fay – that's her at the bow, hauling on the sheets - was courted by the heir to a chemical works in Glasgow. Father was delighted, of course, because it increased our family's fortune, and meant that there would probably be a grandson to take over the shipyard. A week before her wedding in June 1925 Fay went for a swim in the loch there. The sun was setting and I'll always remember her diving into the golden water. But when she didn't surface I ran for the servants. Her foot had fankled on a submerged tree and she drowned.'

'What a dreadful tragedy, losing two sisters in the same way, Miss Farquharson.' Esther hesitated, wondering if she should tell, then decided that it might be a comfort. 'The children say that a young woman in a white dress with red hair comes in to kiss them goodnight.'

'That's Fay. A week after she drowned, I saw her in the drawing-room, and she smiled at me. She comes to me every night to kiss me. That's why I hold on to Glencara. It's far too big, far too inconvenient a house for a single person. But I can't leave my dear sister to wander this large house alone, searching for me, so I'll be here until I'm carried out. Tell the children not to be frightened. They're the children that Fay wanted so much.'

Esther was never visited by the spirit of the drowned triplet during her stay at Glencara. Not that the children were indoors much that summer. She and Annabel took them on nature study rambles, teaching them to identify flowers, to name the birds that were calling in the woods. There were picnics, and open-air dances, with one of the estate workers playing the pipes, and the sole surviving Miss Farquharson watching from a window as the displaced children performed. Esther decided to devise a reel, Miss Farquharson's Reel, dedicated to their generous hostess. She worked out the steps, making the reels flow, like a yacht manoeuvring, and she had three girls wearing balmorals dance in a line, to represent the inseparable triplets. There was a buffet supper before the dance, and the maids had ironed the children's shirts and skirts. Miss Farquharson was the guest of honour, and watched with tears in her eyes as the reel was danced.

At the end a girl came up to Esther. 'Please Miss, the lady with the red hair and the white dress was also watching us.'

'Where was she standing, Kate?'

'By the fireplace, clapping her hands.'

A month later a man in a bowler and long black coat was conveyed along the track to Glencara, to inform the two teachers that the children were being sent back to Glasgow.

'But they love it here. It brings out the best in them. Why can't they stay?' Esther protested.

'Because Hitler's turned his forces on Russia, so there's not likely to be any more major air raids on Glasgow.'

'Miss Farquharson wants them to stay,' Annabel informed their officious visitor with the buckled briefcase.

'It's not Miss Farquharson's decision. In fact they've been too well looked after here. They need to get back to the reality of their position.'

'What's that supposed to mean?' Esther demanded.

'They're abandoned children who need direction – and

discipline.'

The two teachers could see that further argument was hopeless. When they informed the children there were tears, even hysterics.

'I don't want to leave the lady who kisses me goodnight!' one child wailed.

On the Friday night Esther held a final dance, but the children were subdued and seemed to wander aimlessly in the reels they had mastered.

'I hope you'll keep up your dancing,' she urged them, but knew that it wouldn't be encouraged in the Glasgow institution which had, apparently, bars on the windows.

Miss Farquharson invited Annabel and Esther along to her sitting-room for a final pot of tea.

'I'm heartbroken that the children are going,' the sole survivor of triplets confessed. 'This house will be like a mortuary without them.'

But Esther knew that the elegant chatelaine couldn't leave and abandon her sister, who had emerged from the loch days after her drowning, to flit about the house.

'I want you to take this as a memento of your stay here,' Miss Farquharson said, handing each of them a small box. When they opened them in her presence they saw exquisite silverwork Celtic crosses with their names engraved, and 'Glencara, 1942.'

The following day two buses staffed by unsmiling attendants from the institution in Glasgow swayed along the track.

After leaving Glencara with many regrets Esther was sent to a school in Cowcaddens in Glasgow. It was a poor area of decaying overcrowded tenements and the scourge of rickets, but at least the majority of the children there had parents to go home to. She found it difficult in the beginning to keep discipline, and worried about it in the evening as she sat in the bright flat belonging to the bereaved Mrs Armstrong, who was delighted to have her back. Was it her Border accent compared to the children's Glasgow one? At her interview with the headmaster, whose fierce cynical expression had set so that he couldn't shed it when he went home to his family, Esther was ordered: 'if you have the slightest bit of trouble, belt them.' He leaned over the desk littered with the reports of pupils who would come to nothing and confided: 'I had a strategy that gave me a life without trouble before I got out of the classroom as headmaster. At the beginning of every new school year I would pick one boy out of each class and belt him in front of the others to show them: you don't get on the wrong side of me.' He opened his desk. 'Here's a present, a well-used strap,' he said, passing it across to her.

The black leather with the two fangs lay curled on the desk in front of her. Esther was appalled by his brutality, but this wasn't a man to argue with, so she picked it up.

'I need to give you a lesson on using it,' he told her. 'Women aren't as good at it as men, perhaps because their arm isn't so strong, their aim not so good.' He took a piece of chalk from the drawer, laid it on the edge of the desk and picked up the strap.

'Swing it well over the shoulder,' he demonstrated. 'Then bring it down sharp.'

The chalk exploded into powder.

'Here, you try it.'

A new piece of chalk was produced.

'Let your arm go further back, to get the full force of the

swing.'

When she brought down the strip of leather the chalk rolled off the desk and fractured on the floor.

'You'll need to practise, lassie.'

Esther wanted to drop the offensive weapon into a bin, but knew he would ask her if her aim were improving, so she took it and secreted it in her desk. She had prepared a lesson on the Border ballads.

> 'True Thomas lay on Huntlie bank,
> A marvel with his eye spied he.
> There he saw a lady bright
> Come riding by the Eildon Tree.
>
> Her skirt was of the grass-green silk,
> Her mantle of the velvet fine,
> At every lock of her horse's mane
> Hung fifty silver bells and nine.'

One of the boys threw a rubber across the room. She tried not to acknowledge the missile, but then a fight broke out at the back of the class. She shut the ballad book and rushed up to separate them, but received a kick on the shin from a tackety boot.

'Stop this!'

There was sudden silence, and she thought that she had enforced her authority, but when she turned the headmaster was standing there.

'You're having a wee bit trouble, Miss Scott.'

She feared that she was going to be told to belt the brawlers, but instead he asked for his strap back.

'All the boys out, in three lines.'

He took off his jacket and hung it on the back of her chair, then removed his cufflinks and placed them carefully on her desk before rolling up his sleeves. She saw the effect that this preparation was having on the faces of the rows of boys. At the first blow she closed her eyes and held on to the edge of the desk, wanting to cover her ears. Crack, scream, crack, scream: the sequence seemed to go on forever.

'If you have any more trouble with this lot, send for me, Miss Scott.'

The strap was returned to her, the cufflinks restored to the sleeves, the jacket buttoned. They went back to their desks, sobbing, holding their palms in their oxters as if this would draw the fire from them. One girl had been sick at the brutality and had to be taken to the toilet by another. Esther felt that she had let them down. If only she had been able to control the unruly boys, they wouldn't be sitting in front of her, crying unashamedly in front of the girls. The bully of the class silently held up his wrist to show her the livid bruise, not as a trophy, but as a sign that she had failed him. If she hadn't been squeamish about belting them, she would have done far less damage with her weak female arm, her poor aim.

She had no more trouble from that class, not because they were frightened of her, but because they were terrified that the headmaster would be patrolling the corridor (as he did, at unpredictable times), and hear the racket they were making. She tried the Border ballads again, and when she asked a boy to read he mumbled the words. They had been beaten into silence and were learning nothing; not that the headmaster was concerned.

'Most of them are brainless, Miss Scott. They'll be like their fathers, members of gangs. They'll attack people with razors and will steal and cheat. Some of them will no doubt murder. If you can teach them to read and write, well and good. Forget about fine literature.'

Esther felt that she had no talent for teaching, but couldn't confide in Mrs Armstrong, who had been so kind to her, and had such faith in her. But when she went to Miss Milligan's dance class she couldn't conceal her sorrow.

'I've never seen you dance so badly,' the major-domo stated in her usual forthright manner. 'What's the matter?'

'I'm fine, Miss Milligan.'

'You're coming home with me for a cup of tea and a chat.'

Esther was introduced to Miss Milligan's two sisters in the flat they shared in the west end. A cat was playing with a ball of wool on a chair, part of the stock of the production line of warm woollens for those in peril at sea. When they weren't knitting the sisters were driving round the city, collecting old jerseys for the sailors.

'Our boys are almost freezing to death on the Russian convoys,' Miss Milligan told the owner of a large house in Jordanhill.

The woman reappeared with an armful of her husband's golfing sweaters.

'He won't miss these.'

Tea was served in the Milligan house, and under pressure from the interrogation Esther's pent-up depression flowed like a lanced boil.

'You're not a bad teacher, Esther, and these boys are not bad. The headmaster is. He doesn't see that every human being, whatever his or her circumstances, has potential. They're living in primitive overcrowded tenements. Their fathers are away at war and their mothers in making ends meet don't have the time or energy to discipline them. They turn their worries about their fathers into aggression against other boys, because the whole world seems to be fighting.'

'How do I win them round?' Esther asked her mentor.

'What do you mean, win them round? Do you mean on your terms? The people in the Border ballads are a million miles away from their experiences. Many of them will never have seen a field, far less a rural landscape. The girls may be interested in fairies and little people, but not the boys. The Cowcaddens isn't the territory of fairies and knights. Instead of imposing a lesson on them, Esther, let them give you a lesson on their lives. Ask them about their homes, their siblings. Listen to them.'

The following day, when the children were sitting sullen, instead of chalking a sum on the blackboard, Esther asked: 'how many of you have fathers away at the war?'

The class, including the girls, looked startled, and a hand went up tentatively at the back.

'Yes, Thomas, which regiment is your father with?'

'The HLI – Miss.'

'I don't know much about military matters, Thomas, so you'll have to tell me what the letters HLI mean.'

'The Highland Light Infantry, Miss,' was the proud reply.

In the course of that afternoon there were many responses, many different regiments. But two of the pupils, a boy and a girl, hadn't volunteered information, so Esther asked the girl about her father.

'Did you hear me speaking to you, Nancy?' she asked gently.

'My father went to Heaven with the Black Watch.'

The choice of words startled Esther, and there was a lapse of time before she understood. She regretted asking the question, since the girl was biting her lip. But it was as if Miss Milligan were whispering behind her: *don't get flustered. Speak naturally to her. If she's been through bereavement, treat her like an adult.*

'He must have been very brave, Nancy.'

'We got a medal sent to us, Miss.'

'You must bring it in to show us, Nancy. I'm sure we'll all be very interested.'

The only boy who hadn't yet contributed put up a steady hand.

'Ma father's a prisoner of war, Miss. He was captured in the retreat from France.'

'And have you heard from him since, Sam?'

'We had a postcard, saying he was well, Miss, but it didnae say where he wis. We got an address an' sent him a percel wi' food and cigarettes.' He paused. 'Ah hope it reached him, 'cos he canna dae withoot his fags.'

The rest of the class laughed, and Esther knew that she had succeeded in winning them over. There still had to be formal lessons in writing and arithmetic, and simple spelling tests, but at least two afternoons a week were devoted to talk about the war. The medal awarded posthumously to a brave parent was brought in and handled reverently round the class. Photographs of fathers in the uniforms of all the armed forces were passed round, and when the headmaster opened the door he found a quiet discussion going on. That evening Esther took the hated belt out of the school and dropped it into a litter bin affixed to a lamp-post because she knew that she wouldn't be requiring it again in her teaching career. There was another way.

A few weeks later she received a letter from Oban.

'This place with its mountains reminds me of Canada. How about a visit? Love, Gregor.'

Esther told Mrs Armstrong that the Canadian aviator they had both met at the Summer School in St Andrews had made contact with her.

'He's stationed in Oban and wants me to go up to visit him.'

'That could be difficult,' Mrs Armstrong cautioned. 'I have a friend with a family house in Argyll and she tells me that she's having a devil of a job getting permission to go there, because evidently it's a restricted area, and you require a permit.'

'Where do you apply for one?' Esther enquired.

'I'll ask my friend.'

The instructions were conveyed to Esther on the following evening, and she sat at the kitchen table in her flat to fill in the form, explaining that she was a friend of a Canadian airman who was serving in Oban, and would like to visit him. Three weeks later she was sent a permit, and boarded the west-bound train from Glasgow in a station packed with servicemen going home on leave, or returning to the European theatres of war.

Space was made for Esther in a corner of the carriage, cigarettes and even a flask of whisky offered to her. The servicemen drank, sang Gaelic songs, but avoided talking about the hellish places they had come from. They only had a few days home in the peace and benevolent light of the west, and didn't want to convey to their loved ones the dangers they were returning to, against a highly mechanized enemy who had machines which could throw flames for yards, like the breath of a dragon.

When Esther alighted from the train in Oban she saw flying

boats bobbing in the bay. She found the boarding house where she was to stay and deposited her case on the solid bed. She asked a military policeman to help her find her Canadian friend Gregor, and was sent to a large house beyond the bay, the control centre for the flying boats. She was told that Gregor was with 423 Canadian Squadron, piloting a Sunderland flying boat, which was 'on duty' at present, and should be home by the evening. She could leave a message for him, the WAAF told her, so Esther wrote that she would meet him 'at nine tonight under the clock which I saw at the station when I arrived.'

She went to a café for a cup of tea before heading in the fading light to the station. She heard a roaring sound and saw a huge flying boat approaching over a low-lying island at the entrance to the bay. Was this her date for the evening, arriving in style?

When he hadn't showed up at twenty past nine, she decided to go to the boarding house, and she was walking away when he caught her by the arm.

'I've just got in,' he told her breathlessly.

She liked the fleecy boots, the high peaked cap pushed back from his handsome face which hadn't been changed by the dangers of wartime.

'Was that your flying boat I saw coming in about an hour ago?'

'Yes it was. We go out on patrol, shadowing the convoys to make sure they're safe from U-boats.'

'And did you spot a U-boat today?' she enquired.

'We thought we did, and we were going down to depth-charge it when we saw it was a whale close to the surface, so thank goodness we didn't blow it out of the water.'

He took her arm to a hotel on the esplanade and ordered supper. There was a food shortage, but he was a glamorous Canadian who had crossed the Atlantic to help the war effort, so the cook put extra on the two plates.

'How is your sister?' Esther asked as she ate haddock.

'She wanted to come across with me to be a Land Girl, but our parents need her to run the hotel.'

'You started off in ordinary aeroplanes, didn't you?' his dining companion asked, puzzled.

'I did, but luckily before war broke out I switched to flying boats.'

'Don't you miss Canada?'

'I love this place. It's so beautiful, with its mountains and water. It reminds me of Vancouver.'

They were seated at the window and he turned appreciatively to look across the sunset bay, anchored flying boats riding the swell.

'Is it dangerous?' Esther wanted to know, because she was in love with this handsome courteous man whose accent was like a caress.

'I don't think we're likely to meet any German fighters over the Atlantic. The main danger is from a surfaced U-boat firing up at us, but not if we get in first with our depth-charges. The Sunderland's a pretty reliable machine. What about you: what are you doing?'

She told him that she had become a teacher of small children, and that it was a challenging, satisfying profession. Was she still dancing? Oh yes, with Miss Milligan.

'I wonder when the next Summer School will be?' he mused.

'As soon as the war finishes, Miss Milligan says.'

'When I'm flying over the ocean I think a lot about these happy times at St Andrews – and of you of course. I hope you think of me when you're dancing in Miss Milligan's class.'

'I think about you – and your sister – a great deal,' she added earnestly. 'When do you think this war will be over?'

'It's got a long way to run yet. Hitler's got a lot of fire-power. Look at the punishment the convoys have been taking from the U-boats. They move about like sharks. Last week we were out on patrol when we saw a torpedo streaking through the sea. If only we could have shouted to the man on the bridge – get your ship out of the way! But it was travelling so fast and in the direct hit the ship broke in two. We dropped depth-charges where we thought the U-boat had submerged, then went down to look for survivors from the torpedoed ship. There weren't any. It's not the waste of cargo but the waste of men. These were fathers, sons, brothers.'

The creative kitchen produced an apple pie for two, with a modest jug of custard, a rarer commodity than whisky in the town. He walked her home in the autumn darkness to her lodgings, kissing her on the step.

'Will I see you tomorrow?' she asked.

'We'll be out on patrol, but I'll be back in the evening.'

She waited at the railings on the esplanade, watching a flying boat coming in from the west, but a passerby informed her that it was a Catalina. Half an hour later the powerful four engines of the Sunderland brought it down safely, and it taxied across the bay. Esther shielded her eyes against the setting sun to watch the crew emerging from the door in the side.

He's with her half an hour later, and takes her to a different hotel for supper, where the cook is weary of having to provide for airmen with large appetites. Tonight it's rabbit, which Esther has never tried before, but it's acceptable after the sea air. He puts his arm round her waist as he walks with her along the esplanade, away from the town. Airmen aren't supposed to be seen in the company of women, but he doesn't care. He loves her, and has a surprise for her, not a ring, because it's too soon and besides, he wants to follow the protocol of asking her first.

He turns into the large cathedral, and as she follows him she wants to express her surprise. *I didn't know you were a Catholic.* But what does it matter? She has no prejudices with regard to religion.

It's wartime and there are no candles to light. Instead they sit side by side in the front pew. He's praying that he'll survive the war and that they can marry and settle down. Perhaps she would like to emigrate to Canada? If that doesn't take her fancy, he'll gladly stay in Scotland and become a commercial airline pilot.

Her silent prayer is the same: survival for him, and marriage. If he wants her to return to Canada with him, she will. Out there she should be able to teach.

He takes her hand to her lodgings, as if they're already married, and tonight's kiss is longer, more passionate, stretching her out of her shoes.

'I've something for you,' he tells her, taking a paper from his pocket.

She unfolds it to read the title: Miss Esther Scott's Fancy. It's a strathspey, and at the bottom Gregor has written: *Devised by Gregor Macpherson for Miss Esther Scott while on duty with the Royal Canadian Air Force at Oban, Argyll, in 1942.*

'I'll treasure this,' she told him, hugging the paper to her heart.

Esther returned to Glasgow on another crowded train and went back to her Cowcaddens classroom. Careless talk cost lives, certainly, but where was the danger in telling a class of intrigued children about a journey she had made to an unnamed place in the west of Scotland (better to be cautious) to meet a friend, a Canadian who flew a plane which could land on water? The Sunderland she drew on the blackboard had an askew float, and an ominous bulge on the back. There were a whole series of lessons on this theme. She told the totally silent class, all eyes intently on her, how planes took off from this unknown bay and flew out over the Atlantic. Who knew where the Atlantic was, an opportunity to sling a map over the blackboard? The mighty sea was relocated east and north, to Russia, the Arctic, but a girl came out to point out its true place.

'That's Canada. My friend comes from the west coast.'

Fingers snapped. 'Please Miss, did he fly his plane all that way across?'

'I don't know, Tommy, but he's brave enough to have done so.' She moved the brass-tipped pointer. 'This is Vancouver, beside another ocean, the Pacific, much warmer than the Atlantic. There's fighting going on on this ocean also, because Japan is at war with us and America. Can anyone tell me how Japan went to war with America?'

Furious fingers snapped with the answer of Pearl Harbour, so that place of infamy had to be located on the map. The bell went, the lesson to be resumed tomorrow, about convoys protected by flying boats flown by fearless Canadians.

In the evening, if she weren't out dancing in Miss Milligan's class, Esther was writing letters to her Canadian aviator, or listening to the late news on the wireless, then praying before sleep that this terrible war would soon be over, and she could go up the aisle with a groom in the uniform of the Royal Canadian Air Force. She received regular replies from Oban, but with no mention of the flying boat base in case that attracted a German raider from across the North Sea. The lessons moved on to talk about the war, the reassurance to her charges that their fathers would soon be home, and women working in munitions factories and ploughing with tractors would be back with their families.

The Sunderland had gone out to protect the convoy from Halifax, Nova Scotia, in the Western Approaches, a mile of strung-out vital supplies. There were no German predators that choppy day. The flying boat was returning to base when the Canadian pilot was alerted that the far portside engine was on fire. It was too risky, trying to get back to base in Oban, still sixty miles away, so he turned towards the island to starboard. Below was a broad sea loch, with a community at its head. He was bringing the Sunderland down to land on the loch, but too late saw the floating debris, a horsebox from a previously torpedoed ship taking a prize stud out to the safety of India nearly two years before. The obstacle sheared off the float, and a wing struck the rough water. As the airframe began to sink the pilot tried desperately to find a way out, even kicking the screen with his fur-lined boots.

It was Mrs Armstrong who brought her the telegram from Judi in Canada with the terrible news; Mrs Armstrong who comforted her and drove her up to Oban for the funeral, the coffins covered with the Canadian flag, a piper playing a lament. After the interment she asked Mrs Armstrong to wait for her while she went into the Cathedral on the esplanade where she and her sweetheart had sat together, and where she placed the candle she had brought on the iron wheel with a prayer.

The children in the Cowcaddens class could see that their teacher was grieving, so they were quiet and respectful, doing their sums and reading when she asked them. The headmaster's impressed face stopped in the glass pane on the door, nodded, then moved on to the next classroom in search of a situation in which he could exercise his skill at thrashing pupils. Esther didn't trust herself to talk about the war without breaking down, but at night, the submerged Sunderland was under the surface of her dream, a silhouette like a giant bird with a broken wing. Judi wrote an anguished airmail, saying that their mother had taken to her bed at the news, and was unlikely to rise again.

'And you, Esther,' she wrote, 'Gregor was so in love with you and so looking forward to bringing you to Canada. But please don't think that you need to cherish his memory by not having another relationship. That was what my brother would want, for you to be happy.'

Esther took her heartbreak to Miss Jean Milligan's flat in the west end and showed her the strathspey which Gregor had composed for her.

'I like it,' the major-domo told her protégée. 'I'll find a tune for it and we'll dance it at my next class.'

Miss Milligan was always active, collecting sweaters for seamen and cash for the National Savings Association, because this staunch patriot was determined that her country would have sufficient resources to win.

'You remember that very successful International Night which we had last year, when the Poles, Austrians and Indians gave demonstrations of their national dances?' she spoke with Esther. 'I want to put on another dance for the Polish refugees, and this time I want to teach them some Scottish country dancing. I need your help to organize it.'

Esther found herself in a hall with a hundred Polish servicemen and the same number of females from the Glasgow branch of Miss Milligan's Scottish Country Dance Society. The windows were blacked out, light supplied by two storm lanterns which turned the hall into an eerie cavern. Miss Milligan had anticipated that the Poles would turn up in boots, so she had put out an appeal for shoes, and they were lined up on one side of the hall in various sizes and colours. Most of the men found their fit, and those with problematic feet had to dance in their stockings. Miss Milligan began a warm-up session by asking each woman to find a partner and lead him round the hall in promenade hold. She showed the intrigued Poles how to hold the hand of a partner without exercising their strength. Then she called out Esther to demonstrate the parts of the *pas de basque* as she counted out 1, 2, 3. The foreign visitors were encouraged to try. Usually Miss Milligan was critical of the footwork of the men in her classes and teams, but this was wartime, and these were brave men dispossessed of their homeland and now supporting Great Britain.

'Well done!' Miss Milligan complimented the class.

It was time for a simple dance in sets of four couples: set, down the set for two travelling steps, return for the same number, cast off one place, rights and lefts in a square, turn your partner by the right hand for four, then with the left, then six hands round and back. The Poles then taught the Cracow Wedding, a dance of gaiety and zest. At the end they returned their borrowed footwear, and some of them kissed the teacher. Trestle tables were being set up, and sandwiches brought in from the kitchen, with corned beef between the buttered slices, courtesy of an American quartermaster.

As the war progressed Esther felt able again to talk about victory, to sling the map of Europe across the blackboard. She brought in several newspapers, and the children cut out cardboard flags, fixing them to the blackboard with plasticine to plot the Allied advance across Europe. She received the permission of the headmaster to have a party for the children on a Friday in the school hall. Miss Milligan drove round the city bakeries, asking for donations of cakes, and the American club at Charing Cross gave her two cases of Coca-Cola. An accordionist who usually entertained a cinema queue came into the school for five shillings, and Miss Milligan helped the teacher to organize the pupils into sets of six for the Dashing White Sergeant. The headmaster appeared, but when he took off his jacket it wasn't for a belting session, to keep his arm in, but to dance in a set.

On VE Day Esther danced a reel in George Square with a group of like-minded friends, and afterwards they went to Miss Milligan's for a party, where the sisters used up most of the ingredients they had hoarded during the war for a magnificent cake, with a dancing couple (the kilt and lady's tartan sash had taken hours) on the top. The toast in red wine was to 'the health and prosperity of the Scottish Country Dance Society.'

In August Esther attended the first post-war Summer School. Miss Milligan gathered the students around the wireless to hear the official announcement of the surrender of tenacious Japan. Esther rejoiced with the others, but it was sad to think of the men who had enlivened the sets before the war with their footwork and exuberance, but who hadn't returned. Judi made the crossing from Canada, and she and Esther wept over their lost dancing partner. Though the ration books of the participants were collected, there was plenty of food. Miss Milligan gave a talk to her students, reminding them that the spirit of Scotland showed itself in dancing, just as in poetry and music.

'Remember, myself and Mrs Stewart, our co-founder, consulted the oldest books on Scottish country dancing, and sought the opinions of old people who'd performed the dances in their younger days. We didn't just make them up. I'm proud to say that men in the Forces have been doing Scottish country dances all over the world, and I've received many moving letters from prisoners of war in Germany. One man wrote to tell me that he'd been placed in solitary confinement, but preserved his sanity by dancing all the Scottish country dances he had memorized as first man in imaginary sets.'

Esther had a strange feeling of depression as Glasgow returned slowly to its peacetime pace and ways. There had been something exciting and unpredictable in the atmosphere of the sandbagged city, with the patterns of searchlights in the sky, and the mournful warning of the siren. Many of the fathers of her pupils returned, and she saw the excitement in their faces and had them out one by one in front of the class to relate their male parents' experiences. She couldn't forget that the girl in the front row, biting her knuckles, was waiting for her father to return from Japanese captivity. But Esther would never know that he had died of maltreatment and malnutrition, a twelve stone shipyard worker who had shinned up scaffolding like a monkey reduced to five stones of skeletal immobility while forced to help build a railway through the jungle.

In June 1946 Esther was one of the dancers demonstrating the Duchess of Buccleuch's Favourite and other dances in the forecourt of Holyrood Palace for the Royal Family's visit. This led to a request amounting to a command for several dancers to perform in the Throne Room of the Palace, and Esher was in the same set as the King for the Eightsome Reel.

The Summer School of that same year ran for three weeks. Miss Milligan taught the Victory Book, including the St Valery Reel, renamed the Reel of the 51st Division, the prison camp creation by men determined that their love of dancing wouldn't be suppressed by their brutal jailors. In the afternoons European national dances were taught with Irish and Highland. There were people in the corridors of University Hall with teapots and kettles, preparing for parties after the years of austerity, and the common room was crowded for social dancing.

The following year Miss Milligan told Esther: 'We have our greatest chance to demonstrate the delights of Scottish country dancing. We've been asked to dance at Hamden Park for the spectators before the Britain versus Europe football match, and I've put your name down.' In front of a crowd of over one hundred and thirty thousand, the dancers in white dresses, sashes and kilts marched on to the pitch to the pipes and drums of the Highland Light Infantry, and hardened spectators used to rough tackles applauded the elegance and sense of rhythm.

Her mother was ailing, so Esther decided that she had to return to Hawick. She secured a primary school post easily, but found her home drab and depressing after the airy brightness of Mrs Armstrong's flat and the freedom of the city. Having lived with her Glasgow hostess, Esther had changed. Her clothes were elegant, her accent different. Miss Milligan had sent her home with the injunction to spread Scottish country dancing throughout the Borders, so that there would be a class in every community. Miss Milligan had examined her herself and pronounced her competent to be a dance teacher.

'What do you think of that?' Esther's mother asked her, passing the local paper across the supper table.

'I don't believe it!'

> Major Martin Elliot, M.C. has returned to Hawick after distinguished war service. A former mechanic in one of the town's hosiery mills, he enlisted as a private in the King's Own Scottish Borderers at the outbreak of war. An outstanding soldier, he was offered a commission, and soon rose to the rank of Captain. For his bravery in silencing a German machine-gun at the Normandy Landings, he was awarded the Military Cross and promoted to Major. He fought through France, Belgium, Holland, and crossed the Siegfried Line, advancing with his battalion across the Rhine and into Germany. He was twice mentioned in Despatches and received the Croix de Guerre.

Esther sat studying the face under the military cap. She could barely believe that this was the same shy person who had worked beside her in the mill. He had grown a moustache, and his face had filled out, making him very handsome. It gave her a thrill to think that a person could be so transformed by the test of war.

She met him several days later when she was going home from a tiring day at school.

'Shouldn't I salute the war hero?' she asked, but without sarcasm.

'There's no need to do that. Come and have some tea,' he urged, and took her on his arm to the Station Hotel.

He didn't want to talk about his wartime exploits; about those in his regimental company who wouldn't be coming back; about the pitiful refugees they had encountered on their advance across ruined Germany.

'Somehow I don't think you'll be going back to the mill,' Esther hazarded.

'I'm going to work with horses.'

'With horses? But of course, you were our Cornet in the Common Riding. Have you still got your mare?'

'She's been well looked after on a local farm when I've been away. I was riding her yesterday.'

'How are you going to make a living with one horse?' she enquired seriously.

'I had the opportunity to go riding with one of the officers when I was commissioned. He has a big estate in the Borders, and races horses. He's asked me to be his trainer.'

'That's wonderful, considering you hadn't ridden a horse a year before the war.'

'I'm a quick learner. What about you?' he asked, leaning across the table to give her his total attention.

'I'm a school teacher.'

'You say that as if it's nothing, but to get where you are from being a machinist is wonderful. I think we should have dinner on Friday, if you're free.'

'I've started a country dance class on Fridays.'

'What about Saturday?'

She nodded assent.

'Why don't you come to the dance class?'

'Because my feet are safer in stirrups.'

Esther and Martin were married the following summer. Members of the King's Own Scottish Borderers formed a guard of honour at the church, and at the dance after the reception, Miss Milligan, now retired from Jordanhill, took to the floor. It was a few days before her sixty second birthday. She was stout, but she went down the set with her partner with the speed and agility of a twenty year old.

What did the rest of Mrs Esther Elliot's life hold? She danced before the new Queen, and ran a very successful Scottish country dance class in Hawick. Miss Esther Scott's Fancy, the strathspey the Canadian flying boat pilot had composed for her, became a popular dance everywhere. Esther and Martin had two children. The girl, Marjorie, inherited her mother's dancing ability, but the boy, Charles, took after his father and became a horseman and an international show jumper. Major Martin Elliot ran a very successful racing stable, training a Derby winner. Miss Milligan always stayed overnight with the Elliots on her way to cross the Border to visit yet another new branch. Esther's annual holiday was the Summer School at St Andrews. Mrs Armstrong had died and left her twenty thousand pounds in her will, which the Elliots used to build a new house, with paddocks for horses.

There were more and more new dances to master, new faces in the classes at St Andrews. But Esther never lost her love for the Summer School, where she taught for many years, and was one of Miss Milligan's dearest friends.

Piper Through the Meadow Straying

I was aged eight when Aunt Maeve died. She was actually mother's aunt, but that is what I called her. She fell, breaking her hip, and lay for a day in agony before her neighbour found her and phoned for an ambulance. She never regained consciousness in the infirmary, and a week later I went with mother to clear her flat in the Townhead area of Glasgow. It was up two flights of worn stairs in a tenement which, two years later, would be knocked down to widen a road.

Mother opened the lid of a large wooden box, explaining to me that it was called a kist and would have been in Maeve's family for generations. Folded on the top was the shroud she had sewn herself. Mother held it up, noting how beautifully the seams had been hand-stitched, considering that it was a garment no one but the undertakers would see.

Underneath the shroud was a blue waistcoat on which many small medals had been sewn in neat rows.

'That's part of the poor soul's Irish dancing costume,' mother said emotionally.

'Can I have it?' I asked impulsively.

'I suppose so, but we should keep the medals, which look like silver,' she said, handing me the garments.

The next item in the kist was the pleated white skirt she wore with the waistcoat, and below it, a pair of heavy black shoes, with coins attached to the insteps. I slipped off my own shoes and laced up Aunt Maeve's, which fitted me, and when I walked about the coins tinkled like bells.

'They're her dancing shoes,' mother informed me. 'Take

them off and help me.'

At the bottom of the kist was a bundle of papers secured with an elastic band. Mother took them from me, in the hope that one of them was an insurance policy, but they turned out to be postcard views of Chicago.

'Put them in the bin,' mother said, but I sat at the table, going through them. Among the postcards was a programme headed the *World's Fair, Chicago, 1934: demonstration of Irish Dancing*, with a photograph of three women and the same number of men. All of the women had medals sewn to their waistcoats. They were wearing berets with feathers and heavy black shoes and holding hands aloft.

'Is one of these Aunt Maeve?' I asked mother.

She was harassed, having to clear the house, and she glanced at the photograph. 'That's her, second from the left,' she told me abruptly, handing me back the programme. 'I thought you were here to help me, not to waste time over old papers.'

But it wasn't time wasted. I lay on my bed, studying the postcards of Chicago and the World's Fair programme. How could a woman who lived in a dingy flat in Glasgow and who had no money have been dancing in Chicago? The postcards with their skyscrapers fascinated me, and I neglected my homework. I laced on the black shoes and hopped round the room in them, the coins tinkling, chanting: 'Chicago Chicago Chicago.' The following morning, having dreamt of looking out from the top storey of a skyscraper down on a fabled city, I informed my parents at the breakfast table that I wanted to learn Irish dancing. They looked at each other dubiously.

'Lessons will be expensive,' mother cautioned. 'If we agree

you'll have to stick at it – not like the piano.'

She was referring to the lessons I had had when I was six, and which involved two bus journeys across the city to a terraced house on the south side where Mrs Henderson, a large and formidable lady with an unfriendly cat, took pupils. After half a dozen lessons she told my mother: 'your daughter has really no interest in working at scales.' I was relieved, though on the way home mother complained about the wasted money.

'I'll stick at the dancing,' I promised my long-suffering parents.

A phone call was made and I was taken to be enrolled in the Teresa Mathew School of Irish Dance in a hall in Pollokshields, and instructed where to buy the appropriate soft shoes in the city. I was enthralled by the sight of about thirty students, ranging from ones who looked as though they were still toddlers, to teenagers, dancing in an arc to music from a tape. I was led into a smaller room by Miss Mathew to see if I had the co-ordination to become an Irish dancer. I was enrolled in what I would learn was one of the premier Irish dance schools, with six world champions to its credit.

I loved Irish dance and practised dutifully in my bedroom, though when I put on Aunt Maeve's heavy shoes mother said that it sounded as if I were trying to bring down the ceiling.

'You're a natural dancer,' Miss Mathew complimented me, and put me into the Christmas show of the school.

Irish dancing costumes are very expensive, with their embroidery and appliqué, and I knew that I couldn't ask my parents to invest in one. I took Aunt Maeve's blue jacket to the next class in a carrier bag and showed it to Miss Mathew.

'What have we got here?' she asked, most intrigued as

115

she held it up to admire the rows of medals. 'This is surely the apparel of a champion – but someone from the past, judging by the design of the jacket.'

When I told her that it had belonged to my great aunt Maeve O'Byrne, she became excited.

'She was a very famous Irish dancer, winner of many championships. I understand now why you're such a good dancer.'

'I'd like to wear this jacket for the Christmas show,' I told her.

'You couldn't wear it with all these medals, otherwise the audience will think you won them, and it would be a shame to remove them. I'll lend you a costume.'

It was black, with a golden harp embroidered on the shawl. I was to dance the jig Three Sea Captains. I was nervous as I stood, the toe of Aunt Maeve's heavy shoe poised to begin the dance, but once I got going it was as if the footwear had taken over my movements, making them light and effortless as I trebled and battered, crossing the stage with a high kick, and after I had taken my bow Miss Mathew hugged me for 'being a credit to my school.'

I became obsessed with Irish dancing, and if I had been allowed to wear the heavy shoes to school, I would have. They stood by my bed, and I polished them so carefully, as if they were made of the precious skin of an extinct creature. As my steps and confidence improved, despite the increasingly complicated dances I was being taught, I was entered for local competitions on Saturdays, which meant that mother had to drive me there and spend most of the day with me. But I was too young to feel guilty about that, and I loved the atmosphere among my dancing peers as mothers dressed them and brushed their hair, even checking their steps before they went up on stage. Since infancy I had been a shy and somewhat withdrawn child, but wearing these heavy shoes of the champion Maeve gave me confidence, and I seemed to fly across the stage as if my footwear was weightless. I began to collect medals which I stitched on to Maeve's little blue jacket which I wanted to wear, but mother bought me a second-hand modest costume that lacked the intricate embroidery of my competitors.

'One day you'll be a world champion,' Miss Mathew predicted after I had won another silver cup.

The floor of my bedroom continued to reverberate with my treblings and batterings, so mother moved the television into the dining-room. And then she became sick. I find it difficult to write that simple stark sentence, because, many years later, I still feel guilty that I brought it on with the strain I'd imposed on her by having to be taken to competitions, and by disrupting the household with my loud practising. I was twelve, with the dining-room sideboard covered in cups, and yet overnight they lost their lustre and meaning. I wasn't told what mother's complaint was, but I heard father telling Aunt Mary on the phone. Cancer. That word featured in a diagram showing the signs of the Zodiac I had seen in an encyclopaedia in the school library. I was Aries, but mother was Cancer whose symbol was a crab. I didn't like the look of the creature, and when I heard the word spoken I imagined it digging its claws into mother's flesh.

My great-aunt's heavy shoes were put in the bottom of my wardrobe because there were no more practices on the floorboards of my bedroom, no more trips to competitions. Mother became so weak that she could no longer do the housework, and Aunt Mary arrived to help. She warned my brother and me that the house had to be kept very quiet because mother needed to regain her strength and health through sleep. I went about in my stocking soles.

Then, one afternoon when I came home from school, mother wasn't there. I was hysterical, accusing my aunt of not letting me see her before she died.

'She's not dead, you silly girl. She's been taken to hospital, where she'll get the treatment she requires.'

The following week, when we were taken to see her, I saw that my aunt had lied to me. The sign at the end of the driveway said 'hospice', not 'hospital.' I had been in hospital at the age of six to have my tonsils removed, but that place was very different. I was in a ward with other children, but mother was in a single room, and there was no sign of medical equipment. I saw how she was becoming an old woman with sunken cheeks, like the lollipop lady in the yellow coat who took us across the road to school. I saw also the bones through the skin on the backs of her hands as they lay inert on the cover.

I came to dread these visits, because, with the intuition of a child, I knew that she wouldn't get better. This was the first death I was going to have to face. I had cried bitterly when I had lost my guinea pig, but I knew that this one was going to be very different and that, though you can replace a guinea pig, you can't a parent. Yet in a sense she had already departed from our lives, because she was in an institution from which she wouldn't be returning to us.

Since I first opened my eyes to the world mother had always placed a little vase of flowers in my bedroom window, and she remembered coming in to find me trying to climb out of my cot to reach them. But I came to hate the sickly smell of the lilies which father had placed beside her bed in the hospice.

One Saturday afternoon father said to me: 'I want you to get your dancing shoes.'

'Are we going to a competition?' I asked eagerly.

'No, we're going to visit mum. She said you were to take Aunt Maeve's shoes, and your tape and player.'

Mother's voice was very weak, and I had to lean over her bed to hear her request.

'Will you dance for me, darling?'

I sat on the floor and laced up the heavy shoes of a dead champion, and then I selected the music for Piper Through the Meadow Straying. There wasn't space in mother's small room to dance, but the nurses wheeled her bed out into the corridor. I stood, my toe poised, waiting for the music which father was operating. I had put on Maeve's little blue jacket with the silver medals, and I swear to this day that it was not me who danced up and down the corridor of the hospice while mother, raised up in her deathbed by a nurse, watched. It was the spirit of the girl who had occupied these heavy shoes long before me, and whose dazzling steps had earned her the many medals which flashed on her petite jacket as I trebled and battered, spun, kicked high.

At the end, as I bowed, mother's wasted hands came together in inaudible applause. She died, peacefully, they maintained, that evening.

This should be the end of this story, a child who was encouraged by her mother to dance in the face of death, who was being told that the dedication and the performances had to go on. But I didn't wear the heavy shoes again. Our aunt returned home, and father was left with two children to bring up. On Saturdays, instead of going to Irish dancing competitions, I had to help him shop at the supermarket and to clean the house. I wore an apron instead of a dancing costume, slippers on my feet instead of heavy jig shoes. In the early days of our bereavement I cried myself to sleep, but time allocated duties to me that meant that I was too exhausted to weep. Miss Mathew even came round to the house, to implore me to return to her dance school. She told father that she would waive the fees 'because your daughter is a future world champion, I'm sure of that.'

'You must go back; that's what mum would have wanted,' he urged me.

'Maybe next month.'

Months; years; secondary school. I was becoming too old to be a champion, and the shoes were wrapped in a carrier bag in the wardrobe. When I married they moved with me to my new home. Maeve's little blue jacket with the medals was protected by polythene on a hanger in the wardrobe, and one afternoon when I came across it I thought suddenly: *I was too busy dancing to ask mother about Aunt Maeve. Was she ever married*? But the certificates which mother had taken from her aunt's house in order to register the death had disappeared. I intended, the next time I was in Edinburgh, to go into Register House to get a copy of her death certificate, but it slipped my mind.

It wasn't until I was watching a television programme called 'Who Do You Think You Are?' that I thought about Aunt Maeve again. I went to the library and was directed to the local history section, where a most helpful woman told me that I could look up certificates on-line for the payment of a fee.

I found it difficult in the beginning, and wasted money

on false trails, but I did find Maeve O' Byrne and sent away for her death certificate. She was born in Cork City on 5 March 1914. Her mother Lily was a chambermaid, her father Patrick a bricklayer. But what intrigued me was that Maeve was shown as a widow. Then who was her husband? I became more skilled at using the computer for genealogical investigation and asked Ireland to send me her marriage certificate. The letter returned my cheque, informing me that 'there is no wedding certificate for a person of this name, with this birth date, in the records.'

That summer I persuaded my husband that we should take a holiday in the south-west of Ireland, based in Cork City. I took the mystery of Maeve's missing marriage certificate to the library there. A charming woman wrote down as many details as I could give her, and promised to get in touch with me in due course.

A month later I received this letter:

> You asked me to investigate the background of Maeve O'Byrne, your great aunt, who was born in Cork City in 1914. I have been in touch with a member of the local history society, who is an authority on the history of Irish dancing in Cork. This lady, Mrs O'Sullivan, has given me copies of newspaper cuttings showing that Maeve learned her Irish dancing at the Cork Pipers Club under the great Irish dancer and teacher Cormac O'Keeffe. Maeve was considered to be one of the most gifted junior dancers in Ireland at that time. As an All-Ireland champion she was invited to perform at the World's Fair in Chicago in 1934. She was such a success that she was invited to dance the Garden of Daisies on the Major

Bowes Radio Show in New York City, with a microphone at floor level to broadcast her perfect steps. She was presented with a pair of heavy dance shoes, specially made for her, by an Irish cobbler in New York, with coins in the instep for luck, because of the pleasure she had given the Irish community there through her dances.

But Maeve evidently didn't return to Ireland with the rest of the Irish contingent. Mrs O' Sullivan informs me that an old man she interviewed in Cork City some years ago informed her that his brother, who had emigrated to New York, was told that Maeve had gone to one of the southern states of America to dance and had there fallen in with a black trumpeter in a dance band. Mrs O'Sullivan believes that a baby was born, but that they didn't marry. Mrs O'Sullivan has no information as to why Maeve should have ended up in Glasgow, or what became of the baby. But she points out that it certainly ended Maeve's dancing career, because the Catholic Church was very involved in Irish dancing, and an illegitimate child was considered a sin. Mrs O'Sullivan thinks that Maeve might have been barred from competitions, even though she might have put the child for adoption.

With the lack of paperwork and family memories, I cannot see how you will be able to trace this child, assuming that he or she is still alive.

In the Deep South of America, in New Orleans perhaps, did Maeve fall in love with a beautiful black man with large expressive eyes and a genius for improvisation at jazz on the trumpet? Did mother die before having the opportunity to tell me about Maeve's child? He or she may be living in Glasgow, where I am. I could have sat opposite this person on the subway. Is he or she half coloured? Who knows? As for my Irish dancing career, it ended even before Maeve's, but I don't regret it.

Last year I went to the World Irish Dancing Championships in Glasgow. I'm told that some of the costumes cost in excess of one thousand pounds, and that's only a small part of the outlay of turning a son or daughter into a world champion. I sat opposite a group of American mothers as they watched their children competing. The parents were poised on the edge of their seats, willing them to do well and watching the electronic scoreboard as if their lives depended on its outcome. I was glad that I hadn't gone forward in my dance career.

Recently I went into my daughter's bedroom to find her sitting on the floor, trying on Maeve's heavy shoes. I didn't tell her they were for dancing, and took them away to put them up in the loft, with the blue jacket sewn with silver medals, because some things are sacred.

Reel of Three

The Honourable Blythe Campbell took the chair in the hairdressing salon on the Flying Scotsman speeding towards Edinburgh.

'I want it cut short, to here,' she ordered the hairdresser, holding her flat palm at her neck.

'You have beautiful hair, Madam,' the hairdresser enthused, teasing the long blonde strands through her fingers.

'Cut it. I'm going dancing.'

Her hair fell round her shoes as the train passed through the Border country of towers and farms. She felt freer than she had been in years.

'Where are you going dancing, Madam?' the voice enquired as the scissors flashed round her head like a silver bird.

'The Summer School in St Andrews,' she said, easing her feet from her shoes. She had left her husband behind on the platform at King's Cross. He was a Major with the 1st Battalion the Argyll and Sutherland Highlanders, a discontented officer because the Battalion had been on home service for years, based now at Tidworth Barracks in Wiltshire. Major Aeneas Campbell yearned for a posting to a place of sunshine and interesting customs, which is why he envied the 2nd Battalion, stationed in India. He was heartily sick of staring at his own reflection in the regimental silver at Mess dinners, disgusted with the consumption of whisky by his fellow officers and the foul odour of cigars that permeated his kilt. The Major was a proud man, of an ancient sept of the Campbells of Argyll. He had a five-bay laird's house on his five thousand acre estate on the Argyllshire coast, parts of the mansion dating back to the seventeenth century, with the addition of a drum tower, circa 1840, which, he thought, spoiled its character. From his drawing-room window he could see the Bens of Jura. His grandfather had driven his own cattle to market in the south, conversing with his shepherds in Gaelic, but the Major had only a few words of his ancestral language.

His ancestor had fought on the Hanoverian side at Culloden, and his father had fought in South Africa with the 91st Highlanders, bringing home the spear belonging to a Zulu warrior, one of many he had shot. As a boy the Major had been wakened on winter mornings by a crashing sound, as if the foundations of the earth were shifting underneath the house. The gamekeeper was using a sledgehammer to burst the ice on the pool under the waterfall. The next disturbance was a riding crop slamming against the door. Aeneas rose immediately, buckling on his kilt and pulling on the thin shirt before leading his two brothers along the passage with a candle. The piper was already tuning up on the frost-whitened lawn. The patriarch kept time with his riding crop against his kilted thigh as his three sons danced a Highland Fling in their bare feet, and then they were herded through the trees to cast off their garments and enter the jagged hole left in the pool by the sledgehammer. The patriarch stood on the bank, a hunter watch on his palm, timing the morning plunge to exactly ten minutes. Naked, blue, like strange aquatic creatures newly born, the brothers trooped back to the mansion house, to a breakfast of brose laced liberally with salt.

Little wonder, therefore, that Aeneas Campbell loathed dancing, and refused to participate in the activity when he joined the Argylls. He had been introduced to Blythe at a function in London, and when a foxtrot was announced, she held out her hand and asked: 'Shall we?' only to have him tread on her toes. He was convinced that her beauty and his modest means would prevent her from marrying him. She had been photographed by Cecil Beaton for *Tatler*, and named debutante of the year against fierce competition. But several months later he was invited to a shoot at her home in Aberdeenshire. Her father, Alfred Halside, was the principal of an armaments firm that had supplied guns for the Crimean War and made a further fortune out of the first Sino-Japanese conflict. His father had bought a twenty thousand acre estate on Deeside, as close as possible to Balmoral, and when Alfred inherited as a young man he decided to pull down the old primitive mansion with its resident rodent population. He was driven round in goggles and a duster coat in one of the first motors in Aberdeenshire to inspect the new mansions of the area, but decided that he didn't want to replicate the designs of the fashionable architect Alexander Marshall Mackenzie, his two storeyed Mar Lodge with its mullion windows and half-timbered gables, Dinnet House's three storeys with massive crenellations and crowsteps. He had commissioned Robert Lorimer (not yet knighted) to build him a baronial style house on the site of the old one. It had sixty rooms, the public apartments on the first floor, from which one could access the granite loggia that overlooked the loch. The house had its own electricity supply, from a power house fed by the river. The servants had to wheel the meals from the cavernous tiled kitchen along a sixty yard long corridor to the dumb waiter, to be hoisted to the dining-room, whose panelled walls opened to reveal racks for bottles of wine, and shelves for cigar humidors.

It was this house, said to be Lorimer's masterpiece, which Blythe grew up in. She spent all day in the nursery with a governess, and half an hour before dinner was led with her siblings up to the drawing-room, to meet her parents for the first and only time in the day before they went into dinner. She was five when Winston Churchill, First Lord of the Admiralty, his breath tainted by brandy, kissed her goodnight.

On a spring day the following year the three children were led down to the hall and introduced by their father to a fierce-looking moustached man in a balmoral and tartan trews.

'This is Mr Mackenzie, who's going to teach you dancing.'

'They'll need pumps, sir,' the dancing master informed his new employer.

That first day he made them dance in bare feet on Lorimer's sprung floor of boards from the remnants of the ancient Caledonian Forest. He demonstrated the *pas de basque* by dancing the setting step while playing the fiddle. Little Blythe was enchanted, and 'Dancie' Mackenzie, as he was known at all the big houses he travelled round to teach dancing, became a figure of awe and the greatest respect amounting to adoration. She cried when he strapped the fiddle on his back at the end of the lesson and went out to the pony which was his mode of conveyance and for which Blythe stole sugar lumps from the silver bowl in the butler's pantry.

She would be at the window on the stair landing, looking through one of the coloured squares to watch for the arrival of the peripatetic dancing master on his docile mount, and when it snowed and he couldn't make it through the drifts, she was distraught and had to be given a powder by the nurse.

'You're my star pupil,' 'Dancie' Mackenzie confided to Blythe one afternoon when the sun through the stained glass window on the stair was fragmented into myriad colours on the floor of the hall. 'I go round the great houses in Aberdeenshire, teaching adults as well as children, but I've never seen such perfect steps. You must keep up your dancing, because it'll give you great joy throughout your life. In one mansion I go to the ninety year old grandmother joins the children, and dances the reels better than they can.'

In 1920 Alfred Halside was raised to the peerage for his contribution to the Allied victory in the Great War, and asked Lorimer to add a ballroom to his already large house. At a ball to celebrate the title and the new ballroom, Blythe, in a gown of white muslin styled from an illustration in an old painting, performed to an enchanted society audience, including royals, the Deeside Lilt which 'Dancie' Mackenzie had taught her, supplying the music for his most gifted pupil on his own violin. The instrument had belonged to Niel Gow and its mellow sound-box seemed to have retained the maestro's compositions, as if it were his hand, and not the Aberdeenshire dancing master's sweeping the bow.

Blythe's life in the Deeside mansion revolved round dances. She would rise late, have a prolonged bath, the water laced with lavender, then confer with the visiting dressmaker about a new creation for a coming ball. In September 1934 she went to a thrilling Highland Ball at Mar Lodge given by Prince and Princess Arthur of Connaught. After dinner the guests were led out of the Lodge to the ballroom, a separate building about one hundred and fifty yards away, along a pathway of coconut matting, under an archway of flaming torches as pipers played 'Hieland Laddie'. Over a hundred employees on the Mar Lodge estate had been invited to the ball, and Blythe danced a rousing Duke of Perth with a ghillie in brogues. But the spectacle of the heads of hundreds of stags displayed round the vaulted ceiling sickened this passionate lover of animals.

The following year she attended the Ghillies' Ball at Balmoral and danced the Paul Jones, one of her partners being a gamekeeper. She heard about the future king Edward's affair with Wallis Simpson, a married woman, but her father, staunchest of royalists, prohibited discussion of it at table. In September 1937 a house party, including Blythe, motored in two Rolls-Royces to the County Ball in the Beach Ballroom, Aberdeen, the floral crown surmounting the fountain celebrating Coronation Year. She was in the same ballroom that December, among the eight hundred attending the annual ball of the local branch of the Royal National Lifeboat Institution, which was generously supported by her father, though the guns the armaments master manufactured had sent thousands of men to the bottom of the oceans of the world. The dance programmes round the walls were framed in life-buoys, and naval cadets acted as ushers. Blythe would never know that the young naval officer she danced Hamilton House with would go down with the *Hood* in the Battle of the Denmark Strait.

The Halsides, who had begun making swords in a smithy in Lincolnshire, were now regarded as a landed family, part of the exclusive community of royal Deeside. But what they didn't have was old blood, and when his daughter asked Lord Halside in 1935 if he would include Major Aeneas Campbell in his next shooting party, he interrogated her on his pedigree, and once satisfied that this was ancient aristocratic blood, he had his secretary dispatch a gilt-edged invitation, requesting the Major's pleasure.

Alfred Halside admired military men. He himself hadn't seen active service overseas, but instead spent the war in the best hotel in Birmingham, supervising the armaments factory. Hadn't military men such as Major Aeneas Campbell manned the colossal guns his firm had supplied for the Western Front, capable of sending shells miles towards the Huns' batteries and which had augmented an already vast family fortune?

But if he had missed out on front line warfare, His Lordship made up for it by helping to slaughter five hundred pheasants bred especially for execution, the barrels of his twin Holland & Holland guns tailored to his arms hot as he exchanged guns with his personal loader, the spent shells ejected on the forest loam. Major Campbell's tally was fourteen birds, and that night, after a sumptuous dinner of game, Lord Halside invited his guest into his library, to interrogate the Major over substantial brandies about his own estate.

'It's modest, compared to yours, sir.'

'But it's been in the family for a long time, has it not?'

'My ancestor was brought home to it mortally wounded after the Battle of Flodden in 1513. We go even further back, to the Kings of Dalriada.'

Major Aeneas Campbell was back in the Lorimer mansion that Christmas, when he proposed to Blythe. Her father made his future son-in-law gasp at the size of her dowry – plus twenty thousand per year. They honeymooned on the Queen Mary's maiden voyage to America in late May. She had a piece of the cake in the shape of the ship and saw a whale. During the day she played deck-games with her new husband, and in the evening danced while he sat drinking whiskies and smoking Passing Clouds cigarettes.

'Do enjoy your dancing at St Andrews, Madam,' the Flying Scotsman hairdresser said as she went to sweep up the long strands of hair.

Blythe went along the corridor to the first class restaurant lined with mahogany panels, where there were at least six pieces of silver cutlery in rows at each place on the immaculate cloth, as well as napkins in the shape of clerical hats, and bottles of quality wine. While she awaited her order she reflected on the London season she has just left, and in particular the 90th Royal Caledonian Ball which she and her husband had attended, among a crowd of two and a half thousand. Not being a dancer, he had watched from the balcony of Grosvenor House as the Duke of Atholl's Highlanders' pipes and drums announced the dances of the set reels. Though she had 'come out' a decade before, Blythe was among that year's debutantes of Scottish descent, in white dresses and with tartan sashes over their shoulders, who processed with dancers from the Atholl Highlanders and the London Scottish into the vast ballroom brilliant with flowers. Major Aeneas Campbell watched with pride as the dancers in the Sixteensome Reel clapped his wife's dazzling performance. He would have several substantial whiskies in the course of that long night as he looked down on the nobility of Scotland dancing Scottish Reform and Speed the Plough, the men in mess dress, court dress and hunt coats, many of the kilts woven in another century. From the balcony the Major, glass in hand, identified the Order of the Thistle and even a Victoria Cross from the quagmire of Flanders on mess jackets. He wondered, with the territorial ambitions of that bastard Hitler, when the next Ball would take place as he watched Blythe as she went round the square in the Petronella, by far the best dancer in her set.

The Honourable Blythe Campbell took her gold covered diary from her handbag and perused her dancing engagements for the rest of that year while she waited for her luncheon to be brought on the Flying Scotsman:

> 31 August/1 September: Skye Gathering Balls
> 9 September: Aboyne Ball
> 14/15 September: Argyllshire Gathering Balls
> 22/23 September: Northern Meeting Balls
> 27/29 September: Perth Hunt Balls

The way reels were danced at these balls was much looser than the precise steps she had learned from 'Dancie' Mackenzie as a child. She was going to the Scottish Country Dance's Summer School at St Andrews because she found it easy to switch to the strict style demanded by Miss Jean Milligan and besides, she wanted the challenge of learning new Scottish country dances. She had considered taking her maid with her, to live in a boarding house and look after her clothes, but decided that that would be too pretentious.

The Flying Scotsman arrives in Edinburgh. Blythe doesn't have to change trains because her carriage will proceed to Leuchars for Aberdeen. She ponders her life as the steam engine rumbles across the Forth Estuary into the Kingdom of Fife. Tomorrow the Major will go up to his house in Argyll with two fishing officers from the Argylls, though the ghillie reports that the prolonged good spell has reduced the river so much that the salmon are too sluggish to take. Is she unhappy? It's a question Blythe puts to herself as the train runs across land again. Not if she can attend dances and balls, wherever she is, but in Argyll there are very few opportunities to take to the floor, apart from the two balls of the Argyllshire Gathering every September, when she dances until breakfast at dawn, the hall decorated with clan banners draped over respective coats of arms, the lairds, mostly Campbells, wearing sporrans of fox and badger, and even the ferocious face of a wildcat.

Major and the Honourable Mrs Campbell went to a ball at Inveraray Castle, where the grand march was piped in by Lady Elspeth, the Duke's stunningly beautiful sister, who had remained a spinster, partly because she had never met a man who had her fluency in speaking Gaelic, a language she learned, like the pipes she played like a champion. The bachelor Duke Niall shuffled through the Eightsome Reel and cornered anyone who would listen to his account of having seen the Galley of Lorn, crewed by the spirits of his illustrious ancestors, passing above Loch Fyne on its aerial journey to Loch Awe, where the clan originated.

There are sometimes dances in the community hall the Major has erected on his Argyllshire estate, but he doesn't want his wife dancing with the tenants. This frustrates her, and whenever he has to go south, she puts her dancing pumps into the dashboard of the Morris and drives to the hall in the village, where she has a wonderful evening of set dancing, as well as waltzing in the expert arms of a ploughman. But she doesn't tell the Major about this social betrayal, and thankfully no one else does.

Blythe alights from the train at Leuchars Station, and a

porter stands guard over her luggage until the connection for St Andrews arrives. The train is now running beside the golf course on the approach to St Andrews, but she has no interest in the game. A horse-drawn cab conveys her to University Hall, where Miss Jean Milligan observes her arrival and goes to greet her.

'I'm Blythe Campbell.'

Miss Milligan knows who she is. She has a soft spot for titles, and regards Lord James Stewart Murray, heir to the Duke of Atholl, not only as a founder member of the Society, but as a friend.

'I'll get a couple of men to take your luggage up to your room,' Miss Milligan tells the elegant new arrival. 'Do you go to county balls?'

'As many as I can.'

'Then you'll notice that at the balls Scottish country dances now form half of the programme, but when I started our Society with Mrs Stewart fifteen years ago, it was difficult to get a set together for one country dance on the programme. I've put you into the beginners' class until I see how competent you are.'

This is because Blythe supplied no information about her dancing ability when she applied for a place at Summer School. Miss Milligan's error becomes apparent next morning, when the teacher of the beginners sees Blythe's *pas de basque* and informs Miss Milligan over lunch in the pleasant panelled room, its windows open to the exceptional summer, that the Honourable Blythe Campbell should be in the advanced class.

Blythe participates fully in the life of the Summer School. She attends every class, is on the floor for every dance in the common room in the evenings, and goes to the parties that are held in University Hall. Some of the females are intrigued by the polish of her accent and the quality of her summer dresses, but Blythe doesn't want to talk about herself. Dancing has been her obsession since that day 'Dancie' Mackenzie tethered his divine pony outside Lorimer's masterpiece. The talk over lunch and supper tables is about which country will be next on Hitler's list, after his invasion of Austria. But Blythe is in St Andrews to dance, not to discuss such a depressing topic.

At the dances in the common room all the men want to partner Blythe, not only because of her beauty and grace, but also her sense of fun. When Miss Milligan's back is turned, Blythe is quite capable of touching a male dancer's hand *en passant*, as if this is a signal for a later assignation. But the Honourable Blythe Campbell, married to a silent military man with an obsession with rods and guns, isn't looking for romance. She has a husband, however disappointing, and dancing is her life. Nothing must be done to damage her enjoyment.

From St Andrews Blythe proceeded by several trains to Oban in Argyll, where her husband's gamekeeper met her in the Morris. It was an hour's jolting journey to the house, up a rutted avenue lined with trees that were already old at Waterloo. She would like to tarmacadam the avenue out of her trust fund, but the Major says that it would spoil the character. 'To hell with the character,' she bit back. 'What about my poor bones?' But she did insist that the piper was to stop walking round the house and wakening them at seven a.m., a custom that was centuries-old, her husband informed her, but agreeing that the reveille tune could be played an hour later. Blythe also won the battle to replace the sagging floors, the disgusting water closet boxed in with mahogany, like squatting on a coffin.

If the Major weren't out fishing the mile of pools he owned, he was crawling through the heather in pursuit of a stag. Blythe always felt sad when she saw the carcass of the noble antlered beast slung across the pony that the gamekeeper was leading, the meat hung on a hook in the large larder to season it. The Major preferred his venison served rare.

In the autumn evenings in Argyll Blythe sat listening to gramophone records of Scottish dance music, wishing she were in a dance set somewhere. Her husband was either in the gun-room, drawing an oiled rag through the barrels in preparation for the morning's stalk, or he had a jeweller's glass screwed into his eye and was tying a salmon fly. Even from the first day following their honeymoon they had occupied separate rooms, and she was thankful for the privacy. He wanted an heir, but the thought of having to transport children from London to Argyll was daunting, so she told him that they should 'wait a bit.'

Blythe was so thankful when he had to return to his battalion at Tidworth, and she could dance again. At the Aboyne Ball she danced a foxtrot with a Gordon Highlander to the tune 'Have you ever been in Heaven?' played by Tim Wright's Orchestra. After the Scottish season she went south to their flat in Sloane Square, taking taxis to wherever there was Scottish country dancing. She was dancing five nights a week, and would have liked to fill the other two with the same exhilarating activity, except that the Major came to London from Tidworth most weekends. When he wasn't at his club, he brought bridge players to the house, and insisted that the hostess take a hand.

Early in 1939 he came up to London with news that the 1st Argylls had been selected for a tour of special duty in Palestine.

'We'll be active against the Arab rebels,' he told her with

evident satisfaction, because the fighting spirit was in his genes.

When he added that families and wives wouldn't be following the battalion out, she was immensely relieved, having no wish to wilt in the desert while there was dancing in London.

A few weeks later he phoned from Tidworth, to tell her that he was being transferred to the 7th Argylls.

'Is that good?' she enquired.

'No, damn it, it's a Territorial battalion. I want to go to Palestine with my own lot. I've been with the 1st Battalion for twenty years, so why am I being transferred?'

'Why?' she echoed, though she found the topic boring, and besides, there was a new reel to learn for that evening's class. Was this transfer going to cramp her style?

'That's the question I asked the commanding officer. He said that the 7th needed my experience because war with Germany's almost certain.'

'But I thought Chamberlain fixed it at Munich?'

'Hitler's a treacherous rat. No country's safe from his lust for land so that Germany can expand into a great empire ruled by a dictator.'

In July the Major went with the 7th Argylls to Stathpeffer for annual field training. He availed himself of the waters of the Highland spa, but wished that he were in Argyll, on the river, his gamekeeper having reported that the fish were 'plentiful' that summer. He found time to spend the weekend with his father-in-law.

'You saw that Hitler recently launched two brutes of battleships, the *Tirpitz* and *Bismarck*,' Lord Halside said in his library after a sumptuous six course dinner. 'The Germans say *Bismarck's* a ship of thirty five thousand tons, but we suspect that she's much bigger than that – perhaps even the largest battleship ever built.' He led his guest to his massive desk in the bay window and unrolled a drawing. 'We're working on naval guns to knock out the brute, because there's going to be a war, be certain of that. These bloody appeasers wouldn't listen to Winston. so we aren't up to strength compared to the Germans. It's going to be a very different war from the one you distinguished yourself in, Aeneas. No more standing in waterlogged trenches waiting for the enemy to make a move. We've seen what the Luftwaffe is capable of in Spain.'

Blythe was in London, dancing, and the following month she took the Flying Scotsman north, for her second sojourn at the Summer School at St Andrews.

'We're here to dance, not to predict war,' she warned the male dancers. 'Perhaps I should go home early.'

This produced protestations from the males, and the promise that there would be no more talk about war. The men danced the Lochaber Broadswords and Blythe participated in a keep-fit class. Miss Milligan played the new gramophone records that had been made for the dances in Book 12 in her class and praised the 'good tempo'.

On a Sunday morning in September Blythe was listening alone to Chamberlain's announcement about war with Germany on the wireless in the London flat because the Major was up at Stirling Castle, helping to embody the 7th Argylls. There would be no fishing that summer. The next time his wife saw him was at New Year, when he had a few days' leave.

'What's going to happen?' she asked anxiously, because she cared about his welfare, though he could be irritating and high-minded at times.

'I expect we'll be sent overseas.'

'Can't you ask for a transfer to a home regiment?'

His look was one of appreciation of her concern for his welfare, but also surprise at her naivety.

'I have to go, Blythe; that's what I've been trained for. But we should be able to curb Hitler before he gets a grip of Europe.'

The 7th Argylls exchanged their kilts for battledress and sailed for France. Blythe tried to occupy her mind by dancing, but she was anxious about her husband, and her concentration on the floor suffered, and for the first time in her life she began to make simple mistakes. In the spring of 1940 she walked alone in the London parks, then went up to Aberdeenshire to stay with her parents. Her father was following the international situation closely, and doubted if Hitler's army was going to be halted in its tracks. His wife signalled to him that his pessimistic talk was depressing their daughter. 'Aeneas will be fine,' he added hastily. 'He's with the 51st Highland Division.'

In the retreat from France that summer ten thousand officers and troops of the 51st Highland Division were taken prisoner, including Major Aeneas Campbell, captured on the Somme. On the three week long and hungry march through Germany in blister-filled footwear, he thought about his young beautiful wife back home. How was she going to fare during his incarceration?

They arrived at Laufen Castle on the south-eastern border of Bavaria with Austria in the darkness. Their clothes were taken away to be fumigated, and they were given hot showers. A soldier whipped the Major's bonnet from his head and ran clippers over it, leaving bare skull. He wanted to strike him, but had seen men shot on the march for much less.

There were forty other prisoners in bunk beds, four tiers high, in the overcrowded room at the top of three flights of stairs. The Major's sleep was disturbed by snoring, and men shouting out in disturbed dreams. That night the sound of the Rhine Falls beneath his window tortured him with memories of the waterfall on his Argyll river. It wasn't swimming naked as a boy in the hole made in the ice under the waterfall which he was recalling, but fishing the pool for trout on a balmy evening, with his bully of a father dead.

When the London Blitz began Blythe retreated to the house in Argyll. How she missed the sound of her husband's boots on the flagstones of the hall as he went out shooting or fishing, returning late in the day with his prizes, a hare or salmon, to be cooked for supper. Because of the blackout, and the absence of local men in the forces, there were no dances in the village hall. The house was lit by paraffin lamps, and fuel was scarce. The gamekeeper had to drive to Oban and beg a five gallon drum. But there was ample firewood and food, and Blythe began to appreciate the succulence of venison. She went for long walks with her husband's gun dogs, and sat by the log fire in the drawing-room after the cook had served her supper. She realized how fortunate she was compared to those in the cities, and in captivity overseas. The cook made a rich fruit cake, and Blythe drove to Oban to purchase pipe tobacco to put in the parcel with the cake, and a book on salmon fishing to send to her husband in Laufen Castle. She wrote him long letters, in diary form, explaining what was happening on the estate, but being careful not to make him too homesick.

At the beginning of his captivity in Laufen Castle along with hundreds of other officers, Major Aeneas Campbell began to see that his father's strict upbringing of his sons, with the denial of luxuries, and positively no sugar, had been good training. The coffee in Laufen was made from acorns, and the bread ration was four slices of black low quality army bread per man per day. The two meals a day consisted of soup and potatoes. Once a week each man received the minute luxury of two ounces of cheese, a spoonful of turnip jam, and a small pat of margarine. The Major ate dandelions and nettles, but stopped short of joining in the rat-hunts for protein.

The most serious menace wasn't dysentery, but the trigger-happy guards. An officer standing sketching at a window might have made the sentry suspect that he was making an escape map, because he shot the artist dead.

Late that first summer, some fresh vegetables and fruit became available, officers' pay was doubled and food parcels began to arrive, including ones from Blythe. Major Campbell bought a bottle of white wine from the Franconian vineyards, but it was sour, without effect. He would have given a month's pay for a modest whisky. For an active sportsman confined to a fortress life was monotonous and frustrating. Many of the Major's fellow officers seemed to be settling into the ritual of imprisonment. They smoked their pipes as they read, played bridge, or dozed in their chairs. The Major had never been a reader, except of sporting books, and there were a few in the library in Laufen, accumulating from the volumes sent from home. He read the letters over and over sent to him by his wife, as if seeking a hidden meaning. He smoked the tobacco she sent him, and shared the rich fruit cake with fellow officers. Some days, in the inertia of his situation, he stood at a high window, the tumbling falls sweeping his mind down through Europe and across the Channel to his house in Argyll. He now wished that he had spent more time in Blythe's company instead of on the river and moor. He wanted to write, to tell her how much he loved and missed her, but he hadn't been brought up to express such emotions. The possibility of escape was beginning to obsess him. The days spent crawling on his belly through sodden heather in pursuit of stags had made him an invisible presence in the countryside. He circulated among his fellow prisoners, hoping to hear of an escape attempt. Eventually the Major's persistence was rewarded, and he was invited to join an escape party, laboriously scooping out earth. He took his turn in the hole, but the tunnel was discovered, and the guards became more vigilant.

One of the Major's fellow 7th Argylls officers in captivity was Lieutenant Jimmy Atkinson. He sat down beside the Major one evening after their sparse supper.

'I believe your wife's a superb Scottish dancer.'

The Major nodded in proud acknowledgement.

'When we were being marched across Europe to this bloody place I started to devise a dance in my head, based on the St Andrews Cross, the insignia of the 51st. Peter Oliver of the 4th Seaforths has started a Highland dancing class, and we've been working on my dance, with the help of Lieutenant-Colonel Harris Hunter. His wife is secretary of the Scottish Country Dance Society's Perth branch, and he was its chairman. Do you want to come and see it?'

Though he hated dancing after being forced to perform the Highland Fling in sub-zero Argyll by his father, the Major went with Atkinson out of politeness to see the new dance being performed by five male couples in battledress trousers and tackety boots in a hut.

'We've called it the 51st Country Dance, and we tried to send it home because at least it shows our families that we're still alive and active,' Atkinson informed the Major. 'We sent it on letter-cards to several people in the hope that it would reach Scotland, but we were hauled up before the Commandant and accused of sending code. That's what they thought the steps of the dance were. I hope that after we pointed out that it's only a dance, they'll let it go on its way.'

'I'm sure my wife would like to have a copy. She's always interested in new dances,' Major Campbell told the young officer.

The days were long and lonely for the young woman in the house in Argyll, and to break the monotony, in the absence of petrol for the Morris, she asked the gamekeeper to bring the old gig out of the stables, and used it to travel round the houses on the estate, tethering the reins and carrying in the surplus food that the cook had prepared. Some of the old people spoke only Gaelic, and Blythe made an attempt to learn some conversational phrases. In the evenings she listened to her Scottish dance recordings on the gramophone, wishing that hostilities would cease and dancing could begin again, because she felt that her body and spirit had become sluggish through a lack of reels and strathspeys. She tried to devise a dance to dedicate to her husband, a reel that incorporated his activities as a sportsman, but she wasn't gifted in that way. The house was eerie, and she was sure that sounds in the darkness were a resident ghost. She thought she saw a shadow in front of her in a passage, but it might have been nerves. She decided that the house was too drab and gloomy, walls discoloured by centuries of peat and wood fires. The gamekeeper set out for Oban and returned with two drums of white distemper, and a couple of brushes, bought at inflated prices. Blythe tied on a headsquare, put on an old mackintosh of her husband's and began on the drawing-room. It took a week and a whole drum, but she found the swish of the brush on the grimy wallpaper soothing, and slept soundly after a bath. After doing the dining-room she moved upstairs and decorated her own bedroom, until the second drum was empty. She wanted to do her husband's bedroom, but when the gamekeeper drove to Oban there were no more drums to buy.

It was then that Blythe sank into the first depression of her life, staying in bed. The anxious cook brought up trays of broth, which were left untouched.

'I'm at my wits' end,' she confessed to the gamekeeper as she fed him at the kitchen table. 'I don't know what to give her.'

'It's not food she wants, Maggie. It's her husband back. I think I know what will cheer her up.'

The following Friday he tacked black cloth to the windows of the village hall, having put up a notice that there would be a dance that evening. Then he drove to Oban and brought back an accordionist, an old man who played entirely by ear. When the cook brought up the mistress's lunch she told her: 'you'll need to eat up this broth, Madam. There's a dance in the hall tonight.'

'A dance?' she asked, sitting up. 'Who's arranged it?'

'Charlie has.'

Blythe ate the broth. She had a bath and chose the simplest dress from her exquisite wardrobe of dance apparel. She decided that she wouldn't wear the silver bangles she usually adorned her wrists with when she went dancing, and instead of pumps, which would intimidate the people on the estate, she would wear flat shoes. The gamekeeper drove her to the hall, which was lit by two storm lanterns and packed with tenants. The accordionist had his instrument strapped to his chest, the local primary teacher was seated at the piano. Blythe was led round the floor in the arms of the gamekeeper in a waltz of Gaelic tunes, and as a crofter birled her in Strip the Willow the ranks of faces in the set became a blur. She danced a Highland Fling in the centre of the charmed circle of the Eightsome Reel. It was the best dance of her life, and when she returned home she sat in the drawing-room with a whisky, with the music continuing in her head.

Major Aeneas Campbell and some fellow officers of the 51st Highland Division were moved from Laufen Castle to Oflag VII-B at Eichstatt in Bavaria. The Major became involved in a large-scale tunnel project and escaped with sixty-five others, but was recaptured a fortnight later.

In the summer of 1945 Blythe had obtained a new supply of distemper and was whitening the grimy walls of her husband's bedroom. The brush stopped when she saw from the stepladder his approach. She rushed outside and was lifted out of her sandals by his embrace. After a sumptuous dinner of home-killed produce they made love that night in her bed, but he seemed remote.

'Were you badly treated?' she enquired gently.

'Not compared to some. It was the waiting that was the worst.'

He was a changed man. The river was in excellent condition, but some days he couldn't be bothered threading the line through the eyelets on his salmon rod. The gamekeeper told him that a stag with twenty two points on its antlers had come on to the estate, but he wasn't interested in having its head as a trophy for the hall. He hardly spoke with his wife and seemed to have lost interest in life. Blythe went to speak with the local doctor, and was told to give her husband time 'after the trauma of captivity.' She thought that a change of scenery would be good for him, but the London flat had been damaged in the bombing, and the new one they rented didn't seem to appeal to him. She received a note that the Scottish Country Dance Society's Summer School was being resumed in St Andrews in August, after five years of war.

'I won't go,' she told her husband.

'No, you must go. I'm fine.'

Blythe sent a postcard from St Andrews to Argyll:

> The weather here is splendid, and there's plenty of food despite rationing. I was telling the other dancers about you seeing the Reel of the 51st Division being devised when you were a prisoner in Laufen. I have to say, I find it a slightly awkward dance. It's obviously been devised by men. After tea we can do Irish, American Square or Old Time dances, though I prefer Scottish country. I miss you and hope you are feeling brighter.

At one of the dances in the common room a young man came into the same set as Blythe. He was small and thin, as though undernourished, and she noticed that the collar of his white shirt was frayed. When it came his turn to dance she watched him moving round the set as if his feet were barely touching the floor, and when he turned her she seemed to be airborne with him. He asked her to dance the strathspey that was next on the programme, and she felt that they were moving as one body. At the interval she saw him sitting alone and went to introduce herself.

'Willie MacKelvie,' he said awkwardly, taking her hand.

She sat down beside him to find out where he had learned to dance to such an expert level. He told her that when he was a boy his mother had joined a Scottish country dance class in Glasgow, his native city.

'I seemed to take to it straight away, and when we were at home she danced with me to improve my steps. When I was on leave two years ago I went to a dance in Glasgow. Miss Milligan was there, and told me that as soon as the war was over, she was going to restart the Summer School here, and that I had to come. I told her that I wouldn't be able to afford it, and she said: "don't worry about that. I'll arrange a bursary for you so that it won't cost you a penny."'

'Where were you in the war?' Blythe enquired. Though the dancing had resumed, she wanted to find out more about this most attractive young man.

'I joined the Highland Light Infantry at the beginning, because my father had enlisted as soon as war broke out in 1914. I've been in North Africa and other places.'

She could see that he didn't want to speak about his war experiences. She elicited from him in his broad Glasgow accent that he had worked as a waiter before the war. He didn't ask about her, and she didn't volunteer any information, conscious for the first time of her accent and fearing that if she told him that she was the wife of a Major, it would intimidate him.

They danced again together that evening, and afterwards went for a walk in the gardens of the Hall, soporific with the scent from the rose bushes. She wanted to ask him if he had a girlfriend, but that would be too forward. They talked about their mutual love of dancing and how wonderful it was that the blackouts had been taken down in the halls, now that the war was over.

Blythe couldn't sleep in the student's bed, thinking about the new acquaintance she had made. What was it that attracted her to him? His wonderful dancing, certainly; the compactness of his body; the open frankness of his face. He seemed vulnerable, and it was a wonder to her that he had survived the ferocious desert war. He belonged to a different class, a class she knew next to nothing about. Her only contact had been the servants at the Aberdeenshire mansion, and the Argyll laird's house, and dancing at the Ghillies' Balls at Mar Lodge and Balmoral, but she hadn't become intimate with any of them. The young dancer seemed to have an appealing dignity, with his quiet voice and frayed collar, and she wanted to get to know him better.

The following evening Blythe suggested to Willie that instead of dancing in the common room, they should walk into town. Every summer for a week or so the centuries-old Lammas Fair arrived in St Andrews, setting up stalls and amusements on Market Street.

'Why don't you have a try?' Blythe urged him at the gallery where men were leaning on the counter, squinting down the sights of rifles to targets set up among the tempting prizes.

He hesitated, and then took up the weapon. He compensated

for the fact that the sights were crooked, and when the three red-feathered darts thudded into the bull's-eye of the target the attendant raised his eyebrows in surprise. It was a long time since he had offered a crackshot the pick of the prizes.

'What would you like?' the marksman, lethal sniper in the Western Desert, asked his companion.

Blythe surveyed the array. It would be cruel to take a goldfish in a jam-jar, and the glassware looked cheap. She chose a teddy bear which sat on her knee as he took the wheel of the dodgem, the man collecting the fares leaping between the sparking poles on the backs of the cars with the agility of a monkey. She had never been allowed to go to the shows when they pitched in the Aberdeenshire village that was part of the family estate, but now she was revelling in the experience, screaming as they bumped into other cars.

The wooden train they boarded ran into a dark tunnel, lit by luminous skeletons on the walls, and that was when she snuggled up against him, as though she were frightened. When he put a protective arm round her and drew her close she kissed him on the mouth.

'We need to get you back to your Hall before the door's locked,' he reminded her. Only females were allowed to stay in University Hall, and Willie was sleeping in a nearby building with other males.

'There's another way in,' she revealed, leading him by the hand into the garden, indicating the ground floor window which he lifted noiselessly, then put his hand under her buttocks to hoist her into the dim passage she traversed with her footwear in her hands, up the stairs to her bedroom.

The following night, after they had been for a walk on the

beach where they kissed several times, a figure was standing on the stairs.

'You're late,' Miss Milligan reminded Blythe.

'I went for a walk.'

'Well, don't forget that you have classes in the morning. I like my dancers to be fresh.'

As she lay in bed Blythe pondered the major-domo's attitude. The main door of the Hall was locked, so she must have known that Blythe had entered through a window. Why hadn't she scolded her for breaking the rules, when even momentary slipshod footwork in a set made her critical? Did she suspect Blythe was having an affair, or did she really think it was an innocent walk?

On their next walk Blythe asked Willie if he had returned to work after his long absence at war.

'I'm out of work.'

He told her that Guido, the proprietor of the Italian restaurant he had worked in, had promised him that he would keep his job for him. But when Italy entered the war in 1940 Guido's restaurant had been attacked, the plate glass window smashed, *Italian Traitor* written in red paint across the frontage. He was on the *Arandora Star*, bound for Canada with other Italian and German internees and prisoners of war when it was sunk by a U-boat.

'So what are you going to do?' Blythe asked.

'I've tried other restaurants, but they don't have any vacancies. With the rationing business isn't good.'

'Can't you do something else?' she pursued the topic.

'I'm not trained to do anything.'

Blythe and Willie didn't make love at the Summer School. It

was too risky, using her room. If they were caught, they would be banned permanently by the major-domo. Instead they arranged a rendezvous in Glasgow, with Blythe booking a room at a small hotel in the west end.

'How are you managing without a job?' she asked her new lover after the satisfying consummation.

'It's not easy.'

'I'd like to give you money.'

'I couldn't take it,' he said resolutely.

She knew that would be his answer, but it was a test of his integrity.

'I've been thinking, why don't you open a place of your own?'

'I've only got seventy pounds of savings.'

'Suppose I put up the rest of the money?' As he was about to protest she put her hand over his mouth. 'Don't say anything. It can be a proper legal partnership. I've been wondering if Oban would be a suitable place. It's only an hour from where I live, but the disadvantage is that there's no Scottish country dancing there, and we both want to keep that up. There are classes in Glasgow and I could come down regularly.'

'I don't even know if you're married.'

She knew that the question had to come, sooner or later.

'I'm married to a Major in the 7th Argylls who was with the 51st Highland Division in France and who spent the war as a prisoner, though he did try to escape. Since he came home he's been depressed and very difficult to live with.'

The man lying beside her was silent. She belonged to a class he hadn't much time for, and he had found some of the officers in North Africa arrogant and careless with men's lives. But he knew how fortunate he was to have someone so stylish and affectionate.

'I'll stay for a few more days and we'll start looking for premises tomorrow,' she pledged before turning to him again.

But when they met next morning she had changed her mind.

'Glasgow's not particularly suitable for me, because if I say that I'm coming down regularly, my husband will be suspicious. On the other hand, Edinburgh wouldn't raise any questions.'

They took the train through to the capital and began their search. They were walking along Rose Street after a frustrating afternoon in which they had viewed two unsuitable premises when they saw a For Sale sign on a building. Blythe took her lover to the selling agents in Queen Street and was assigned a clerk to show her over the property.

'I forgot to say that the flat's included in the sale,' the lawyer called after her as she was going out the door.

'The flat?'

'The flat above the shop was the owner's residence.'

The clerk brought these keys also. The shop would require being stripped back to the bare walls, and the cracked window replaced, and when they went upstairs they saw the primitive grate in the kitchen.

'What do you think?' she asked Willie.

'It's got a lot of potential, but it must be very expensive.'

Blythe went back with the clerk to put in an offer for both premises, and a phone call later was the owner.

'I know it's not very comfortable, but you can live in the flat until it's done up,' she told her lover. 'The first priority is to get the restaurant up and running.'

They stayed the night in Edinburgh, and the following day Blythe signed the necessary papers and wrote the cheque from the account in which she kept her own money separate from her husband's. Willie stayed in Edinburgh to arrange for the tradesmen to begin work in turning the run-down shop into a restaurant. He had no experience, but trusted in his intuition. His lover had put faith in him, and he couldn't let her down, so he slept on the stained mattress upstairs and cleared the ashes from the choked grate in the kitchen to cook for himself.

Blythe returned to the house in Argyll, to her depressed husband. His fishing rods remained in their racks, and instead of walking the hills with his two retrievers he sat in the drawing-room, staring out to the Bens of Jura, as if these three peaks held deep significance for him, a significance he couldn't express to his wife when she came up behind him and put her arms round his shoulders. The truth was that the war had shown him the unpredictability of life. He needed an heir to keep the line going, but didn't know how to raise the subject with his wife.

'Why are you not out on such a fine day, darling?' she asked with genuine concern.

'I'm resting.'

She wanted to say: *you rested for nearly five years in prisoner of war camps*. But he had become touchy. He had always been temperate in the amount of alcohol he consumed in the mess, but now he was drinking whisky before lunch. The case of twelve bottles which the gamekeeper had brought from Oban a fortnight before was down to one.

'Why don't you go down to London for a week?'

'I don't like London now.'

'Then we have to give up the flat,' she said decisively. 'I

prefer to go through to Edinburgh for my dancing. It's more convenient and less expensive.' She didn't tell him that she had already bought a flat there. He must never know of its existence.

'That's fine,' was all the reply.

'Then I'll go next Monday for a few days.'

'Where will you stay?'

'I'll find a small hotel.'

She found the transformation of the shop into a restaurant well under way. Willie himself had decorated one of the bedrooms in the flat and installed a new double bed. They went together to a Scottish country dancing class but didn't dance with each other and afterwards walked hand in hand through narrow Rose Street.

'It's so atmospheric,' she enthused over the street lighting, the click of heels on the cobbles, a woman in a slouch hat with a bag under her arm in a doorway. 'It's hard to believe it's so close to the bustle of Princes Street.'

But some nights, as the city quietened, the trams running to the late night schedule, Blythe began to have doubts as she lay in bed beside her exhausted lover. She was betraying her husband, who was alone in Argyll, probably still sitting up, drinking whisky, watching the Bens of Jura in the moonlight. She should try to discover why his personality had changed so much, instead of consorting with a former waiter who was now her business partner as well as her lover. What had happened to Aeneas in the prisoner of war camp? Had he been beaten up by the guards for some minor offence? Had the inertia of imprisonment caused clinical depression?

But she had made a choice, and there was no going back. The man lying beside her was her lover, and the building work below had to be completed, because to resell it as it stood would mean losing money. Besides, she wanted to do something for him, and she saw the difference in his personality and his fulfilment as he planned the new enterprise, looking at fittings.

'What shall we call it?' he asked over the simple supper he had cooked for her on the range.

'I've been thinking, but I haven't come up with anything that sounds suitable. Have you?'

'Blythe's?'

'Are you serious?'

'Who would know? It would be a secret between us.'

'I don't want to tempt fate,' she cautioned.

Over the bottle of wine they decided on the Rose Repast. He wasn't sure about a Black Watch tartan carpet, but she overruled him, and thought they should go for more stylish tables and chairs. They drew up the wine list together, and she left it to him to interview and hire staff, because she couldn't afford to be associated with the venture. He chose two good looking waitresses, a blonde and a redhead. The cook was from a quality city hotel and was worth the money, he assured his partner.

On its opening night, publicised in the evening newspaper, Blythe dined alone at a corner table while her lover showed customers to their tables. They ran out of roast duck, and every table took two bottles of wine. The culinary critic in *The Scotsman* was full of praise for the décor, the quality of the food, the slickness of the service. Blythe noticed that success was changing Willie. He was becoming more confident, more outgoing. The shy person she had met in the dance set at St Andrews chatted to his customers, but never staying long enough at a table to make it look as if he were favouring them above the other diners. He was different also when he came upstairs to the flat towards midnight after another packed-out evening in his white dinner jacket and bow tie, looking like a film star. His love-making was gentler, more considerate, as if the experience of serving his clients with a quality dining experience was being extended to her in bed.

She didn't want to go home to Argyll, but knew that she couldn't stay away for more than a week at a time without rousing her husband's suspicions. Though he was still depressed, she found that now she could tolerate spending time in the Argyll house, so long as she knew that in a fortnight she could return to Edinburgh and her lover for another fulfilling week. So she collected the empty whisky bottles and allowed him to come into her bed, but found his attempts at an heir clumsy.

Blythe Campbell's life became a ritual between Argyll and Edinburgh, dining once in the week at a corner table in the restaurant, but without disclosing to the other diners that there was something more than courtesy between herself and the proprietor who stopped to chat with her on his round of the tables. The restaurant was making money, and after he had a salary and the expenses of the flat were paid, the balance was ploughed back into the business, with an assistant chef recruited, the blonde waitress made the manageress and another one hired. Blythe loved sitting at the open window of the flat, listening to the evening activity on Rose Street, people going in and out of pubs, and leaving the restaurant below full of praise for the dining experience. Sometimes a drunk saw her sitting at the window and waved up to her.

Blythe reckoned that now the busy restaurant was running

smoothly, it was time to put her husband in order, so on her first night home after another week in Edinburgh she asked him abruptly over dinner, as he was refilling his glass from the decanter by his hand: 'why are you drinking so much, Aeneas?'

His hand stopped momentarily, but tilted the decanter.

'Because I like whisky.'

'That's a childish reply and you know it. Something happened when you were a prisoner of war and I want to know about it if I'm to help you.'

'Nothing happened,' he insisted, because he couldn't tell her of the humiliation in Laufen of unravelling the wool of his holed jersey and socks, and being instructed to knit new ones, referring to a diagram on graph paper on how to turn a heel.

But there had been much worse. After being recaptured following his escape with the other sixty-four from Eichstatt, a Gestapo officer had put a pistol to his head, and he had said his prayers. But the trigger hadn't been pulled.

'Are you looking forward to the Summer School at St Andrews this year?' she asked her lover as they were drinking a sweet wine after midnight at the open window of the flat as the city became hushed, the last pair of heels retreating along Rose Street.

'I can't go.'

'Why not?'

'Because I can't close the restaurant for the week. We need to maintain our clientele.'

'Can't you leave Sandra the manageress in charge?'

'She hasn't the experience to be left alone. But you go.'

But it was different from the previous years she had arrived at St Andrews. University Hall had lost its appeal with the absence of her lover, and she didn't concentrate in Miss Milligan's class for thinking about him in Edinburgh. On the evening of the third day, during the social dancing in the common room, she went to Miss Milligan with the fiction that she had received a telegram informing her that her husband was ill, and she needed to return home.

'That's a great pity,' the major-domo responded. 'Incidentally, have you seen anything of that young soldier from Glasgow who's such a beautiful dancer? I need him for an international demonstration team.'

Did this shrewd woman know something she shouldn't?

'I haven't seen him for ages,' Blythe lied.

Instead of going home to Argyll she drove to Edinburgh, parking her car on Hanover Street before hurrying along Rose Street. It was after midnight and the restaurant was closed. The door to the flat was open and she went up the stairs. She opened the door at the top. The bedroom was directly opposite and she saw the startled face of the blonde manageress over the heaving shoulder of her lover. As he turned his head she went back down the stairs again, leaned her forehead against the wall as if to draw strength from the stone, then hurried back to her car, where she took the packet of cigarettes she used rarely from the dashboard. What should she do? Confront him? He had betrayed her when he thought she was safely at the Summer School. Somehow that seemed a violation of the dancing that had brought them together and which they loved as much as each other.

Blythe turned the ignition and drove back to Argyll. A deer leapt out in front of her, but there was no danger because she was going so slowly, as if she had mechanical trouble or a slow puncture. She didn't want to go back to the five-bayed house by the Atlantic, but where else could she go to? She pulled into the pillared entrance to an estate and slept for two hours. The sun was brightening the Bens of Jura when she reached the house. The Major was in a deep sleep induced by drink, and when he came down to breakfast was startled to see her.

'Why are you back so early?'

'I wasn't enjoying the Summer School.'

'But you adore dancing.'

'People go off things, Aeneas. How have you been?'

That afternoon she wrote to her former lover.

> Because I encouraged you to open the restaurant I don't want to be vindictive and to draw out my money since that would cause you problems. Instead I'm proposing that you pay me one thousand pounds – a quarter of what I put in – and you can own the restaurant lock, stock and barrel. As for the flat, I'm not going to be so generous, providing a nest for you and your floozy, so I'll sell it.

Because of the way he had been brought up, when all complaints and confessions had been stifled, the Major didn't tell his wife that the trauma of the pistol applied to his temple after his unsuccessful escape attempt had contributed to his drinking. He could hear his father's voice, though the veteran of the Zulu War was long since in his grave. 'I brought you up to fend for yourself, teaching you fieldcraft, how to live off the land, yet you go and get caught by these bloody Huns.'

The Major continued to pour the rents from his estate down

his throat, and to retreat more and more into himself. He and Blythe fumbled through a form of love-making, but there were no children from their union. Did his gun go off accidentally while he was crossing the fence?

As for Blythe, she lived on in the five-bayed small laird's house. It was in a pitiful state. As the ceilings came down because of the rotten roof, she retreated from room to room without having repairs done, though she was still a wealthy woman. She couldn't keep staff because of her temperament, and didn't practise personal hygiene. She had gone religiously to the best hairdresser in Oban once a fortnight, but now cut her hair in handfuls herself. She smashed her Scottish country dance records and threw her dancing pumps on a bonfire of autumn leaves, watching the toes curling up and blistering. She never returned to St Andrews since the night she defected, and she never went back to Edinburgh since that night she discovered her lover in bed with his manageress. Once, visiting the doctor's surgery in Oban, she picked up a magazine devoted to the Scottish upper classes and read a eulogistic article on the Rose Repast, 'with Mr William McKelvie the urbane proprietor of what for many people is one of the best restaurants in Scotland, if not in Great Britain. He and his wife Sandra, an elegant blonde, are pictured preparing the restaurant for the evening.' Rather than wait for her appointment, Blythe walked out of the surgery.

The Lindy Hop

The American troops who disembarked from the liner *Queen Mary* which had been converted to a camouflaged troopship in World War II brought Camel cigarettes, nylons and Hershey bars to Glasgow. They also brought the Lindy Hop. 'It don't mean a thing/If it ain't got that swing,' Ray Nance of Duke Ellington's Band crooned between blasts on his trumpet. No one can remember when this social dance, a fusion of jazz, tap, breakaway and the Charleston was first seen in the ballrooms of Glasgow, but it was certainly danced in the Barrowland, where there were many romances between the GIs and citizens.

The Lindy Hop didn't disappear when the Americans returned home, some with Glaswegian brides, others who didn't know, or didn't care, that they were fathers. Its movements were incorporated into other dances, and there were stalwarts who kept dancing it. Swing Dance societies were formed, and young people began to take an interest in the Lindy.

Mandy Graham was taken along to a swing society dance when she was eighteen by a friend. She loved the energetic movements to the beat of the big band sound – actually a recording of 'I've Got a Gal in Kalamazoo' by Glenn Miller and his Band, said to be the greatest exponents of swing music. Mandy's obsession with the Lindy Hop wasn't only with the dance, but also with its accessories – the shoes, the dresses. As a modern young woman she called the jewellery she bought 'bling.' It wasn't hallmarked gold or silver, but coloured baubles of glass and plastic clustered on a necklace. As for dancing dresses, since she couldn't find what she wanted in the stores, she went on eBay and began to bid for dresses of 1940s vintage. They were expensive, and in the beginning she was beaten by a late bid, but she became adept at the strategy of keying in a bid in the closing seconds of the on-line auction.

She also purchased dresses from a shop in the west end of Glasgow called Retro Grotto. The title didn't really live up to the range of stock in the cavern of the shop which was run by a woman who modelled the garments she was selling. One day she would be wearing a long blue dress, the next a daring little number. When a customer wanted to buy she went into the curtained cubicle and removed the desired article.

Mandy became friendly with the proprietor, who was called Stella. Isobel was her real name, but that was too prosaic for a shop which specialized in such unusual garments. Stella's first task after opening the steel shutter to her shop in the morning was to peruse the death intimations in the *Herald*. She wasn't being morbid, or looking for the demise of a relative to see if she might inherit. She was scanning for the passing of women of a certain age and in certain areas only because some of them would have kept the garments of their youth. She had sent a circular to most of the lawyers in the city, intimating that she was prepared to clear the residences of the deceased of garments. In some cases the family preferred to do this out of respect for the departed, and perhaps also because they hoped to come across items of value, though no one wanted fur coats or stoles now. But widows and spinsters who had no known relatives, or whose relatives were overseas, also died, and the lawyer winding up the estate was anxious to find someone to clear the house of furniture and clothes, provided there were no costs involved, so that the property could be sold, and the substantial bequest sent to look after stray cats.

So Stella's unmarked white van was parked outside tenements and villas throughout the city, and in the driveways of suburban bungalows. Clothes that weren't saleable were bundled into black sacks for charity shops, but surprisingly often she opened a wardrobe, to be assailed by the reek of mothballs, to find herself rummaging through a rail of garments which the departed had perhaps purchased for a party, or a wedding dance, and never worn again. In the bottom of the wardrobe she might find strapped shoes of a pre-war style, and a handbag last carried on an arm in a shopping excursion to Sauchiehall Street in the summer of 1947, when the world of fashion was beginning to recover from the war. The dresses were folded carefully and put with the shoes into the large case, which was then wheeled out to the van. The garments would be hung on the railing behind the counter in Retro Grotto. Then Stella would boot up her computer and send an e-mail to favoured clients, announcing that she had 'fabulous new items just in which you must come in and see before I put them out for sale on the railings.'

Mandy lived in a one bedroom flat in Wilton Street, Glasgow, in an elegant building which had once been an entire town house. She was on the top floor, where the nursery had been, and she loved the vista from the windows of her sitting-room. Her grandfather had given her the deposit to purchase the flat, and her parents had helped to furnish it. It was bright and cheerful, with white walls, and a kitchen of cream cupboards and a built-in oven and hob. The bathroom was tiled in black and white, with a power shower and lights recessed in the stippled ceiling.

Mandy walks down Belmont Street in the morning in a smart dark costume and elevated heels, protected by a transparent umbrella according to the weather, and boards the subway at Kelvinbridge. She usually has to stand, and one morning when the man behind her put his hand on her buttocks, she turned slowly, shook her head and removed it as if it were the limb of a naughty infant. When she comes up out of the earth on Buchanan Street she hasn't far to walk to the glass-walled edifice of the stockbroking firm where she works as secretary to the senior partner. She ascends in the glass box of the elevator to her fourth floor office and boots up her computer, opening her personal e-mail. There are ten overnight messages, six of them immediately recognizable as spam. She doesn't require discounted airport parking, and she is not interested in the intimation that she has a bequest of ten million dollars lying in an Argentinean bank, all that will take to release it being a payment of a thousand dollars.

At this hour of the morning the traditionally attired secretary is interested only in e-mails with the suffix Retro Grotto.

Dear Mandy, I found a wonderful cache of retro dresses in a house in Clarkston. When can you come? Love, Stella.

At 12.30. Grateful Thanks & Love is the immediate reply.

Mandy sits all morning with headphones, transcribing the correspondence that the senior partner had spoken into the micro-recorder, the most important component on his glass sheet of a desk. Mandy, who always types with her shoes off, is quick and accurate. She presses the button and through the wall the letter slides out of the tray on the laser printer on the partner's desk. He signs it and she collects the batch for dispatch. These are confidential letters that cannot be trusted

166

to the web, in case a hacker discovers the extent of a client's investment portfolio.

At 12.20 p.m. Mandy descends in the elevator. It's quicker to take the subway than a taxi in this congested city of fraught and dangerous drivers. Mandy's elegant heels click up the steps at the Byres Road subway. She crosses to Retro Grotto and is allowed access to the railing for favoured clients behind the counter. Mandy loves the dresses she's fondling, perfect for doing the Lindy Hop in. She holds one up to the neon tube to admire the cute bow at the waist, the high frilled hem, very daring for the time it was stitched, probably by hand, given the quality of finish.

Mandy buys two dresses for which she pays one hundred and forty pounds with her Switch card. They're costly, but if they came up on eBay, they would start a bidding war which would probably go beyond that sum.

'I almost forgot: I have new shoes in,' Stella informs her as she hands over the carrier bag of purchases.

Is this a subtle sales technique to tempt further the young swing dancer? The carrier bag is set down and Mandy steps out of her elevated heels. Stella brings an armful of footwear, the pink strapped ones, still in their original box, and perhaps never worn, irresistible. Sixty more pounds are extracted from the Switch card, and Mandy is thrilled as she descends into the underground to return to the office, where she will eat a healthy snack at her desk. She checks her mouth in the discreet hand mirror to make sure that no flecks of lettuce are adhering. The face in the glass is a very pretty one, the lips having been accentuated with a modest lipstick, because this is an office in which the elevator brings up elderly sedate clients (some accompanied by their chauffeurs) to confer with their stockbrokers, and who do not like garish cosmetics or the showing of too much leg. Mandy's short hair is naturally blonde, so no treacherous dark roots show. Her eyes are blue, her expression placid. But this short inspection of her face in the little glass is deceptive, because Mandy becomes a different person when it's a dance night.

She's going swing dancing. Having immersed herself in the bath for fifteen minutes, she's now putting on the pink dress she purchased at a price from Retro Grotto two days before. It looks even better than when she tried it on in the shop. The straps on the pink shoes are undone carefully. She puts a white towel like a wimple round her neck to protect the dress from the makeup she's now applying, very different from the subdued colours she wears at work. Her lipstick is scarlet, the eye shadow black. Mandy looks like an outsized doll, but one which many men would dearly love to sit on their knees. Her legs are shapely, seams on the nylons (she is faithful to the era by wearing a suspender belt), her figure in full proportion.

Glasgow has become a much more civilized and safer city since the time when Mandy's dress was high fashion, when rival gangs clashed with razors and even swords, turning the streets into a battle-ground, with bloodshed and fatalities, the mounted police protective of their horses in case their burnished flanks were opened up with a blade. Still, it's safer to take a taxi to the dance venue.

In the hall Mandy arrives as the swing band – trumpet, saxophone, nest of drums, a guitar – is testing the acoustics. Other dancers have arrived early, the women in similar dresses to Mandy's, though the men are casually dressed, in denims and sweatshirts. Mandy is swung, spun, lifted by the waist, and slid along the floor on her heels. The hem of her retro dress circles her waist, the knickers pink and frilled, but not provocative. The music from another era pulses through her body, her head thrown back, arms wide as if she's about to receive a lover.

But Mandy didn't have a boyfriend. On the first working day after the festive season holidays a red rose was waiting on her desk when she traversed the snow-bound city in fur-lined boots and thermal jacket. She cupped the bloom in her hands to inhale its fragrance, placing it in a glass of water. The same gift appeared the following morning, until she had to take in a vase from her flat. Who was this admirer who must have paid considerably for such freshness and colour in the prolonged sub-zero spell, when the streets of the city were sheets of ice, and one of the partners was snowbound at his country mansion for a week, his vital internet artery severed?

After a dozen, the roses stopped, but only to be replaced by individual stargazer lilies of such potent fragrance that they made the recipient light-headed and caused her to make transcription mistakes in typing the senior partner's patronizing correspondence with his clients. Overcome with curiosity, Mandy came in an hour earlier and stood in the adjacent office, watching through the glass wall for her floral gift benefactor. It was one of the partners, a flamboyant man who drove a Jensen and who lived in style south of the river. Mandy knew that he was married, with two children, and she presumed that he was on the hunt for a mistress while maintaining the sanctity of the matrimonial home. He didn't see her watching him laying down the lily, but it appeared on his desk ten minutes later, and thereafter there were no more furtive blooms.

The man who asked her to dance was wearing a white tuxedo jacket with a black bow tie and black trousers, his dress incongruous but intriguing among the other men on the floor. He was also an expert dancer, his two-tone black and white shoes executing the correct moves according to the choreography of the Lindy Hop. When the band stopped he asked his partner if she would like a soft drink, and when she assented he took her arm and led her to a side table while he went to the bar. When he returned with two chilled glasses and straws he introduced himself as Colin Munro, and she disclosed her name in return. Mandy wasn't one of these people who question a person about their employment and background: rather, she let them tell her as much as they wished. When Colin asked her what her profession was, she liked the use of that word, and told him that she was the assistant to a partner in a stockbrokers' office.

'You must be good with figures.'

There being no innuendo in the remark, she told him that she wasn't a dealer in shares, and that she took instructions from the senior partner and typed his correspondence with his clients. Colin told her that he was a lawyer in a city centre practice, specializing in wills and trust funds, and they discovered that their offices (he was in St Vincent Street, in a building of architectural merit which the developers' ball hadn't been allowed to smash down) were only two streets apart.

When the band started up again they took to the floor, and stayed on it together for the rest of the evening, only becoming aware that the other couples had sat down to admire this beautifully attired couple whose moves were in perfect co-ordination, and at the end they received rapturous applause.

Colin takes her home in a taxi, but she doesn't ask him up

for a late coffee, because it doesn't seem appropriate for a first meeting. Usually she cannot sleep for a good hour after the exhilaration of an evening's dancing, and will go on to YouTube and watch her favourite film of all time, *Orchestra Wives* with Glenn Miller and his Band, made in 1942, and in particular the scene where the barman and the girl go to a swing dance of such exuberant energy that Mandy rises from her Habitat sofa and dances by herself. When she switches off her laptop she has a relaxing bath followed by a cup of herbal tea which will not induce insomnia, but tonight she sits up in her white towelling robe, meditating on the evening. It's far too early to tell herself that she's in love, but she's certainly interested in the elegant lawyer with the repertoire of perfect steps for the Lindy Hop. But isn't he too perfect, like Fred Astaire in the 1936 classic musical *Swing Time*? Colin seems to have everything, an important profession, immaculate clothes, and a perfect sense of rhythm.

She had given him her e-mail address, and, sure enough, when she reads her mail in the office, there's a message from him, thanking her for the 'wonderful evening' and asking if he can take her out to lunch the following day. For the rest of the day this highly efficient young woman seems to be super-efficient, typing at speed, and accurately, the voice of her boss she hears through the headphones connected to the little silver recorder, a letter to a large investor in Newton Mearns who has a portfolio worth three million, and who is being informed that part of her investment is being moved into 'more lucrative shares, because we are confident of the continuation of the phenomenal development of information technology.' It's a phrase the elderly widow doesn't understand when she opens the envelope the following morning at her low-fat breakfast because of her arterial problems, but she's quite satisfied with the size of the dividends which she receives regularly but which she cannot spend, and which are reinvested.

The following morning when she boots up her computer in the office Mandy has a message from Stella at Retro Grotto.

'More fabulous gear in! See you at lunchtime?'

What is she to do: cancel her lunch date with Colin and cross the city to the Retro Grotto? Or go out with Colin and perhaps lose a stunning dancing dress? She decides that her new friend must be a priority, so she e-mails Stella to say that she will come in at five forty five, just before the shop closes.

If Mandy isn't crossing the city to Retro Grotto, she is having a plastic tub of carefully selected salad ingredients at her desk, followed by a smoothie. But today she's sitting in Sloans Restaurant in Argyll Arcade, listening to its history from her host. It's one of the oldest restaurants in the city, and generations of professional men have hung their lum hats, bowlers, soft hats and umbrellas on its stands. Mandy is studying the menu as if it's a text which she must give her full attention to, but she doesn't fancy haddock.

'I will have the salad, thank you,' she says eventually, closing the menu.

'Will you have a glass of white wine?' Colin asks.

'No thank you,' this teetotal young woman tells him, even refusing quality champagne at the office party because she believes that her life doesn't require the stimulus of alcohol and besides, it's dangerous to have drink in one on the dance floor, because the Lindy Hop is energetic, sometimes frenetic, and accidents happen to the inattentive and tipsy. She will have tap water, and he will have the same.

Colin talks about his lifestyle. He has a flat in Kelvin Court, the fashionable pre-war complex on Great Western Road, which he inherited from his grandmother. It has a concierge, and the rooms are elegant. She must come to see it.

'Where do you live?'

She sees no reason why she shouldn't disclose that she has a small flat with interesting views of the city in a converted town house in Wilton Street.

Inevitably the conversation moves on to the Lindy Hop. He wants to know how long she's been dancing, and she calculates three years. He has been doing it for seven, having been enticed while at university to a swing dance class organized by a postgraduate female.

'I'd done – or was forced to do – Scottish country dancing at school, and at the first swing dance class I sat watching and thought: this is a crazy way to dance. There are no set steps, and you could do damage to yourself or to your partner. The postgraduate – her name was Hilary – taught us the swingout step first of all and I saw there were definite movements which one had to learn. I'm like you, I became addicted to it and now I never miss a class or a dance if I can help it.'

There was so much to talk about with regard to the Lindy Hop that there weren't any long silences over lunch, and when he walked her back to her office they arranged that he would pick her up in his car for the dance class the following week. The woman who ran the class insisted that one didn't remain with the same partner for the evening, so Mandy only danced once with Colin. She had already decided that when he took her home, she would invite him up to her flat. She didn't have to clean it, because the woman who did that had been in the previous day, but she put a fresh hand towel on the chromium ring in the bathroom and left out cups and saucers for two on a tray, together with several biscuits, gluten free, because Mandy was most careful about what she put into her mouth. The man who came with pails of hot water and mops in the back of a van to wash down the stairs wasn't due for another week, so Mandy did this chore.

'You have a very pleasant place here,' Colin complimented her as she invited him to sit down in the swivel arm-chair from which she watched selected programmes on the small television shut away in the black cabinet.

'I'm happy here,' she confirmed, and went into the open-plan kitchen to make coffee. The type she drank was made from roasted barley and chicory because dancing gave her the stimulus that caffeine never could, but as a concession to her guest she had bought a packet of quality ground coffee which she put into the glass percolator with the plunger. He told her that the biscuit was 'very tasty,' and she gave him a short talk on how wheat bloated the body. Putting on weight was one of her greatest fears, and every morning after her shower she stepped on to the scales. But she knew that she mustn't bore her guest – after only three meetings, really her first boyfriend – with her thoughts on the junk food being consumed by a nation of overweight people who would in turn cost the overstretched health service unaffordable billions. Instead she asked him about his family.

His father was a doctor in Helensburgh, and their house with its views of the Clyde estuary was only a stone's-throw from the Hill House, Charles Rennie Mackintosh's modern masterpiece.

Colin had been schooled at Kelvinside Academy in Glasgow, which meant a very early start by train from Helensburgh.

'I didn't get home until after six in the winter, when it was dark. My mother met me at the train in her car. We had supper, and after an hour of homework it was time for bed. But at least I got sailing in spring and summer.'

Mandy had had a much more modest upbringing. Her father was a teacher of geography in the same state school which she had attended on the south side of the city, together with her younger brother Sam. They had a semi-detached villa of five apartments in a medium-priced road. But her guest didn't ask her about her background. Instead he issued an invitation to sail with him the following Saturday. There would be several other people on board, with his father as helmsman because it was his boat.

'What should I wear?' Mandy asked.

'Yachting wellingtons.'

'I'll buy a pair.'

'What size are your feet?'

Why was this pertinent? But she disclosed that they were six.

'I'll check the size of my sister Sue's wellingtons when I get home. She's in America, but you can use her yachting gear if it fits. I'll pick you up at nine thirty if that's convenient.'

She rose at seven and heard on the radio the weather forecast for inshore yachtsmen. The wind would be force four. Was this too strong? But Colin didn't ring to call off, so she dressed in blue trousers and a thermal top, with a cute blue knitted cap which pulled down over her ears. Colin's father was a quiet spoken, well built man with a vigorous handshake. She was introduced to two crewmen, Peter and Billy, and the five of them climbed into a rubber runabout with an outboard. The yacht Mandy was helped aboard was one of the substantial classic craft of the Clyde, built for racing in a famous yard down the estuary. She sat huddled in the absent Sue's blue waterproof jacket as the sails were hoisted. Everyone on board was busy but herself, but she was commandeered to sit out on the gunwale to counterbalance the boat, over at an angle, its spinnaker ballooning. Mandy found the experience exhilarating, but also somewhat frightening, thinking that she was going to be pitched backwards as the boom swung.

After the strenuous sail she was driven up to the imposing residence, built by William Leiper on the hill above Helensburgh where the mother, attired in a silk trouser-suit, served the monkfish by candlelight. Mandy found the dining experience intimidating, with the silver cutlery set out in rows on either side of her place-mat, with its illustration of a yacht race on the Clyde. The hostess enquired about her background and profession, and Mandy had the impression that she was being appraised as a suitable wife for the son, who smiled encouragingly across the table. Afterwards there was coffee from a silver pot in the very large drawing-room in which the guest counted four sofas, with room for more, and many cushions, including a row on the window seat overlooking the water. Rather than be rude and ask if the brew was caffeine-free, she drank from the dainty cup with the gold band.

'You made a big hit with them,' Colin revealed as they drove back to the city.

She wasn't sure if she liked that phrase, but she pleased him by telling him that he had nice parents. The following week,

176

after the dance class, he took her to his flat in Kelvin Court. It was the residence of a bachelor, with tubular steel and leather furniture, and a glass coffee table on which a map of the Clyde estuary, with its ports, was engraved. He told her that it was 'unique,' and that he had commissioned a city artist to make it.

Suspended at the window was a five feet long model paddle steamer which she admired.

'My grandfather had it made. It's a copy of the one he used to commute to Glasgow on. He was in the tea import business.'

Several of the paintings on the wall, by the Scottish Colourists, had also come from his family home. But Mandy wasn't at ease in this flat as she sat on the black leather sofa to be served a fruit tea, since he knew her tastes, and he had also bought a gluten-free cake. The flat was too clinical for her taste, perhaps reflecting his profession as a lawyer.

Mandy knew that it was only a matter of time before he asked her to stay the night. Did she want to retain her virginity? This was the question she pondered at her desk in her office above Glasgow, the voice of her boss stopped temporarily in her headphones as she stared out over the rooftops of the transformed city, distinguished Victorian buildings demolished to make way for elevations of cement and smoked glass. Shouldn't she tell him that she would rather wait until marriage? But was that trying to pressurize him into proposing? Would it be better if they remained dancing partners and good friends? These were questions she knew she would have to resolve, and the decision came sooner than she expected. After the next dance class, he extended the invitation to stay.

'Tonight?' she queried, really stalling for time.

'Yes.'

'But I don't have anything with me.'

'We can pick up whatever you need at your place.'

'I need more time. Maybe next week.'

On the night before the next dance class she packed a suitcase, as though she were going on a journey. It contained her night attire, toothbrush, cosmetics, clothes and footwear. He carried it down to his car and put it in the boot before driving them to the Lindy Hop class. Mandy felt that she danced clumsily because she was nervous about the coming night, and for the first time she was grateful when the class ended. Her case travelled with them up in the smooth elevator in Kelvin Court. It was the first time she had been in his bedroom, and the double bed made her wonder if he'd had female overnight visitors before.

Having sweated in the Lindy Hop, the guest took a shower and put on her white towelling robe. She sat on the bed while he also showered. Though the slatted blinds were closed, there was still light coming into the room, laying bars across her body, as though she were imprisoned in her anxieties. What was this going to be like? Was there going to be pain and blood? He had bought protection and turned his back on her as he rolled it on with inexperienced fingers. Their limbs seem to meet clumsily, and when he penetrated she reacted as if in pain. And then it became very pleasant.

Mandy and Colin are now lovers at ease with each other. They stay at each other's places over weekends - when they aren't down in Helensburgh, where it has to be separate bedrooms in Leiper's mansion. She finds the house gloomy, almost eerie, and doesn't like having to rise in the night to go to the bathroom down the corridor. The parents treat them as a couple who will marry and give them grandchildren, and on the yacht she is being trained as an essential member of the crew. They seem to dance even better, now that they are physically and emotionally conjoined. After an exciting race in which they commandeered the wind to cross the line first, Colin's father broaches two bottles of seriously fine champagne.

'What holidays do you get at Christmas, Mandy?' Colin asked his lover.

'The office takes ten days.'

'Over Christmas and New Year?'

'Both.'

'In which case I can go ahead and make the booking for the Lindy Focus.'

'What's that?' she asks, intrigued.

'It's a big Lindy Hop convention I found on the net. It's held in Asheville, North Carolina, at the end of December and beginning of January.'

'In America?' she says, startled.

'Have you not been there?'

'No. Have you?'

'I was in New York two years ago with my sister and had a fabulous time. I'll book the flights and the hotel.'

Mandy is nervous about such a long journey over an ocean, her flying having been restricted to weekend flights to Paris and Rome with girls from the office. But it's for dancing, and she'll be with the man she knows she loves.

They have a large room with a bed that could hold two couples in the Crowne Plaza Hotel in Asheville, but are seldom in it because there are five intensive nights of dancing and four days of classes at the Lindy Hop camp, with tuition from the best swing dancers in the world, and the opportunity to participate in high level competitions. Back in Glasgow dancing stopped at ten o' clock, but in Asheville the hundreds of participants dance throughout the night. Mandy and Colin are exhilarated rather than exhausted when they ascend in the elevator to their hotel room with the rising sun. Instead of resting they go down to a healthy breakfast of freshly squeezed juice, and wheat-free cereal, because she has converted her lover to her healthy ways.

They see wonderful costumes on both sexes on the dance floor, and are taught new moves. After the first evening they decide that it would be better to seek different partners. Mandy has a muscular black dancer, his hair in dreadlocks, in a sweat shirt emblazoned with the invitation *Wanna Dance, Honey*? and yet his grip at her waist is so gentle as he lifts her so that she can see over the swaying heads of the dancers to the vibrant swing band of trombones, trumpets, thrilling drums, such wonderful vintage tunes, 'In the Mood,' 'Tuxedo Junction.'

'If only it could go on forever,' Mandy remarks wistfully over an early supper before the evening's dancing.

'Yes, it would be wonderful to live in a world of dance,' her lover concurs. 'To rest in the morning with no work to go to, then prepare for the evening's dancing.'

'The world would be a better place if everyone danced,' Mandy believes.

She finds it hard to express her feelings and observations about dancing. She has never witnessed a quarrel at a dance, never had a confrontation, and has only experienced courtesy and joy. But when the swing band members lay their instruments in their cases, and the lights of the dance hall are snapped off, there's a dark unpredictable world to go out to, a world of suffering and violence, of infidelity and sorrow. And, of course, dancers get old and no longer have the energy or suppleness to perform the swingout and the other movements of the Lindy Hop. Better to enjoy what one has at present and not anticipate the future.

The New Year's party is the highlight of the Lindy Hop camp. The participants come attired in flamboyant costumes and comical hats, and there are dancers in the garb of great dancers of early eras. For this special occasion Mandy is wearing a tartan dress which she bought in Glasgow. She had the hem raised to above her knees, and has a white cockade affixed to the right shoulder of her becoming blouse. Colin is wearing his kilt and a velvet evening jacket with high collar and black bow tie. The brogues on his feet are patent leather, and his stockings match his kilt.

Their national dress causes a sensation on the dance floor and the others make a circle to watch them perform.

Someone shouts: 'A Scotsman has to wear something under his kilt for the Lindy Hop!'

Mandy's underwear matches Colin's, with the St Andrews Cross embroidered. When it shows as he spins her there is deafening applause. Just before the bells of midnight he opens his sporran and produces a small black box, slipping the engagement ring on to her finger.

'Let's get married in the spring!' he says as the first of the artillery of champagne corks are fired to the ceiling. They put through a call to their parents, telling them the news.

In the dawn they link arms with the others in 'Auld Lang

Syne' and promise that they will return the following year, when they'll be man and wife.

Instead of going up in the elevator they decide to go outside the hotel, to inhale the air of the new year of promise. They take a walk along the street, her arm in his. This is when a man emerges from a doorway. He's high on drugs, and he plants himself in front of Colin.

'Why are you wearing a skirt, man?' he demands.

'It isn't a skirt; it's a kilt.'

'Don't mess with me, man. You're one of these queer folk who're neither man nor woman. That's not what the Lord intended. He made man and woman separate and distinct.'

'I don't want to discuss theology with you,' Colin tells him, pushing him aside.

Mandy screams when she sees the flash of a blade.

Did Mandy Graham ever do the Lindy Hop again? Yes, because she hopes desperately that one night she'll see before her a man as handsome and elegant as the one she lost in the first sunrise of the new year in North Carolina. Besides, dancing is a way of forgetting.

The Ceilidh Howff

Norman MacIsaac brought to Glasgow from the Western Isles a variation on the Highland Schottische not seen in that city before. It consisted of clockwise and counter-clockwise movements, with light footwork, and was copied by many. This was in the early 1970s, when there were still dance halls in Glasgow. Norman's father, who had worked in the shipyards during the war, told his son about the Institute in Elmbank Street which was a haven for Highlanders in the city, a most elegant building with carved panels, and a cook who knew how to produce black puddings to perfection.

But Norman was too late to visit this mecca, to demonstrate his Schottische there. The Institute had moved a decade earlier to Berkeley Street, in a building with art deco features. This is where Norman taught his variation on the Schottische to a generation of young women who put on decorous dresses and a limited amount of lipstick to go in search of husbands, preferably with Highland accents, and Gaelic. He was there every evening when there was a dance, and on special occasions he would put on his kilt and the patent leather brogues which his father had bequeathed to him. He was on the floor for every dance, and was noted for the careful way he held a partner by the elbow as he birled her down the set in Strip the Willow, whereas his contemporaries left them with bruises at the end of the night.

Norman travelled to the dance halls on a motorbike which he serviced himself, because he worked as a mechanic, having, since the age of ten, been able to repair the temperamental tractor on the family croft. The city centre garage he worked in serviced some limousines. It was a privilege for Norman to open the bonnet of a Rolls-Royce, to reveal the superb engine which he tuned until it had the perfect tone of an accordion in a Highlanders' Institute Band. As he worked Norman would whistle pipe tunes which he was used to dancing to in the Canadian Barn Dance. He was an accomplished player of the mouth organ, and sometimes could be prevailed upon to give a tune at a works party.

When he first arrived in Glasgow he lodged with a Gaelic speaking widow, a relative of his mother's, in Knightswood, but when the neighbours began to complain about his motorbike arriving home late from dances, he moved to a small rented flat in the east end, where the citizens had learned to live with noise from locomotive works and Orange bands. He chained his machine to railings and at the weekends unscrewed the mirror, because there were still gangs roaming the streets of Glasgow. However, they never put a razor or any other blade near his tyres.

Where else in the city, apart from the Highlanders' Institute, could Norman have chosen to dance? He had arrived in the city too late to partake of soft drinks only between dances at the Dennistoun Palais. There was the cavernous Barrowland, but Norman wasn't into jiving and the Twist. The Plaza with the fountain in the centre of the polished floor was for dedicated ballroom dancers, some of whom competed in tails and long gowns for trophies. Norman was a ceilidh dancer and so was not interested in the strict steps and formal sets of Scottish country dancing. What about the Locarno in Sauchiehall Street? The cashier in the garage had persuaded the mechanic to take her to a Halloween Hop there, but to him dancing wasn't standing swaying to the music and besides, the drinks were expensive.

One afternoon when Norman was speaking to a fellow Gael whose Triumph convertible he had just serviced, he was informed that the Highlanders' Institute was going to close. Norman took this news very badly and lay on his bed brooding that night. Where was he going to go for his dancing? The big Highlands and Islands associations in the city didn't hold regular dances. Did it mean that he was going to have to move back to the Islands in search of a regular venue? (This was a serious consideration).

For the night of the last dance in the Highlanders before it closed its elegant doors Norman put on his kilt and his father's patent leather brogues. He danced his variation of the Schottische with a pretty young nurse from Lewis, whose feet co-ordinated with his own to the extent that a Gaelic wit sitting out compared them to a four-legged creature hopping round the floor. At the end of the evening there was an emotional 'Auld Lang Syne' with linked arms and tears. Norman thought it courteous to offer the affable nurse a ride back to her quarters on his pillion, but she declined politely, fearing that she would get engine oil on her new white shoes. However, instead of a parting kiss she gave him the invaluable information that a new ceilidh house was going to open in the city.

Norman made it his business to find out where it was to be located, and when its doors were to be opened. He discovered from a feature in the evening paper which he was reading with his supper that it was to open in a building which had been a meeting hall on the waterfront. Norman tilted his motorbike on to its stand half an hour before opening time, and was disconcerted to see that there was a hundred yard long queue stretching along the river. As he went to its end he was hailed by former patrons of the Highlanders' Institute.

'You'll be lucky if you get in, Norman!' they taunted him.

But Norman has patience and hope. He waits in the chilly autumn night by the dark Clyde until the queue begins to move. When he reaches the door an arm bars the way.

'No more,' he's told abruptly.

But Norman knows, even from these two abrupt words, that this man is a Gael. He appeals to him in Gaelic, and the arm drops to admit him. The dance hall consists of a wooden floor surrounded by an assortment of tables picked up at various city auctions by Peter and Isabel Menzies, the proprietors. Both denizens of the Highlanders, including the original one in Elmbank Street, they recognized the need for a ceilidh place in the city following the closure of the Berkeley Street premises. The hall they have leased was used by a religious organization, and a dance band is sitting where hot gospellers, in the style of Billy Graham, who visited Glasgow twenty years before, incited the congregation to commit themselves to Christ. On the tables are bottles with candles stuck in them, and at the opposite end from the band is a bar with a gantry offering several choices of whiskies.

The floor is heaving for the Gay Gordons, the first dance in the Ceilidh Howff, as it's called. The band used to play in the Highlanders, and Norman likes the lift they give to the pipe tunes they're playing. None of the four players – accordion, second accordion, fiddler, drummer – has music in front of him, because reading it would impede their expression, and they have played these sets of tunes so often that their fingers deliver them automatically.

Norman will dance every dance this evening, including a particularly energetic Eightsome Reel in which his partner is a teenager who is an accomplished Highland dancer, because she does the Fling in the centre of the circle. At the interval Norman drinks an orange juice, and thinks that this new venue is truly wonderful. He wends his way back to his flat on his motorbike and returns to dance the following night with the same enjoyment, because the Ceilidh Howff opens on Saturdays as well.

Why did it attract so many young people? Because many of them were of Highland descent and dancing was in their genes. In the middle of the nineteenth century their ancestors had been cleared from their townships to make way for sheep, and instead of going on emigrant ships had walked their families south, seeking work in the cities, particularly Glasgow. Some of them were successful, learning skills in the shipyards and the locomotive works; others swept the streets and took in washing, grateful for any work. The various Hebridean islands and mainland communities formed Highland associations which not only preserved their native Gaelic, but also arranged entertainment like dancing. An organization like the Lewis and Harris could attract nine hundred dancers to the massive floor of the St Andrew's Halls, with many unable to obtain tickets.

They danced quadrilles and the Lancers, and did the correct arm turns in the Reel of Tulloch because they took a pride in their ability to dance, as well as turning out in kilts and long gowns, signs that they had prospered in the city. They certainly weren't averse to a quickstep being slipped into an evening's programme, and some of them had been known to shout in an Eightsome Reel. Some took their enthusiasm too far.

Norman MacIsaac's father told him of an occasion when he was at a dance in the old Highlanders' Institute in Elmbank Street. In turning his partner in Strip the Willow a police inspector had caught her sleeve, ripping it off. When the woman complained that it was a new dress bought for that night, he grasped the other sleeve and pulled it off. 'They're equal now, and you won't sweat so much,' he told her in Gaelic. She was so convulsed with laughter at his effrontery that she didn't rage, but at the last waltz he gave her a goodnight kiss, and five pounds towards a new dress.

Norman had been attending the Ceilidh Howff for six months. He was getting to know some of the young women he began to partner regularly because they had perfect balance for birling, or else moved round the floor with grace in a Gaelic waltz. But he found it more difficult to find a Schottische partner who co-ordinated with his clockwork and anti-clockwork turns, and he was often disappointed. His toes were trodden on, and one of them even kicked him on the shin with a particularly sharp shoe as he was steering her round. That was why he was delighted when a new presence appeared in the dance hall on a windy November night. She was very good looking, with short black hair, and her blue dress boasted a most pleasing figure. He decided to take her up for the Schottische, and found that she anticipated the turns he made.

'Where did you learn to dance like that?' he enquired when the music stopped.

'I'm from North Uist.'

'And I'm from South Uist. You must have Gaelic,' he spoke in his native tongue.

'So what?' she answered him in English.

'What do you mean?' he asked, perplexed.

'What good is Gaelic to me in this city?'

'There are still plenty of people who speak it – and are proud to do so.'

'Count me out. If I went for a job and spoke in Gaelic, would I get the position? So you're from South Uist?' she said, eyeing him as she pulled a cigarette from a packet. 'You'll be a Catholic.'

'We *are* allowed to dance.'

'Everyone's allowed to dance. Do you come here every weekend?'

'Since the night it opened.'

'My, but you're keen,' she remarked, expelling smoke.

'I love dancing.'

'So do I. And I like the way you do the Schottische. Most people make a mess of it, hopping round the floor, trying to keep in time to the music. What's your name?'

'Norman MacIsaac.'

'I'm Rhoda MacCodrum, and I'm dangerous,' she cautioned as she transferred the cigarette to her other hand to shake his.

'How do you make that out?' he queried. He had never met a woman who spoke like her; not the accent, but in the phrases.

'They say that the MacCodrum women are seals by day, but that at night they come out of the sea and change into women to seduce men.'

'I never heard that said.'

'It's an old Gaelic legend.'

'I don't believe that sort of stuff,' he told her resolutely.

'What sort of stuff would that be, Norman?'

'Things like second sight.'

'My granny had it. She saw the funerals of the living, and one day when she was down at the pier she met a man with fish scales on his face. She said he would drown soon, and the next week his boat capsized.' She lectured the Schottische exponent with a raised finger. 'There's more in heaven and on earth than we know about.'

A waltz was being called, and he went to find a girl called Alison whose timing suited him to perfection, but three dances later, he asked Rhoda up for a Canadian Barn Dance. At the end of the evening she proposed that they share a taxi home.

'I came by motorbike,' he explained.

'Then I'll go on the pillion – unless you have someone else in mind for that position. I live in the west end.'

She clung to his waist, dress billowing round her dancer's legs as they rode by the dark river. She had told him that she lived in the Hyndland area, and he pulled into the kerb to ask her which street.

'Just drop me here. I need some fresh air, the dance hall was so stuffy. Will I see you there again next Friday?'

'I hope so.'

When he had chained his bike in the east end street he went up the tiled close to his first floor flat, thoughtful about his encounter with the feisty North Uist girl who didn't like to use her native tongue because she considered that it made her seem backward. Despite this rejection of her culture he was attracted to her, and before he went to bed, and to unwind after the dancing, he sat in the lounge with a mug of cocoa and his ruminations. He was twenty seven. Most of the mechanics in the garage of below his age were already married or living with someone. They teased him about going to so many dances, yet not being able to find a partner for his bed. He took it good-naturedly because that was his personality. Rhoda wasn't only a fine dancer; she was also good looking, with an attractive personality, which is why, as he brought engines back to life in the garage the following week, he looked forward to Friday. If she asked for a pillion ride, should he invite her back to his abode? Being a bachelor flat, it was untidy, but on the Thursday evening he picked his clothes off the bedroom floor, and put his underwear in the blue bag for the laundry. He hoovered the lounge and used bleach to try to remove the stains in the bathroom.

He drove to the Ceilidh Howff three quarters of an hour before it was due to open. A queue was already forming, but he was close to the head. By the time the first dance (nearly always the Gay Gordons) was called, Rhoda hadn't turned up. His disappointment affected his dancing, and he was out of phase with the music in the Military Two Step. His speciality the Schottische was being announced when he felt a hand on his shoulder.

'May I have the pleasure?' Rhoda requested.

They were first on the floor, and perhaps because their dual timing was so perfect, the half turns so gracefully executed, other couples in the crowded place chose to sit out and admire the demonstration rather than take to the floor. Norman had never experienced such a feeling of exhilaration as the dance came to an end. He had read somewhere that Red Indians danced themselves into a heightened state in their rituals, and Norman had the feeling that his senses had become even more acute, as if the appealing perfume his partner was wearing was making his head float. He saw her beauty with a new clarity and felt the yielding embrace of her body in his arms, as if they were coupled in intercourse.

He danced several more times with her that evening, including the best Eightsome Reel of his life, and as they were going out to his motorbike he invited her back to his place. *What will she think of the flat?* he was asking himself as her arms circled him from behind, and he felt her breath on his neck.

'I love these tiles,' she told him, running her fingertips over the wall as he led the way upstairs. 'They're very artistic.' And, when he took her into the lounge and he had ignited the gas fire, she complimented him: 'you're very cosy here.'

When he offered her coffee of the instant variety, she asked if he had 'anything stronger.'

He was teetotal himself, but kept a bottle of malt whisky for rare callers from the island. She refused water with the dram and had a second one as they talked. She wanted to know about his life in the city, and what his interests were, apart from dancing.

'I listen to records.'

'What kind of records?' she pressed him.

'Gaelic singers.'

She pulled a face. 'I prefer Presley singing "Blue Suede Shoes" to a woman whining on about her home island.'

He didn't pursue this argument, but put her remarks down to her opposition to her culture. Perhaps something had happened to her on North Uist as a child. But when he asked about her upbringing she was vague, saying only that her family were 'crofters.'

'What do you work at in Glasgow?'

'I'm a beautician in a fancy city centre store. I help well-off women who have nothing better to do to choose lipsticks and face creams, for which they're charged more than a person earns in a week.'

'So you don't like your work?' he hazarded.

'It's a job, and the surroundings are pleasant. You told me you're a mechanic,' she changed the subject.

'It's a job.'

That conversation being exhausted, they sat in silence. She leaned over and helped herself from the whisky bottle.

'I wish you had some decent records to put on instead of that Gaelic drivel,' she told him. 'Do you have a radio?'

He fetched it from the bedroom and she tuned it to Radio Luxemburg. She kicked off her shoes and began to sway her hips to the beat, then held out both her hands to pull him to his feet.

'Come on – move it!' she shouted.

The provocative twisting of her hips so close to him was arousing him, and he tried to use his hand as a shield to cover his embarrassment, but her hands were linked round his neck now and she was pulling him close, towards the sofa. The priest at home had been warning him since adolescence that fornication before marriage was a sin, but he couldn't resist those firm hands.

'I may as well stay the night,' she told him, gathering up her dress and heading naked for the bedroom.

Norman had never missed a morning Mass in his life, but his new lover was still lying beside him at nine o' clock, when he should have been seated in church, getting the blessing of the priest. This perplexed him. It had been his first experience of sex, and it had been wonderful; but he was also conscious that he had committed a sin which he must confess. But if he did so the priest would not only give him decades of the rosary as a punishment, but also warn him not to sin again. It would, of course, be fine if he married her, but he had only known her for a fortnight, so it was an absurd thought. He was as careful with his decisions as he was with the engines of customers in the garage.

'Are you not working today?' he asked when she appeared from her prolonged bath, her hair sleek, like a seal's coat.

'Saturday's my day off. What am I getting for breakfast?'

'All I have is porridge.'

She pulled a face. 'Then you'll have to take me out, won't you?'

They walked to a café, where she ordered bacon and eggs and several cups of coffee before reaching for her handbag, as if she intended to pay, but it was to show that she had to go.

'I'll see you on Friday,' she told him, and she was gone, without a wave as she passed the window.

He had hoped that he would have her company for the rest of the day. They could have shopped together and bought suitable fare for supper, preparing it together. But his vision of domesticity, of places laid for two at the table in the kitchen, and another session in bed, was replaced with depression. He realized that he had slept with a woman he knew so little about. She had asked him questions about his life, but had volunteered no information about herself. That made her even more enigmatic and appealing. On a Saturday he played football in a team with other men from the Islands, and seemed to have derived strength and skill from his night of passion because he scored two goals.

Norman went back to the Ceilidh Howff that evening, but

though he was up for almost every dance, he wished that Rhoda were there, and for the first time sat out the Schottische because he knew that he would never find a partner like her. Usually he changed his bedding on Sunday morning, but her perfume still pervaded the sheets, and he left it because it seemed to send him into a sound repose of erotic dreams.

She was back on the dance floor the following Friday and rode home with him on his pillion, and after the wonderful sex he proposed that she should move in with him.

'I don't think that would be a good idea,' she replied, reaching for her cigarettes.

'Why not?'

'Because I have commitments.'

He waited to hear what these were.

'My mother lives with me. She was widowed last year and didn't want to stay alone on Uist, so she came down to Glasgow. She's a great help because she does the shopping and keeps the flat clean and tidy, but she doesn't like sleeping in it herself.'

'What about last night?' he asked.

'What about it?'

'Well, she was alone in the flat.'

'No, she was staying with her cousin in Knightswood. That's why I'm here.'

'What about next Friday?'

'I'll tell her that after the dancing I'll stay with a friend, rather than come home late. She'll go to her cousin, who's grateful for her company because she's also a widow.'

'Could she stay the Saturday night too so that you can stay here?' he appealed.

'No, because she goes to church on Sunday morning.'

'Don't you have to go with her?'

'Look, is this an inquisition? I'm here and I'll be here every Friday night, so long as you want me. Why don't you leave the future to take care of itself? That's the trouble with you Catholics: you want everything laid out, to know if you're going to heaven or hell. Here we are, talking, and I'm starving.'

'I got in bacon and eggs,' he told her proudly.

'You're learning, Norman.'

They danced together every Friday night at the Ceilidh Howff, and their Schottische became a demonstration, filmed with a cine camera by visitors whose ancestors had been sent across the ocean from Scotland and who would project the Schottische on to the lounge walls of their Canadian homes, so that neighbours could appreciate the vitality of Scottish dances. When it was raining the young woman on the pillion of the motorbike wore a transparent plastic cape which billowed behind her as though she were an angelic presence about to take off into the firmament. The sex seemed to get better and better until they were one in ecstasy, as when they danced the Schottische. She always checked that he was taking precautions, though he would have liked to leave it off so that she would become pregnant and committed to him.

'I think we should get married,' he proposed beside her.

'Don't spoil it.'

'Why would getting married spoil it?' he asked, taken aback, as with so many of her answers.

'Because I have a mother to consider.'

'She could live with us.'

'My mother's a very private person. Can't we just enjoy each other's company and leave the future to take care of itself? Who knows what might happen?'

He had to accept this, but it depressed him. One night a week wasn't sufficient for him, and it wasn't only for the sex. He liked her company, her unpredictable answers, the different potent perfumes on her unblemished skin, the energy of her body beneath him, the beautiful geometry of her breasts as she emerged from the bath, a towel round her head like a turban. Some nights, sitting by his gas fire, he thought of what she had told him about the seal legend associated with the MacCodrums of North Uist. She was like that creature. She emerged on a Friday night to delight him with her dancing and the appeal of her body and then she disappeared for the rest of the week, sliding into her own world, a world he knew so little about.

During the Glasgow Fair holiday in July he always went home to South Uist to see his folks, but this year he decided to stay, because he saw so little of Rhoda and didn't want to be parted from her. He made the excuse to his parents that he was saving up for a new motorbike. On the Friday Rhoda didn't appear in the Ceilidh Howff. He was worried that she was ill, but he had no phone number or address for her. The following morning he took the subway into the centre of the city and went into the cosmetics section of a store in search of her. All the women behind the brightly lit counters of expensive products were good looking and immaculate. He stopped and asked a striking blonde in a blue costume if someone called Rhoda worked there.

'I don't know that name, sir. Ask at the next counter.'

He was directed to six counters, but no one knew a Rhoda who was a beautician. He was advised to try another store on

Argyle Street. The women and the counters looked the same, and the result was the same. There were no more high-class stores to go into.

He went to the dance hall that night, hoping that she might appear. He declined the invitation of a woman to partner her in the Schottische, though he had danced with her before and found her steps accorded with his. For the first time he wasn't enjoying a dance. The Howff had lost its appeal, and there was no longer anticipation as the band prepared to call the next dance. He didn't wait for the last dance, but before midnight went down to his motorbike. He was throttling by the river, saddened that there weren't arms round his waist, when a car on the outside lane swerved towards him. He was going at speed, and had to take action to avoid a collision. The wall loomed.

Norman MacIsaac was in a coma. His parents came down from South Uist to sit by his bedside for a week, but were advised by the consultant to return home.

'If there's any change we'll phone you,' he reassured the distraught couple. But he didn't tell them that Norman was in what was now being called a 'persistent vegetative state.' The X-rays showed injury to the brain, and the spine was damaged. It might be a kindness to the patient and his family to switch off the life-support machine.

It was a summer evening before Norman opened his eyes again, welcomed back into the world with a Gaelic waltz. The person bending over him wasn't Rhoda MacCodrum, but Mary Henderson, the nurse he used to dance with in the Highlanders' Institute. She had been playing him the tape of Bobby MacLeod and his Band for days.

'Don't you recognize me?' she asked.

He didn't, but he thought she was most attractive in her starched blue uniform, with the little watch inverted at her white bust.

'Where am I?'

'You had an accident on your bike. This is the Southern General Hospital in Glasgow.'

He seemed to have lost his body from the waist down.

'It was a bad accident.'

When the consultant came on his rounds it wasn't the time to tell the patient that he would never walk again. Two days later a policeman came in to ask him for details of his crash, but he remembered nothing.

'Has Rhoda been in touch?' he asked the nurse.

'Rhoda? No, nobody of that name.'

What Norman will never know was that it wasn't an accident. Rhoda MacCodrum, like the seal turned woman for purposes of seduction, wasn't what she seemed. She was from North Uist, certainly, and she was a lapsed Gaelic speaker, but she wasn't a beautician. Nor did her mother, nervous of being alone at night, live with her. She was the mistress of a notorious criminal the police couldn't stick anything on because he was too clever for them and might have gone to university and become a respectable citizen. When Rhoda (it was her real name) told him that she was going dancing on a Friday night he consented because he had business in the city, extorting protection money, but when she said she was staying overnight with a friend he became suspicious. One of his employees sat outside the Ceilidh Howff and watched her emerging with a man whose pillion she climbed on to. He followed them and reported to his boss that they had entered a tenement in the east end. It was too risky, to go into the tenement, because the sounds of a beating could be amplified by the stairwell. The criminal, known as Angry Malky, told his mistress that she wasn't going back to the dance hall, a decision she accepted with unusual meekness because she was entirely dependent on him for her clothes, cosmetics, and restaurant meals. Besides, to disobey would mean the back of his hand – or worse. So she stayed at home. watching television while the criminal's man waited in the car outside the Ceilidh Howff. He tailed the bike with the empty pillion along the waterfront until an opportunity presented to force the rider against the wall that ran by the dark river. He sped away without waiting to see the consequence.

Norman MacIsaac was told eventually that he was a paraplegic. He would never walk again, far less ride a motorbike or dance. It was the first time since childhood that he cried, but Mary Henderson comforted him. 'We'll work together on this and have a waltz together.'

It took months before he was on his feet; many more before he could take a step. But Mary Henderson was there to hold him. The St Bernard's Waltz is a simple dance: three steps to the man's left, two back to the right; two backwards, then two forwards, before turning the lady under your arm. The three steps left took a year to achieve, the others six months. Tonight Mary has brought a portable player into the ward, with a recording of Bobby MacLeod's Band playing a selection of Gaelic airs for a waltz. The first tune is the 'Uist Bridal Song' and Norman, in the arms of Mary, takes three steps to the left, hesitates, then takes two to the right, back and forward. He can't yet raise his arm to turn her under, but he holds her tightly instead.

'We'll do a Schottische yet,' she whispers to him as the ward staff, including the sceptical consultant, applaud.

Everything is Pleasing at the Plaza

All the residents of the Sunset Court Nursing Home in a leafy enclave of Edinburgh had pleasant rooms overlooking lawns and flowerbeds, but rather than have them sit in isolation they were brought into the large lounge of the former convent, where the nuns used to pray, though the chapel fixtures had been removed when the building was converted into a home for the elderly and infirm. Some of them were in wheel-chairs; others were supported on zimmers as they were helped to the bathroom. The woman in the high-backed chair in the corner had been a noted artist, but she sat all day with her head between her knees, sedated in her dementia.

The television was on most of the time, but few of them paid it any attention. However, on a Saturday evening after tea a resident was wheeled forward, his chair parked in front of the set. He watched the show *Strictly Come Dancing* attentively, nodding and smiling at a quickstep or foxtrot, and sometimes covering his eyes with a palm at some of the more creative moves, as when women were lifted or slid between their partner's legs.

Robert Hunter was ninety nine years of age, and had been in the home for four years, following a stroke. Though he had lost the power of speech the nurses who dressed him knew that he liked to wear a collar and tie with a jacket, with shoes instead of slippers with Velcro fasteners on his feet, as most of the residents wore. His lawyer had sold his client's detached bungalow in Craiglockhart to help pay the considerable cost of the nursing home. There were no known relatives, and when the lawyer sent a junior to clear the house before the sale she was looking for share certificates and other documents in case the client had funds which the lawyer wasn't aware of. The entire contents of the house, furnishings and clothing, were cleared by a charity, which put the photographs and other papers into black sacks for disposal. The woman came across a box of medals which she took in good conscience to the lawyer, who sent his assistant with them to see what a jeweller in Rose Street specializing in second hand and antique items would pay for them.

'They're dance medals,' the jeweller announced, appraising them through the glass screwed into his eye. 'They're gold and silver, but their main value is in scrap metal.'

The lawyer accepted the jeweller's offer of thirty pounds, and the medals were melted down and went into trinkets in the shapes of the signs of the Zodiac to hang from bangles.

Robert Hunter was a teenager at the Royal High School when a glamorous couple stepped off the Flying Scotsman to bring the Charleston to Edinburgh. It was discovered in 1923 among black dock workers in Charleston, North Carolina. In October of that year it was introduced to the world at the New Amsterdam Theatre by the Ziegfeld Follies and at a tea-dance in London at Ciro's Club by Robert Sielle and Annette Mills, names that mean nothing now, but who were stars in their day in tail coat and flouncy dress. Robert had been too shy to ask girls up at the school dances, but when his mother coaxed him along to watch a demonstration of the Charleston in Edinburgh, the schoolboy discovered what would be his lifetime's abiding passion. He enrolled for instruction in dancing the Charleston at an Edinburgh ballroom and was told by his teacher: 'you're not only a natural dancer, Robert; you're exceptional.'

The Charleston became all the rage throughout the land, danced by couples who didn't have Robert's control. It was considered a dangerous activity and condemned as vulgar by those who preferred the sedate waltz. Doctors issued dire warnings about fractured ankles and paralysis resulting from trauma to the body through the frenetic moves of the dance. Innumerable bruises were treated with poultices, and females wept over ruined stockings. But the dance would be modified to a safer, more graceful version called the Flat Charleston, with the feet remaining on the floor. In time the dance would be absorbed by the quickstep, and there were no more bruises or ruined stockings.

When he left the Royal High School Robert went to Edinburgh University to study classics. He had become such a proficient dancer that he answered an advertisement for dance instructors for the Marine Gardens, Portobello. When he saw the extent of the ballroom he gasped. It was almost one hundred yards long and twenty six yards broad. Settees placed round the perimeter could, it was claimed, accommodate several thousand without a squeeze. No alcohol was the strict rule, but tea and soft drinks were placed behind the settees.

Mr Fraser the manager asked the applicant to dance a waltz with one of the instructresses, who was wearing a blue dress with white squares.

'You'll be joining us,' she told him confidently as he steered her round a portion of the floor within range of the gramophone with the large horn which the manager was playing. 'I've never danced with anyone I've felt so – so co-ordinated with.'

Robert explained to the manager that he was a student and

so couldn't be at the ballroom every night it opened, but they came to an arrangement that he would be available for four nights, which included the weekend, the busiest time. When he was told that he would be paid a pound a week, plus twopence for every dance, he smiled, not at the paucity of the pay, but because he loved dancing so much that he would have worked for nothing.

This quiet, elegant man with the erect carriage wore an evening suit and a wing collar with black tie, like the rest of the brigade of instructors. He sat in a roped-off circle, waiting to be asked. Some evenings the floor was crowded with close to two thousand dancing to the New Rialto Orchestra with Leslie D. Jeffries leading on the violin. As he went round the floor with his paid-up partner, Robert Hunter truly believed that he had arrived in heaven on earth. He loved the atmosphere, the rhythm of orchestra and dancers, the elegance of the ladies, the formally suited men.

But he does not know that he is being watched from one of the settees. The lady is wearing a white fox fur round her shoulders, the clasp at the creature's mouth holding its tail. Her dress, which reaches to her ankles, seems to belong to a more modest age, and her shoes were fashionable before the Great War. Mrs Drummond-Murchison is a widow of mature years who was married to one of the richest men in Scotland, and by the grace of family coal mines in Midlothian, proprietor of a mansion at North Berwick. As a child Sophia loved to dance, but her husband had no interest in, or aptitude for it, and refused to let her go alone to the ballrooms of Edinburgh. She has had to wait until his death to satisfy her yearning. The period of mourning is now over, and she is in the Marine Gardens, looking for a partner.

She sees Robert Hunter passing and she lifts a finger. Her chauffeur, who is standing behind the settee, leans forward to receive his instructions. Her gloved hand indicates that the chauffeur is to go and arrange that she dances with the chosen instructor.

Ten minutes later the rich widow is in the arms of Robert Hunter, and loving every step and turn of the waltz. This is what she has been dreaming about for years, and it's been worth waiting for, putting up with a philistine husband who shoots defenceless wildfowl and shouts himself hoarse at rugby matches. At the end, as her dancing partner bows to her, she presses a pound note into his palm and tells him: 'I shall be here next Saturday and will expect to dance several times with you.'

The Rolls-Royce pulled up at the Marine Gardens the following Saturday evening, and Sophia went to see the manager. She explained that the style of dancing of Mr Robert Hunter suited her particularly, and she wished to avail herself exclusively of his services for an hour this evening, and for Saturday evenings into the foreseeable future. The manager was perplexed. It was the strict rule that instructors and instructresses must not become familiar with those they were teaching, for a liaison would bring the ballroom into disrepute; on the other hand, Robert was a young man and this formidable lady in the fox stole in front of him must be past fifty, despite the skilful application of cosmetics. A lady of this bearing, and such obvious wealth enhanced the status of the establishment.

'Of course, Madam,' he said, bowing, and called Robert out of the roped-off instructors' area (known as The Paddock) to tell him about the arrangement.

But Mrs Drummond-Murchison didn't only want to dance waltzes with the accomplished instructor: she also wanted to learn new dances, and in particular the tango, having made the chauffeur drive her four times into Edinburgh to see Rudolph Valentino performing the exotic dance in *The Four Horsemen of the Apocalypse*, not daring to tell her husband about her excursions, since he considered the Italian-born actor to be a gigolo.

When Mrs Drummond-Murchison suggested that he teach her the tango, Robert Hunter wasn't fazed. He had danced it many times before, but always avoided making it sexually suggestive. He proposed the Argentinean Tango, and Sophia assented. She liked the imperious resonance of the name, so he went up to the leader of the New Rialto Orchestra and requested that dance. Sophia was a gifted dancer and by the end she had mastered the steps in the arms of a superb teacher.

After an hour of being continually on the floor the rich widow from North Berwick presses three pounds into Robert's palm. They have danced a dozen dances, so he is only entitled to two shillings, but his pupil insists. She will see him next week.

They began the following week's session with a One-Step, a smooth walk of one step to every count of the music, followed by a foxtrot (to the tune 'I'll See You in my Dreams'), and the Amelia Waltz. When quadrilles were announced, they went into a set. That evening Robert received five pounds.

'It's very generous of you, but please take it back,' he pleaded. 'It's an honour to dance with you.'

'The honour is mine,' the widow told him, closing his fingers round the banknote.

That Christmas the wealthy widow and expert instructor performed an Argentinean Tango that had dancers sitting out on the settees applauding in admiration. At the end of the evening she didn't put money into his hand, but instead gave him her arm to lead her out to the limousine, the chauffeur following behind.

'This is a small token of my appreciation,' the widow announced when they were out in the frosty night air of Portobello.

Robert had his hand out for the gift, but she pointed to a Morris car parked beside her Rolls-Royce.

'I can't accept that, Madam,' he said in perplexed astonishment.

'Why not? You've given me more pleasure than I've had in years. Have a happy Christmas, and I'll see you here on the third week of January, on the Saturday evening, because I'm going to Switzerland for the festive season,' she told him, extending her gloved hand.

As the Rolls-Royce pulled away the dancing instructor stood with his hand on the roof of his incredible Christmas gift. He couldn't return it, and he certainly couldn't tell the manager about it, because he would definitely think that he and Mrs Drummond-Murchison were having an affair. He hadn't learnt to drive, so he left the car at the Marine Gardens and went home by bus as usual. However, the following day he returned with a friend who drove the Morris back to Edinburgh and promised him lessons in the new year.

Robert was still living with his parents in the west end of Edinburgh, and they were astonished when he took them out to show them the car. How could a student afford this? When he explained that it was a gift from a wealthy dancing partner at the Marine Gardens, they were sceptical, but kept to themselves the suspicion that he was having an affair with this mysterious obviously wealthy woman.

When the new Plaza Salon de Danse threw open its doors in the Morningside district of Edinburgh in September 1926, Robert went along on one of the nights when he wasn't committed to the Marine Gardens. The floor was semi-floating, on shock absorbers, and a soda fountain quenched the thirst of the dancers. There were afternoon dances at 1/6d, evening dances ranging from 2/6d on Mondays to 5/- on Saturdays, from 8.p.m. to 11.30p.m. On Friday nights, when dancing went on to 1.a.m., evening dress was 'essential.' The slogan of the new ballroom was: 'Everything is Pleasing at the Plaza.'

Robert danced to Lionel Murray's London Band. There was no alcohol on sale, but the beverages offered included Horlicks and Bovril. Robert didn't think he needed either to send him to sleep or to build up his strength. He was twenty years of age, at the height of physical fitness through his dancing. Robert was conscious of his posture, on and off the floor. He was both relaxed and at the same time faultless in the execution of his dancing steps, and most considerate of a partner who didn't possess the same skills. He would spend decades on the dance floor, but would never tread on a partner's foot. A classics scholar, Robert wondered if Plato had been a dancer, because the great philosopher had written: 'The dance, of all the arts, is the one that most influences the soul. Dancing is divine in its nature and is the gift of the gods.'

To Robert dancing was like inhabiting another world. It was about decorum; about moving one's body in perfect timing with the music; it was a feeling that one took away from the ballroom and induced dreams of waltzing with a perfect partner, but without sexual innuendo.

Robert went to yet another Edinburgh ballroom, the Palais de Danse in Fountainbridge, on the first evening of 1927, having been excused duties at the Marine Ballroom, Portobello, Mrs Drummond-Murchison being away in Switzerland with wealthy friends. A crowd of eight hundred danced the Charleston among scores of coloured lights and lanterns, the walls festooned with evergreens. The huge Christmas tree in the centre of the ballroom was loaded with toys for the children's party, and the lights were lowered for the exquisite waltzes. Robert drank an energizing glass of lemonade, but denied himself a slice of festive cake, because putting on weight was detrimental to one's dancing. He was setting down the glass and preparing to seek a new partner for a foxtrot when the manager approached him.

'I was watching you dancing the Argentinean Tango.'

It wasn't a rebuke for holding his partner too close in that suggestive dance, but an expression of admiration.

'It's one of my favourite dances,' Robert told him.

'I'm looking for gentlemen to be dance partners.'

'I'm sorry, but I'm already an instructor at the Marine Gardens at Portobello.'

'I'll give you half again what they're paying you.'

'You have a beautiful ballroom here and a wonderful band, sir, but I can't leave the Marine. Now if you'll excuse me, I'm going to look for a partner for the foxtrot.'

'If you change your mind, they'll always be a place here for you. I've never seen such footwork.'

The following week, when Mrs Drummond-Murchison made her stately entrance into the Marine Gardens, in her white fox stole, her chauffer walking behind her like a servant at the court at Urbino, she had news for her dancing partner.

'My birthday is next month.' (She didn't disclose which one it was). 'I've decided to hold a party. I've hired the entire Marine Hotel at North Berwick, so that my friends can stay there. I want you to come, to make up the programme and be the master of ceremonies – and dance with the ladies, of course.'

Robert knew that the invitation came with a generous gift, but that wasn't what made him accept. He wasn't attracted romantically to his gracious dancing partner, but he was very fond of her, as if she were a favourite aunt. He explained to the manager of the Marine Gardens that he wouldn't be available that night, since he had a function on.

'Have you booked a band?' he enquired of Mrs Drummond-Murchison.

'I've reserved Mr Tim Wright's Band, having been to hear it at the Assembly Rooms.'

Robert had danced to this band, and had found it a harmonious experience. He knew, however, that Mrs Drummond-Murchison would have to pay a considerable sum for this much-in-demand band. The Marine dance instructor had become a competent and careful driver, and when he parked his Morris outside the Marine Hotel and entered its elegant interior he saw evidence of the wealth of his dancing partner. There were flowers of many varieties and colours, some of which had been imported from the continent by that increasingly popular mode of travel, the aeroplane. Mrs Drummond-Murchison had chartered one from a Croydon Airport based company. Her chauffeur was the only passenger across to Holland, and when he returned every seat and the hold were filled with blooms from greenhouses in the Low Countries. In the Marine Hotel pollen gleamed like gold dust on the sleeves of Robert's evening jacket as he made his way to the ballroom, Mr Tim Wright's Band already in place. The strings of the banjo had been tuned, the saxophone checked for tone, the violin's pegs given a slight adjustment. The pianist was at the grand piano, the drummer comfortable behind the high hat.

It wasn't only the chandeliers which dazzled the master of ceremonies. They reflected the jewels, mostly diamonds, worn by the ladies. Their dresses had been fitted to their figures in Paris and Rome by kneeling seamstresses, pins between their lips, perfection in their fingers. Some of the male guests had bought their white tuxedo jackets in business trips by liner to the Land of the Lindy Hop. Robert even saw a tiara, an arc of fire on an immaculately coiffured head.

He had prepared the programme very carefully in consultation with his patroness. She wanted to lead the evening off with a Viennese Waltz, one of their specialities at the Marine Gardens. The Ladies had been provided with slim printed cards of the programme, with a dangling pencil to pin to their waists so that they could write the names of their partners against each dance. Robert's name was written against the Viennese Waltz on the birthday celebrant's card. This was because she wished to set a standard for the evening and also, frankly, because she wished to show off in front of her guests. So when Mr Tim Wright's Band struck up he led his patroness on to the floor and took her in his arms.

Did this shrewd lady who kept in constant touch by

telephone with her stockbroker to check that her massive investments were achieving maximum return know that this demonstration of a classic waltz would intimidate her guests and that only two other couples would venture on to the floor with faltering steps as she was swept round, the tulle at her waist attached like a blue rainbow to the smallest finger of her right hand, head slightly to the side like a Roman goddess who has no desire to look at real mortals?

The master of ceremonies saw her strategy, which is why he chose an anxious looking spinster, heir to a pharmaceutical fortune in Switzerland, to be his partner for the Argentinean Tango. She too had salivated over Valentino's tango on the screen in a cinema in Berne, daring to wish that she were in his arms. But this man she was now dancing with at her friend's birthday party in North Berwick was so elegant, so considerate, the way he steered her round the floor, giving her confidence with every complicated step, her virginal thigh close to his, but never touching, her head turned to the side in a dance she would long recall in her lonely feather bed in the canton.

There was an interval for the banquet of exquisite food, including a wild boar, gunned down in a forest in Bavaria and flown to Scotland, to be roasted on a spit, with a large apple inserted between its jaws. Passing the laden tables, behind which were white-jacketed waiters with silver serving utensils, Robert chose sparingly of this lethal spread. He refused the salver of tulip-shaped glasses of vintage champagne and instead drank apple juice as he sat by invitation at Mrs Drummond-Murchison's table, sensing, from the way the other privileged guests were watching him, that they suspected he was her retained lover, a thought that amused rather than distressed him, for his conscience was as clear as his complexion.

He danced twice more with his patroness in the second half, and was at the back of the circle watching her cutting the cake which had been wheeled on to the dance floor. At the top of the white confection a couple in ballroom hold had been sculpted in sugar, the man in an evening suit, the woman in a gown encrusted with edible sequins. At the end of the evening he arranged the guests round the floor with linked hands, and as they sang 'Auld Lang Syne' the birthday celebrant bowed and smiled in the centre.

'Thank you for a wonderful evening,' she enthused as her master of ceremonies draped the full-length mink coat round her shoulders. She opened the little jewelled bag and passed him an envelope.

The chauffeur carried the presents – including a brooch by Cartier, perfume by Caron, and a Mont Blanc pen - in armfuls out to the Rolls-Royce, and Mr Tim Wright's Band put their instruments into their cases. Robert stood under the chandeliers, wistful that such an exceptional evening was over. Before he retrieved his coat and white silk scarf he opened the envelope and found a cheque for one hundred pounds. There was also a note: 'Dear Robert, I will see you as usual next Saturday evening at the Marine Gardens. Affectionately, Sophia.'

Robert Hunter had graduated from Edinburgh University with a 1st Class Honours in Classics and trained as a teacher, bringing to the classroom the same calmness, the same quiet discipline which he displayed on the dance floor. If a pupil whispered to a neighbour while the classics master was reading from *De Bello Gallico*, all he had to do was to look up to regain silence and attention. When he walked between the desks while they were doing a test it was with the same graceful gait he used while perambulating a dance floor in search of a partner. His life was a long slow stylish waltz, and, like a muted saxophone, his tone was never raised. It seemed that he was leading two separate lives, that of a classics teacher in a private school in Edinburgh, and in the evenings, a dance instructor in the Marine Gardens in Portobello, or a dancer in the Plaza Salon de Danse and other Edinburgh venues of a certain standard. He was invited to the Plaza, to the wedding of a dance acquaintance, but it was a very different affair from Mrs Drummond-Murchison's birthday ball with its masses of flowers and its Black Forest boar. Robert sat down with forty other dancers (strictly couples) to the usual wedding menu in the Plaza. It cost four and sixpence per head and the spread included: tea, coffee, assorted sandwiches, muffins, cake, shortbread, a selection of pastries, biscuits, plain and chocolate, fruit and wine jellies with cream, trifles, fruit salad and aerated waters, otherwise lemonade. The guests made considerable inroads into the selection, and afterwards, when dancing started for the evening, the bridegroom, a clerk in the City Chambers, led his wife in her pillbox hat, on to the floor, for a Viennese Waltz, and Robert partnered the bridesmaid, a sallow skinned young woman from Canonmills who had no aptitude for dancing, and whose weight was augmented by three helpings of trifle. When an attack of heartburn came on, she had to sit down before the end of the waltz, but couldn't resist another shortbread fantail.

When Robert wasn't dancing he was at home with his parents, listening to big bands on the wireless. This evening it's the Ambassador's Orchestra from the Marine Gardens, Portobello, and, eyes closed, Robert is on the floor of the ballroom with his patroness. He began to venture further than Portobello in his Morris in search of dances. One evening of clear skies he drove through to Glasgow. In those days motorized traffic was light compared to our time, but he was nervous as he entered the city, finding himself opposite a horse hauling a cart. Fortunately the animal was blinkered and used to the congestion, and went on its way with sacks of flour for Bilsland's Bakery so that next day the citizens might have bread. At this time there were eleven major ballrooms in Glasgow, compared to Edinburgh with five. Since London had fewer than this, Glasgow was considered to be the capital of dance in Great Britain, if not in the entire world. Wasn't it Jack Diamond of the city's Dancing Academy who, along with a Mr MacNaughton and partners, first demonstrated the Argentinean Tango in the McLellan Galleries on Sauchiehall street in 1913, inspiring a half column in the *Glasgow Herald*? Hadn't the battalions who marched through the city to war a year later carried its irresistible tempo in their heads, their feet marking out the tricky steps in the trench until the lethal shell arrived? And back in Glasgow, many young women received as tactful gifts from sweethearts and spouses the best selling manual *The Tango and How to Dance It* before being invited to the latest craze, Tango Teas.

Robert Hunter's destination that mild evening in another world was the Albert Ballroom. He had come to this hallowed dance place on pilgrimage because he had read about the Warren family who owned the Albert. The patriarch was John Warren, assisted by his wife Annie, and their two sons and two daughters had been raised in an environment which Robert considered to be blissful, an elegant ballroom, which, in its early days had advertised: *Gentlemen, one shilling, Ladies, invited.*

Robert has come through to watch the Warren dynasty giving an exhibition dance of the Argentinean Tango. The males were immaculate in swallow-tailed coats and white gloves, the ladies in ankle-length gowns. The patriarch's son John was partnering Miss Dorothy Dawn, who would become his wife. But the patriarch wasn't dancing with his wife Annie. Their daughter Jessie, divine exponent of the Royal Empress Tango, had died several years before at the age of eighteen, and her heartbroken mother Annie would never dance again.

It wasn't envy that the demonstrator from the Marine Gardens felt as he watched the Warrens going round the floor of the Albert; it was gratitude that there were such dancers to learn from. When the spectators were invited on to the floor Robert requested the honour of dancing with the patriarch's daughter Anne. This was the age long before transmission of traits and talents through genes or environment were talked about, but as he danced the most fulfilling tango of his life, Robert speculated that there was some kind of inheritance of grace and co-ordination in the Warren clan.

One evening, gracing with his presence the Fountainbridge Palais in his native city, Robert asked up for the foxtrot a young woman whose gold shoes matched her hair and the belt at her waist. A pair of golden monkeys dangled from her ear lobes. Her footwork rivalled that of Anne Warren, but several times her thigh made contact with his. Usually when the dance finished he followed protocol by leading his partner back to her seat, bowing to her and thanking her for the privilege without learning her name. But this young lady held out her hand.

'Kitty Dawson.'

He shook hands, giving his own name.

'You're one of the instructors at the Marine Gardens, aren't you? I've tried several times to get a dance with you, but there are always women in the queue in front of me. Who is that woman you always dance with on Saturday nights?'

Robert considered this to be confidential, and made the reply: 'a lady who likes to dance.'

'Are you looking for a partner?' she enquired.

This intelligent man who could see the subtleties in questions in classical texts was taken aback.

'Do you mean for the next dance?' he asked.

'No, I mean for competitions.'

'I don't enter competitions.'

'You *must*,' she urged. 'You're such a beautiful dancer and there are fabulous prizes to be won.'

This is how Robert Hunter acquired a dancing partner. Kitty Dawson was twenty two years of age and worked in the lingerie department of Jenners' imposing store on Princes Street. At first the manager had been dubious about taking on a girl with such a distinct dialect (was there a touch of Irish in it?), and a plain way of speaking. But she became one of the most successful sales persons in the fashionable emporium, persuading shy ladies that their husbands would appreciate the latest short silk negligees from Paris in the privacy of their New Town houses and suburban villas.

Robert was also intrigued by her guileless directness. Perhaps this was one of the qualities which made her such an exceptional dancer, but a risky one at times, because she flounced her skirts in the Charleston and showed too much silk stocking in the tango. They won competitions in these dances and in more sedate ones such as the foxtrot and the Viennese Waltz. Kitty bought her spectacular dresses from a shop in Lothian Road, but under a special arrangement: when females came up to her on the dance floors of the city and asked where she had bought the garment, she delved into her bust to produce a card giving the address.

After competitions, when Robert drove her home to her single room in Stockbridge, there would be two gramophones on the back seat, their prizes for the evening. They had already won four each since the start of their partnership six months earlier, and Kitty had put a notice in the evening paper, advertising them as 'unwanted dance competition prizes, most reasonably priced.' On both their dressing-tables were medals in gold and silver, but not bronze, because they were one of the two best couples in the capital.

'We should go through to Glasgow to compete,' Kitty suggested one evening as she was being driven home after the triumph of a major competition in which they had each won genuine gold watches, hers for her dainty wrist, his, with a chain, for his waistcoat.

'We wouldn't get back until late,' he cautioned her.

'What does that matter?' she challenged. 'I don't need much sleep. In fact after a competition I'm so alive that I can't sleep. I've seen me sitting up reading until it was time to go to work.'

'What do you read?'

'Love stories. I tried my hand at one, about a girl who falls in love with a dancer, but the magazine I sent it to sent it back with the comment written on red ink across the top: too *risqué*. Bloody cheek. Anyway, there's a competition in the Albert Ballroom in Glasgow next Wednesday.'

'I can't go. I'm on duty at the Marine Gardens.'

'Dancing with the mysterious lady with the fox fur stole?'

'That's on a Saturday,' he informed her defensively.

'You don't give much away, do you, Robert? How do your pupils learn from you?'

'What do you mean?'

'Do you actually tell them anything, or do you say, as one of my teachers used to say: open your textbook at page sixty two, and if I hear so much as a whisper – I was always being punished. So if Saturday and Wednesday nights are hallowed, I'll need to look for competitions on other nights.'

She reported that there was a competition in a new ballroom, the Locarno in Glasgow on an evening that Robert was free, and that they must go. He was dubious, because he was teaching the following day, and was usually in bed by ten thirty, but she was persistent. The ballroom on Sauchiehall Street was lit by electric lanterns and could accommodate up to a thousand couples. There were two supper rooms, and a garage for a hundred cars in which Robert parked his vehicle. The eighteen alcoves round the ballroom had been painted with mythological figures by Maurice Greiffenhagen of the Glasgow School of Art.

Leslie D. Jeffries was conducting the Locarno Orchestra as Robert and his partner took to the fabulous sprung oak floor. The competition was the quickstep at which Robert and Kitty excelled. But there was a male competitor Robert hadn't seen before in his visits to the ballrooms of Glasgow. His name was Farquhar MacRae. He had all the qualities, the footwork, the captivating rhythm of a champion, and it was he who was presented with the gold cufflinks as first prize, his partner with a bracelet in the same hallmarked metal.

Kitty was despondent on the way home to Edinburgh.

'That's the way it goes,' her driver told her philosophically. 'Glasgow has some of the finest dancers in the country. Competition's always going to be stiff.'

But on their next foray, this time to the Dennistoun Palais, they beat Farquhar MacRae into second place and won canteens of silver plated cutlery. It was on the return journey from this success when Kitty announced: 'I suppose we should get married.'

The equitable man at the wheel almost lost control of the vehicle.

'Well, we dance so well together, and we get on well.'

In his classes, even when he was asked a testing question by gifted senior pupils who would go on to take 1st Class Honours in classics, Robert was never stuck for an answer. But on this occasion, as he drove home, he didn't know how to explain his feelings to the young woman awaiting a reply at his side in the small intimate car. He could explain his situation to himself, but not to another, because it sounded so selfish. If he married Kitty, he would have the one dancing partner, because she would prevent him from devoting the hallowed hour on a Saturday evening to Mrs Drummond-Murchison at the Marine Gardens. He needed variety, different females for different dances. For example, Kitty was without rival for the Charleston, but his North Berwick patroness would always be his choice for the Viennese Waltz. Dances, like people, had different personalities, risky, sedate. Dancing has its own philosophy, its own mores and customs. One should not mix dancing and seduction, because the latter would destroy the purity and joy of the former.

A woman could ask a man to dance with her, but she

should never propose marriage, in Robert's estimation. Kitty was forward, sometimes crude, but always appealing, and endowed with a shapely graceful body, at least as far as dancing was concerned. But he didn't love her. It wasn't that he had homosexual leanings. Perhaps he didn't need sex because he experienced sufficient joy through the act of leading a partner round a ballroom floor.

'I don't think that would be a good idea,' he had to respond eventually.

'Stop the car!'

They were on the outskirts of Edinburgh by now, and he assumed that she was either feeling squeamish, or needed to shed the lemonade she had drank in the Locarno.

'What's wrong with me?' she demanded to know as he reluctantly switched off the engine.

'Nothing at all.'

'Then why did you hold me the way you did in the tango competition tonight?'

'It was you who came so close to me.'

'That's because the tango is a sexy dance. Do you understand that? That's why some women have orgasms when they watch Valentino dancing it in *The Four Horsemen of the Apocalypse*. I've seen that film six times and it still makes me weak. You're far too sedate, due to your dancing with that rich bitch in the fox fur stole. I serve that type in Jenners. They don't have a romantic bone in their bodies. They buy woollen knickers down to their knees, and I bet they haven't had sex with their husbands for years and years. Robert Hunter, you're a lovely dancer, but dancing isn't everything. There's a life beyond it, of marriage, children, holidays – yes, sex. You have a straight spine on the dance floor, Robert, but perhaps it's too straight. You need to bend sometimes. I'll make my own way home.'

She opened the car door and before he could open his door and go after her she had disappeared out of his life.

Robert never danced in competitions again. He continued to attend the Marine Gardens every Saturday night, to dance with Mrs Drummond-Murchison. She felt safer than the fiery Kitty Dawson. His North Berwick patroness continued to bestow her generosity: a gold tiepin from Hamilton & Inches, on which she had had engraved a waltzing couple. Theatre and concert tickets arrived by post, and the Rolls-Royce brought at Christmas a plum pudding studded with fruits, into which had been poured half a bottle of Courvoisier. The fact is that, though she was old enough to be his mother, the North Berwick resident was a little in love with him. After her crude husband, Robert was the epitome of exemplary manners and grace. He was calm, he was loyal, a partner one was proud to accompany round the colossal Marine Gardens dance floor. When they sat out a dance on a settee, she told him intimate details and asked his advice. He was what she had always wanted, a good listener, not a loud mouth like her late husband.

Robert was promoted to Head of Classics in his school, which gave him added responsibilities, but he still attended the Marine Gardens four nights a week, and Mrs Drummond-Murchison continued to arrive by chauffeur-driven Rolls-Royce on Saturday evenings. Her hour of bliss in the expert arms of the classics master, dancing the waltz Daybreak to Jeffries's Rialto Orchestra was now extended to two with the blessing of the manager, who was anxious that if he refused, the couple would transfer to a rival ballroom like the Fountainbridge Plaza.

But Robert noticed that his partner was becoming slower, and also looked pale. For the first Saturday evening in years she didn't turn up. Instead the chauffeur appeared with a note, inviting him to lunch at the North Berwick residence the following Sunday, 'provided that you are free of another engagement, of course. Adam will collect you at 12 noon.'

Robert went out on to the street to meet his conveyance because his parents would quiz him as to why he was stepping into a limousine. He enjoyed the drive in the back to North Berwick. The architecture of his partner's large house overlooking the sea appealed to his tastes. The door was answered by a butler in a swallow-tailed coat who marched up the stairs in front of him, leading him into the library where the hostess was sitting beside an iron basket of blazing logs. Robert made a rare exception by accepting a sherry. The high-backed chair he sat in opposite Mrs Drummond-Murchison was the most comfortable he had ever occupied.

'I apologize for not coming to the Marine Gardens last Saturday, but I have not been well. I have cancer, which the consultant told me is terminal, meaning that I may have three months left. He suggested that I go to America in search of the most advanced treatment, but I told him that I wouldn't enjoy crossing by liner, however comfortable.'

Robert Hunter was a scholar of Greek culture, and that race in antiquity had kept their emotions in check. But he found his eyes filling with tears at his dancing partner's calm statement about her demise. In fact he was so overcome he crossed to sit beside her on the sofa, holding her hand.

'It's kind of you to care so much, Robert.' It was the first time she had spoken his Christian name. 'But I'm not so young, and I've had a privileged life compared to the majority of people. Oh, there are things I lacked, but they weren't material.' (This wasn't the time to reveal the emotional frigidity of her late husband). 'I want us to have one last dance, so I'm going to come to the Marine Gardens next Saturday.'

They answered the summons of the gong, beaten by the butler, to go through to lunch in the impressive dining-room overlooking the Firth of Forth. But the guest had no appetite for the perfectly cooked turbot, and the silver cutlery felt heavy and clumsy in his hands. He saw how little his hostess ate.

The following Saturday Mrs Drummond-Murchison arrived in the Portobello ballroom in a dress which had had to be taken in because of her loss of weight, and which made the female dancers sitting on the settees round the floor gasp as its beauty. The hundreds of sequins sewn on the white silk dazzled them.

'I have only the strength for one dance,' she told her partner.

'What would you like?'

'The Viennese Waltz.'

Robert takes the request to the orchestra. They are the first on the floor, and very few couples join them because the watchers from the settees sense that there is something exceptional and almost spiritual about the spectacle. They will never again see the Viennese Waltz performed like this. Robert knows that he had never danced so expressively, despite the sorrow of the occasion, and the woman sweeping round in his arms, a pillar of light from the reflective sequins, forgets about the finality of the malignancy; forgets also about her age; about the disappointments and despair of her marriage. She is young again, and a whole life is ahead of her with all its choices.

When the dance stopped the couple held hands and bowed, and the watchers on the settees rose and applauded. Robert gave his arm to his partner as he led her out to the Rolls-Royce for the last time.

'May I come to see you?' he asked through the open window, after he had settled her in the opulent interior.

'I don't think that would be a good idea. Thank you for a wonderful time, not just tonight, but all those years we've danced together.'

He watched the tail lights of the limousine receding and saw her head framed in the back window. Other women were waiting to dance with him, but he excused himself and went out to his Morris, his head on the steering wheel as he wept.

A month later he saw the intimation of Mrs Drummond-Murchison's death in *The Scotsman*. 'Funeral private.'

Two months later he received a letter from her lawyers.

> I have the pleasure of informing you that our client the late Mrs Drummond-Murchison has left you the sum of five thousand pounds in her will. A cheque for this amount will follow shortly.

Robert Hunter decided that he had lived long enough with his parents, and with the legacy from his late dancing partner he bought a detached bungalow in Craiglockhart, convenient for the school he taught in. There was a garage for his Morris, and an adequately sized garden. He had three bedrooms, of which one was devoted to his dancing gear. The wall-length wardrobe he had had fitted contained his dancing suits, satin collared, swallow-tailed, and below them was a rack for his dancing shoes. The dressing-table drawers contained his evening shirts and black ties, and on its top he laid out the gold cuff links he had won, beside the tie-pin which his late patron had given him.

Even dancers age. Robert Hunter was celibate, contented, without salacious dreams. (Perhaps Freud should have taken up ballroom dancing). Robert ate healthily, drank sparingly. He considered offering a home to a West Highland terrier, but decided that it wouldn't be fair to the animal, since he was out dancing most evenings in the week. But he no longer went to the Marine Gardens, and he no longer worked as a dance instructor. Exempt from war service as a teacher, Robert served as an air raid warden in Edinburgh. But dancing in the capital was blighted temporarily when the doorman of the Princes Ballroom, Princes Street, sustained an injury to his head when he was attacked by a Polish soldier armed with a revolver.

Robert had a circuit of ballrooms in Edinburgh which he patronized: the New Cavendish at Tollcross West; the Embassy Club in Queen Street; the New Locarno in Slateford Road. They were all different, with distinctive bands, and he never had a mediocre evening's dancing because of his disposition.

Robert saw Kitty, the dancing partner who had proposed to him, at a bus stop on Princes Street. She had put on considerable weight, and the legs were no longer those of a champion Charleston exponent. He was sure she saw him, but made no sign of recognition as he passed, and he felt a momentary pang of remorse about not marrying her.

From the 1960s onwards the ballrooms couldn't compete with television, the new form of entertainment which meant that you didn't have to leave your home. The Marine Gardens had closed at the beginning of the Second World War; the Fountainbridge Palais went as the 1960s were drawing to a close. The Plaza, Edinburgh, called the last waltz on a chill spring evening in 1975. The previous year the Albert in Glasgow, where he had seen the legendary Warren family dance, had been destroyed by fire.

Robert Hunter was saddened, but philosophical. On evenings when he would formerly have been out dancing, he spent in his garden, showing a gift for growing roses, passers-by stopping to compliment him on the colours and heady scents. Once a year he cut blooms to take to the last resting place of his dancing partner in North Berwick. Her house was flatted, the Rolls-Royce shipped to America.

On winter evenings Robert watched *Come Dancing* on television. He thought about the competitions he had been in against the Warrens and the suave Farquhar MacRae. Grateful for the memories, he switched off the set and slept soundly. He retired from teaching and had over thirty years of trouble-free health before a stroke put him into the nursing home. The staff only suspected that he had been a ballroom dancer when he nodded and smiled at brilliantly executed waltzes and tangos in *Strictly Coming Dancing,* but covered his eyes at some of the antics.

Robert didn't reach his century to merit a royal telegram. Two months short of it, he passed away, peacefully in his sleep. *Strictly Come Dancing* had finished its run. He had left instructions with his lawyer that a classic recording of tunes for the Argentinean Tango was to be played in the crematorium, and that his ashes were to be scattered over the grave in North Berwick of his dancing partner, patroness, and dear friend.

Gay Abandon

As Miss Jean Milligan fixed her old fashioned hat in the mirror of her Glasgow home on the morning of her retiral from Jordanhill College in 1948, a brooch at her throat, the spinster of sixty-two saw a person who couldn't accept a sedentary life of knitting needles, a cat on her lap. There would now be more time to devote to her beloved Society, to travel abroad to inspect branches, and to encourage the formation of new ones. The Society had over eleven thousand members, but Miss Milligan would never be satisfied. If she heard that Madge Wildfire's Strathspey was being danced to bongo drums in Africa, she would probably have endured the dangers of the forest to make sure that the steps were accurate.

But it wasn't bongo drums that the young generation would be listening to in the 1950s. It was a man who had made a simulated guitar out of cardboard as a boy who would set the frenetic pace for the decade on the dance floors of America and Britain. Bill Haley and the Comets recorded 'Rock Around the Clock' in 1954, but it only stayed in the charts for a week. However, his version of 'Shake Rattle and Roll' entered the British singles charts in December of that same year, becoming a Gold Record. Not that Miss Milligan was tuned into Radio Luxemburg to listen to it: she was too busy teaching her Glasgow class Lady Louisa Macdonald's Strathspey from the Society's Book 18, to be published the following year. A couple of miles from the hall where the doyen of Scottish country dancing was demonstrating the sedate steps of the strathspey, the denizens of the Barrowland Ballroom were beginning to rock.

In 1957 Miss Milligan visited Montreal, and was treated to a dancing display. She was particularly impressed by a young man in full Highland dress, including Glengarry bonnet, who gave a demonstration of 'Maclain Ghasda' ('Hieland Laddie').

Tearlach Gunn's ancestor had brought the steps of the dance with them when they were cleared from their north of Scotland home in the mid nineteenth century, some of them forcibly carried out to the emigrant ship by thugs hired by the laird, desperate for the sake of his economic survival to replace his clanspeople with more profitable sheep. The *Martha* was infested with rats, the barrels of dried herring, the main fare for the reluctant passengers, so over-salted that it had left them with a fierce thirst, forcing them to drink the polluted water. Some developed diarrhoea, choking the water closets and filling the sleeping quarters with a sickening stench despite the ventilation at the bulwarks.

Even though their own minister, the laird's ally in the evictions, had stayed behind, the emigrants held a service on the deck of *Martha* every Sunday morning, the old schoolmaster reading from the Gaelic Bible, his trembling hand holding down the gilt-edged pages against the wind, leading the singing of the psalm.

The vessel had run into a storm, ferocious even in those violent latitudes, the timbers groaning as if at any moment they would splay and the Atlantic pour in. Many of the passengers, vomiting over the sides of their bunks, would have preferred this, as if it were an eternal punishment imposed for their sins. Their vomiting became an epidemic, and those who rolled out of their bunks were dead before their bones broke on the boards. The heads and limbs of some of the sufferers were grotesquely swollen, like freaks in a fairground.

Hundreds of sick people were lying on other anchored vessels, waiting their turn to discharge at Grosse Isle, because they had to be certified clear of disease before they could proceed to Quebec. When *Martha*'s turn came to tie up at the island, ropes were stretched across the deck so as to leave a passage in the middle. A doctor was stationed on each side of this passage and only one person from the newly arrived ship was allowed through at a time.

Tearlach Gunn's family survived the voyage, though a son of sixteen died. One of the stories that would be recounted in Gaelic by Tearlach's great-grandfather Samuel would be of the sight of hundreds of coffins of assorted sizes piled behind the emigration buildings. He would recall how they had trekked to eastern Quebec, where the distribution of land became a ceremony. The men had drawn lots for a place in the procession and Samuel by divine intervention was first. He had an axe in his hand and when he began to move he started to sing the 23rd Psalm, 'Is e Dia fein a's buachaill dhomh,' 'The Lord is My Shepherd.' He moved singing through the wood, the jays taking off at their first encounter with a human in the dense cover of the eastern Quebec forest, and a bear robbing a bee's nest stopping to listen, his gigantic paw sticky with honey within the tree. Samuel marked a tree with his axe, and the men coming behind him with their axes took up the psalm. They sang this six times as they walked through the woods, and the leading man made another mark. They were walking a square, and the marks on the trunks represented their grant of land from the British American Land Company. But this had already been decided on a map. The Hebridean emigrants wanted to walk their new territory singing, because at home everything was done to singing.

They had to sleep out in the forest for seven nights until some kind of shelter was erected, the logs squared with the broad axe. The Indians watched with helpless bewilderment as they were dispossessed of their ancestral land by those who had also been dispossessed in Scotland. The emigrants cut down lumber and burned it to sell the ashes for potash, planting round the stumps which they left to rot in the ground. The women were tormented by black flies as they cooked or sat in the shade, spinning wool for winter garments while the men improved the cabin, splitting timbers to make floorboards and building a loft for sleeping quarters.

Spring was deceptively short, the season to plant potatoes, but only when there was a new moon, because they had brought with them across the ocean a fear of planting the crop when the moon was on the decrease. When Samuel dug the first crop from the cleared soil in autumn there was a moment of dread in his heart that the potato in his fist would be diseased like the one he had dug up in his old home across the ocean, but when he split it with his knife it was snowy white.

In the first summer men came from earlier settlements to help build a barn, and oxen were used to clear the land of stones, an essential chore that would go on for generations, the stones piled into cairns by the field's edge until a use could be found for them in a land where all building was of timber. Samuel loved the clear cold days of autumn, with the brilliant red maples standing out against the endless skies. He was learning to recognize the wildlife of Quebec, some familiar from his native place. Red squirrels flowed up trees; a wolverine passed with her cute cubs. He heard the black-capped chickadee calling out its own name, and within a week one was eating out of his hand.

One morning they woke to snow piled up to the windows, and work outside had to cease. It was so cold that the settlers huddled by their stoves, yearning for the Hebridean winter, with snow a rarity. But the Indians, now accepting the white man's presence, arranged a moose hunt on snow-shoes, and the moon was in the sky when the men returned with their coats scarlet from the packs of meat on their backs.

In the starry nights neighbours waded through the drifts, bringing their fiddles and bundles of newly baked bread for the ceilidh round the stove. The Gaelic songs they had brought across with them brought tears, but there was also a new composition by Samuel, who had a reputation as a bard, and when he recorded in an angry song about the brutality of the laird's hired horsemen and the old woman drowning from the boat, the assembled company were back in the bay from where they had sailed.

In some of the houses of people from other islands there was no dancing because they were strict Presbyterians and would not consort with the devil. But Samuel had been taught 'Mac Ian Ghasda' as a child, and he taught it to his grandchildren, the boards reverberating under his home-crafted shoes.

Samuel's great grandson Tearlach was demonstrating this same dance to Miss Jean Milligan in a hall in Montreal a hundred years after it had been brought to Quebec, and she was enthralled. She went backstage to congratulate him and to ask if he had ever tried Scottish country dancing.

'I haven't heard of that style of dancing, ma'am.'

Though she was an elderly woman, Miss Milligan blushed at the deference of his address. This was exactly the kind of young man she wanted to recruit. He was slender, and he was handsome in Highland garb, his dark hair short and neat. The doyen of Scottish country dance favoured decorum, though dancing was also about release.

'They're hoping to form a branch of the Society here next year, and I do hope you'll join,' she told the Canadian dancer. 'I run a Summer School for Scottish country dance in St Andrews in Scotland, and it might be possible to assist you financially to come to us,' she informed him. As always she was looking ahead, since good dancers were usually good teachers. It was all very well to recruit, but they had to be taught if the movement were to survive.

Tearlach was a student of English Literature at McGill University. His parents were still on the land in eastern Quebec which Samuel had ploughed into a farm, after the boulders had been hauled away, using the muscular power of oxen. They had acquired two adjacent farms belonging to settlers who wished to retire and whose children had no interest in working the land, wanting to work with adding machines, not ploughshares.

His prosperous parents supported Tearlach at university, and he went home in the vacation to help with the harvest and to dance 'Mac Iain Ghasda' at ceilidhs. He was close to his parents, but not close enough, nor courageous enough, to tell them that he was attracted to his own sex. There were beautiful sexy female students at McGill, but it was the males whom Tearlach watched as he stirred his coffee at the refectory table at McGill. It had to be at a distance, however, and he daren't make contact with them in case he was mistaken about their sexuality. Homosexual acts were illegal in Canada; not that he wished to indulge in that way, but it would be fulfilling to have a platonic partner. If he met someone it would have to be kept from his parents, because as well as Samuel's broad axe having become an heirloom in the family, fixed to the wall it had helped to create, his big Bible on whose flyleaf family names and marriages had been written in black ink since the seventeenth century, was still read from by Tearlach's father every Sunday evening.

He would never forget that night when he was sixteen when his father had chosen a text from Leviticus. 'If a man lies with a male as with a woman, both of them have committed an abomination; they shall be put to death; their blood is upon them.' His father had lifted his eyes from the page and looked at his son, and Tearlach wondered if he suspected and that this was a warning to him to suppress his feelings, otherwise suffer damnation from parents as well as deity. The only time he felt free and relaxed was when he was dancing. He took Miss Milligan's advice and joined the Montreal branch of the Scottish Country Dance Society, now with the prefix Royal. Tearlach found the company congenial, and the footwork came easily to him because of his skills at Hebridean solo dances. But he sensed that there was no one in the class of the same sexual inclination as himself.

The law firm which occupied an entire building in Charlotte Square, Edinburgh, was one of the oldest in the city, and claimed to have acted for David Hume. The rooms were panelled, and the senior partner's, which overlooked the private gardens in the Square, had a massive mahogany desk. The inkwells on it were capped in sterling silver, and the ivory knife he used to open his mail was in the shape of a shark's serrated teeth. Walter Stevenson-Napier claimed descent from the author of *Treasure Island* and other classics, and the trust funds he administered were worth many millions. He was a generous patron of the Edinburgh Festival.

He lunched each day with other lawyers at the New Club on Princes Street, and was a member of the Royal Company of Archers, and each year drew his long bow in the Silver Arrow competition on the Meadows. His only son Bruce had been educated at Fettes and Edinburgh University before joining the legal firm. He was twenty six, and his office, at the back of the building, was much more modest than his father's. It went without saying that one day he would occupy his father's office.

Bruce is supposed to be looking over the title deeds to a property in exclusive Ann Street which a client wishes to offer for. But he's daydreaming. He wishes he were far away from his desk, up in the Highlands at the family holiday home, where he loves to walk the hills. He hates the dreariness of the law, a life of dusty documents and clients whose only interest is in acquiring more wealth. Being a lawyer is about confidentiality, but he has a personal secret which he daren't divulge to anyone: he's attracted to men. Recently his parents gave a dinner party for selected friends, to celebrate his father's thirty years as a lawyer, ten as senior partner. The dining-room table was laid with the silver which Walter Stevenson-Napier had inherited from his own father, who had been senior partner in the same firm, because comparatively new money was becoming old, mellowing like the light from the candelabra reflected in the mahogany. The choice malt whisky on the sideboard was locked in a tantalus.

One of the guests had brought up the name of Francis Cadell, famed for his brilliantly coloured studies of Iona, in particular the pure sand, the aquamarine ocean.

'My father bought the painting for a few pounds from the artist in the 1930s, when Cadell was on his uppers,' the guest disclosed. 'I had it valued for insurance purposes last year and was told that it would fetch five figures at auction.'

'My father knew Cadell, but never liked him,' the host pronounced from the head of the table. 'He was a rampant homosexual and used to go importuning among the low life on Calton Hill. He got what he deserved, a good thrashing. Merrilees the Chief Constable had the best idea: round up the perverts in this city and give them a one-way train ticket to London to join all the others down there with their filthy habits.'

His son Bruce was staring into his consommé as the diatribe proceeded. He wanted to get up and proclaim to the table that it didn't matter if Cadell – or anyone else for that matter – was a homosexual. What mattered was their worth as a person. But Bruce lacked the courage, because he knew that his father would accuse him of having shamed the family and would probably disown him.

There was a young man in the office to whom he was attracted. His name was Thomas and he worked in the accounts department. They were on nodding terms in the corridor. Bruce would have liked to stop to speak with him, but there was a strict hierarchy in the office, with the senior partner as the deity, and his son would only draw attention to himself by conversing with a junior with whom he had no business. He considered slipping the clerk a note, suggesting a meeting one evening, but it was too risky.

At that time homosexuals in Edinburgh seeking partners had very few places to meet. However, a new restaurant cum bar, The Trysting Place, had opened in Howe Street, and it was attracting what would later be called a gay clientele. Bruce heard his father fulminating against this 'Edinburgh Sodom,' saying that the city fathers should never have granted it a licence. 'It's places like that that corrupt youth,' the senior partner raged. But his son, in an evening of bravery or recklessness, went for a drink at The Trysting Place and saw women as well as men who were attracted to their own sex. How could he tell? They were middle-class, and they dressed in the same clothes as their heterosexual peers. He saw the yearning in their faces, their eyes, as they sipped cocktails. It was a safe haven, but as soon as they stepped out into the streets of Edinburgh any sign of their sexuality could be met by insults and beatings.

All this, including the tyrannical father, made for a most unhappy young man as he sat in the notable building in Charlotte Square, which represented all the traditions of the Athens of the North: elegance, durability, conformity with neighbouring properties, because the layout of the New Town was about conformity, the same astragals, the same stones from which residents used to ascend into their carriages. This was the claustrophobic society from which Robert Louis Stevenson had fled to the freedom of the South Seas.

Bruce's only release from his unhappiness and frustrations was in Scottish country dancing, which he had discovered at school. While most of the other boys complained that they would rather be playing more rugby than prancing round the floor in reels, the senior partner's son loved it because it allowed him to express the freedom he craved for. To strap on a kilt and lace up pumps was to leave behind the striped suits and polished shoes of the law office. Here, on the dance floor there was no hierarchy, because, when he joined the Edinburgh branch of the Society, his partner could be a gynaecologist or a bus conductress. Social status didn't count on the dance floor.

On an early summer's evening he excuses himself from the formal family dinner and goes upstairs to put on his kilt. He drives into town and parks on Princes Street and goes down into the Gardens. He can hear the band testing their sound levels in the bandstand below the castle as he goes down the path to the concrete area, an open-air dance floor. The Flowers of Edinburgh is announced, and he quickly finds a partner and a place in a set. He particularly likes this dance because it closes with a poussette in which you hold your partner's hands and move round in a square to change places. The co-ordination of feet and music is difficult in the poussette, and some cynics claim that Miss Milligan made up the movement and didn't take it from tradition.

After the exhilarating evening Bruce would drive down to The Trysting Place for a coffee before going home to that strict cheerless house where his father's bowler hat confronted him on the stand in the marble-floored hall. When the Society's classes resumed in the autumn the secretary asked if anyone wished to go to Summer School in St Andrews.

'I won't be coming to Aviemore next year,' he informed his parents at breakfast the next morning.

The Scotsman was lowered to reveal his father's face.

'Why not?'

'Because I want to go and dance at Summer School in St Andrews.'

'We always go north as a family,' his father reminded him in his bullying tone. 'Don't you get plenty of dancing during the year?'

'Let him go next year, dear,' his mother interjected. 'It's good for him to mix, and he may meet a suitable girl.'

In February 1962 another new dance, The Twist, arrived in the Barrowland Ballroom, Glasgow, from America, inspired by Chubby Checker's hit 'Let's Twist Again.' The new dance soon spread like a fever among the young generation from which Miss Milligan required to attract Scottish country dancers. Her style of dancing was formal, with strict footwork, whereas in the Twist the performers responded to the frenetic music with swivelling hips, sometimes hoisting their female partners above their heads. Which sage described it as a dance in which you endeavoured to stub out a cigarette with your toe while trying to dry your back with a towel?

That summer of 1962 Miss Milligan had to contend with another change to tradition at the Summer School in St Andrews. The Victorian elegance of University Hall now had a new extension called the Lumsden Wing, and the Scottish country dancers were the first residents. Miss Milligan was saddened because the dining-room in which she had presided from the dais was now closed, with meals taken in the much larger new dining-room in Lumsden. As a lover of most things old, from dances to decorum, Miss Milligan was saddened by the change.

But there was a big attendance at Summer School, including the young man she had met in Montreal. Tearlach Gunn had managed to persuade his parents that his services, helping out with the harvest on the farm, could be dispensed with for a fortnight. He wished to go to dance in Scotland.

'You can also do some research into the family,' his father advised him, having agreed to pay the air fares. 'Copy the names from the family Bible.'

Miss Milligan gave him a warm welcome to St Andrews, and he was put into a demonstration team in the Younger Hall. Bruce Stevenson-Napier from Edinburgh was in the same team. The young lawyer had already noted the presence of the Canadian dancer in University Hall. Their bedrooms were on the same floor, and they passed with signs of mutual interest. They spoke in the common room on the second day of their arrival, introducing themselves, each knowing by a subtle signal what the other desired. After the evening's dancing in the common room they sat together, chatting, describing their individual lifestyles. Tearlach was teaching a course on English romantic poetry in a college in Montreal where the students were attentive and interested.

'Lucky you. I work in my father's law firm in Edinburgh.'

'Which I gather you don't like.'

'I hate every minute of it. Sometimes I want to rise from my desk and throw the title deeds into the wastepaper basket. But I can't. I'm been groomed for the senior partnership, as they say.'

'You could walk away from it,' his new Canadian friend suggested.

'To do what? My qualification is in law. I would have to go back to university, and my parents wouldn't support me. I suppose I could serve behind a bar, but it wouldn't be very fulfilling.'

'At least you would be free.'

'It's hard to be free, if you mean to be oneself in Edinburgh. My mother expects me to bring home a girl from a good solid Edinburgh family with money and status. A doctor would do very nicely. But I'm not interested in women.'

'Nor am I, but my parents don't push me. I live and work in Montreal, and they're a long way away in the country, so I can arrange my life the way I want.'

'Do you have a friend?'

It was a leading question, but Bruce knew that he could risk it. It would be years before the word partner would become part of the world of the homosexual.

'I don't. I'm a teacher, so I have to be careful with my relationships. Montreal's quite a traditional place.'

They knew they had to be careful at the Summer School, because most of the dancers were couples. But on their walks along the deserted West Sands they held hands, and on the last night of the School Bruce went to Tearlach's room.

'Are you going to come back next year?' he asked his Canadian friend.

'I hope so, but it depends on my parents paying my air fare. What about you?'

'I'll certainly be here,' Bruce pledged.

But that was a year away, and though he wrote regularly to Tearlach, he still felt lonely and isolated. He heard two of the typists in the office giggling as one told the other about going into a bar in Rose Street with her boyfriend.

'We didn't realize that it was a place where nancy boys met.'

'Nancy boys?' the other queried.

'Homosexuals. One of them approached Charlie, and he told him if he didn't bugger off he would punch him in the mouth.'

Bruce noted the name of the Rose Street bar, and decided in his desperation to go into it. He bought himself a sherry (he wasn't a drinker) and sat at a corner table. The bar was busy, and he recognized instinctively his own kind. One of them, sitting three tables away, was staring at him. Bruce was sure that he was wearing make-up. As the man smiled encouragingly Bruce saw to his horror that it was one of the partners in his father's firm, a married man, because Bruce had met his wife at a Christmas party in the New Club. Bruce abandoned his drink and fled out into the narrow street. On the way home his fear that the man would report him to his father heightened into a phobia.

'What's wrong? You look very pale,' his mother said when she met him in the hall.

'I'm fine, just a bit tired.'

'Maybe you're doing too much dancing.'

Bruce feared going into work the next day, and when the partner met Bruce in the corridor he nodded and smiled, transmitting the silent message to Bruce: *I know about you now*. But Bruce also knew about him.

He found that his frustration was interfering with his pleasure in dancing, and in the class he felt sluggish and made simple mistakes. He considered using the office phone to make contact with Tearlach in Canada, but that was too risky. It was a long time until the next Summer School. Should he tell his parents that he was taking a holiday to Canada? Certainly he had enough saved, but his father would say that he had already used his annual holiday entitlement by going to St Andrews. The office shut for a week over the festive season, but that wasn't long enough to cross and re-cross the Atlantic, and spend sufficient time with his Canadian soulmate.

In Montreal Tearlach was experiencing the same frustration. He had to be so careful, because he was a teacher. Some evenings he left his lonely flat to go for a drink in a nearby hotel. He was sure that some of the young men drinking together had the same inclinations as himself, because there was a subtle signal even in a glance. One of them brought his drink across to Tearlach's table and introduced himself as Simon. He was a fair haired young man practising as an architect in Montreal.

'Why don't you come across and join our group?' he invited the school teacher.

He was introduced to the other four, discovering that they were all professionals, one of them a doctor. It didn't have to be voiced that they were all homosexual. They were being watched by the barman polishing glassware behind the long counter.

'That guy could be a police informer,' Simon cautioned.

'What do you mean?' Tearlach asked nervously.

'He'll phone the police and say that we're soliciting. We'd better get out of here.'

Tearlach went with the others up in the elevator to the doctor's fashionable flat in the new building, its glass walls giving panoramic views of the city. The young teacher felt uneasy about the situation, but accepted the drink handed to him by Simon. He didn't come to consciousness until dawn was brightening the window, and found himself lying naked beside the doctor.

'What happened?' he asked, leaping out of the bed.

'You had one too many,' the doctor told him. 'I had to put you to bed.'

The question he was really putting was: what did you do to me? But he didn't know how to formulate it, and because he had no recollection since the time he was handed the drink, which must have been spiked with something, he had no proof. If this had been his physical initiation, it was a traumatic experience.

'I need to get to school,' he panicked, pulling on his trousers.

In Edinburgh Bruce Stevenson-Napier heard of another bar in which homosexuals congregated. It was up a flight of steps in the Old Town, in a historic close where prostitutes had kilted their skirts in the time of Robert Burns's visit to the capital to arrange the publication of his poems. The bar was old fashioned, with a mirror advertising the ale of a defunct brewery, and instead of optics fixed to bottles on the gantry, the drams were tipped from brass measures. Bruce didn't think it was the type of pub where one ordered a gin and tonic with a slice of lemon, so he settled for a lager. He carried his drink to an unoccupied table heavily scarred where generations of drinkers had laid their cigarettes on the edges.

A young man slid into the seat opposite him without introduction. He was wearing a donkey jacket.

'You look as if you're wanting business.'

'I beg your pardon?' Bruce enquired.

'That's what they all say,' the youth said. 'Five pounds in the close, ten if I'm coming back to your place.'

This must be one of the rent boys his father had fulminated against, saying that they should be castrated. His face lacked affection or desire. His body was a commodity he was selling, without knowing anything about the person he was servicing. Bruce got up to leave. He was hurrying down the steps when he felt the hand on his shoulder.

'You walked away from me.'

He was dragged into the side alley, the buttons ripped from his jacket to get at his wallet. Then he was kneed in the testicles and punched in the face before being rolled down the steps.

When he opened his eyes in the hospital bed his mother was sitting beside him.

'What on God's name happened?'

'I was robbed.'

'Where?'

'In the Old Town.'

'What were you doing there? Your father warned you it's a dangerous place of criminals and perverts.'

He was too weak, too much in pain, to offer an explanation.

'What a mess your face is in!' his mother lamented. 'And we're having a dinner party next Saturday.'

He didn't ask for a mirror. He wanted to sleep, not only to repair his damaged body, but also his bruised heart. Instead of being a pleasure, was his sexual inclination an affliction, connected to the disgusting and the violent, without love or tenderness?

A fortnight later, still bruised, he was sitting at the family dinner table.

'What were you doing in a sordid bar in the Old Town the night you were attacked?' his father demanded.

'I was having a drink.'

'There are many decent places to have a drink in Edinburgh,' his father reminded him. 'You could have gone to the New Club; that's one of the reasons I made you a member.'

'I wanted a change.'

'How do you know he was in a pub in the Old Town?' his

mother asked her husband.

'Because I phoned the Chief Constable and told him my son was attacked, and I wanted the perpetrator brought to justice. He phoned me this afternoon and told me that my son was in a bar which has a notorious reputation as a place of congregation for homosexuals. The barman remembered him talking to a rent boy. I said: "that can't be my son," but the Chief Constable said: "it was, Walter, because I showed the barman the photograph you gave me, and he was certain." Is this true?'

Bruce stood up, though he was still unsteady on his feet.

'Yes it's true. I'm a homosexual and I went looking for company because you can't find it in the so-called decent part of Edinburgh because everyone's frightened and ashamed of it.'

His father stood up. At first his son thought that he was going to come round to strike him. Instead he gripped the edge of the table and heaved. The Spode china, the hallmarked silver, accumulated over the years to give the family status in Edinburgh society, but without an heir now, cascaded and smashed as his wife screamed.

At the Summer School in St Andrews in 1976 Miss Milligan demonstrated her 'new knees' as she was supported between two of her 'boys.' The two visitors from Canada are not in this photograph in the Younger Hall, but they were present. Walter Stevenson-Napier had seen his dreams of a continuing legal dynasty destroyed by the admission of an only son's 'perversion' he could never come to accept. Bruce took a flight to Montreal and shared Tearlach's apartment. He went to McGill to train in Canadian law and became a member of a successful practice. In the more liberal 1970s, homosexual partnerships began to be accepted.

Miss Milligan considered the two men from Canada to be among her best dancers, and she persuaded them to become teachers of Scottish country dancing. One of their examiners was Esther Elliot from the Borders, who had been attending Summer School since 1936. Relaxing in the common room with a company of dancers, she reminisced about the war years in Glasgow.

'What was Miss Milligan like in those days?' someone asked.

'Mrs Armstrong, the lady I lodged with and who was so kind to me, told me a story about Miss Milligan. On the first night of the Clydebank Blitz the inhabitants of the building in the west end where the Milligan sisters lived went down into the cellar for safety. They heard the patter of feet on the stairs, and this figure clad in a brown fur coat appeared. Miss Milligan didn't have a steel helmet, but she made do with a tea cosy on her head, with an enamel basin on top, kept in place with a scarf tied under her chin. Instead of a bottle of whisky Miss Milligan had brought a jar of barley sugar. "Good for the nerves," she told the company as she passed round the jar.'

Miss Milligan liked to quote from Longfellow's *The Song of Hiawatha*:

> 'And the night shall be filled with music,
> And the cares, that infest the day,
> Shall fold their tents, like the Arabs,
> And as silently steal away.'

She died on 28 July 1978, aged ninety two, as the Summer School was under way. The death notice in the newspapers stated: 'cremated privately on 31 July. (No letters, please).' Surely the exquisite Miss Milligan's Strathspey is a far better memorial than a tombstone.